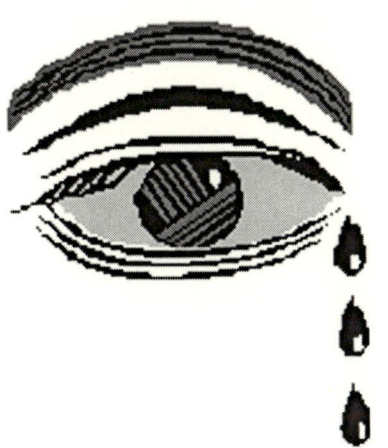

A CRUEL TWIST OF FATE

A CRUEL TWIST OF FATE

By
Jack Stahl

E-BookTime, LLC
Montgomery, Alabama

A Cruel Twist of Fate

Copyright © 2010 by Jack Stahl

All rights reserved. No part of this book may be reproduced or transmitted in any form or by any means, electronic or mechanical, including photocopying, recording, or by any information storage and retrieval system, without permission in writing from the copyright owner.

This is a work of fiction. Names, characters, places and incidents either are the product of the author's imagination or are used fictitiously, and any resemblance to any actual persons, living or dead, events, or locales is entirely coincidental.

Library of Congress Control Number: 2010924986

ISBN: 978-1-60862-150-7

First Edition
Published March 2010
E-BookTime, LLC
6598 Pumpkin Road
Montgomery, AL 36108
www.e-booktime.com

PROLOGUE

In an interview with Red Barber in July of 1946, Leo Durocher, then manager of the Brooklyn Dodgers, made an observation about his hated, cross-town rivals, the New York Giants. In his observation he stated that the Giants had some nice guys on their team, but nonetheless would finish last in their division. The headline writers of the day twisted Durocher's words and quoted him as making the statement "Nice Guys Finish Last." As time passed by the context of that quote was narrowed to mean that people who lead a good life, are solid citizens and who have high moral standards generally ARE NOT those who become successful in love and/or in life. The conception that people with these personality traits will get run over by more aggressive individuals who do not live by such a high moral code has become generally accepted by the public. In short, in all of life's scenarios the law of the jungle rules; the strong survive, the weak finish last.

If you are a nice guy that doesn't necessarily mean you are doomed because there are always exceptions to every rule. At least that's what I thought. But what I thought and what I found out were two very different things.

SAGAMORE, PA

The lifeline of the early coal towns was the gleaming track of a coal-carrying railroad. Coal was king in those days and as railroad companies like The Buffalo, Rochester and Pittsburgh Railway laid their tracks, shanty towns of hastily built cabins sprouted up and dotted the landscape. Most of these towns were owned by mining companies and Sagamore, named after a New York State Indian chief, was one of these towns. The Wiggins Mining Company, headquartered in Bentlcyville, PA had seized on the opportunity to buy the land and build the town of Sagamore from scratch shortly after it was announced that the BR and P Railway was building a spur from their main line that would intersect with this parcel of real estate. The original town consisted of ninety double houses, a church, a post office and a general store. Each double house measured twenty-eight by thirty feet and had five rooms on each side. It is in this little mining town that my story begins.

John Stalkovich and his wife, Meta had immigrated to the United States from Poland in the early part of the decade of the 1920s. At the processing center in Ellis Island, when John was asked to recite his name, he said, "John Stalk." He altered the spelling of his surname as many other emigrants did in hopes that a more American sounding name would enhance his chances for success in his new world. After a series of odd jobs and living from hand-to-mouth for over a year John heard about the opportunity for a job as a coal miner in the little town of Sagamore. When John and Meta arrived in Sagamore, Meta was pregnant and when John met with Tom Wiggins; owner of the Wiggins Mining Company, Tom seemingly took pity on John and Meta's family situation and offered John a position in his company. But it wasn't all pity on Tom's part as Tom was a crafty business man and knew that with a little one coming into John and Meta's life, John would have to work and wouldn't be another drifter who earned a few paychecks and then moved on. After signing on, Tom inquired about John and Meta's financial status. How much money did they have? Where did they plan to live? The answers to Tom's questions were, "Enough to last for a few days" and "we don't know." Tom offered to advance John enough money to get him situated and told him that he had a half of a double house available for rent and that he and Meta could move in that very day.

John and Meta were elated. Tom, "Thank you so much, but how can I pay you back for the advance and how much rent will we have pay for the house?"

"Don't worry John, just sign here and I'll make arrangements to take the proper amount out of your check every month." John was overwhelmed with Tom's generosity and he and Meta felt that the dreams they had when they left Poland in search of a new life in America had finally come true.

"Tom, we'd like to celebrate our good fortune by having a good home-cooked meal in our new house. Where might we go to buy some food?"

"John, you and Meta don't have to go anywhere. We have our own store in our little town. Every employee of Wiggins Mining has an account at the store. You can use cash at the store but if you ever find that you are short of cash, arrangements will be made to deduct a portion of your paycheck until your bill is paid."

> *"You haul 16 tons and whadaya get?*
> *Another day older and deeper in debt.*
> *St. Peter don't you call me cause I can't go*
> *I owe my soul to the company store"*

During the first month John and Meta were as happy as they ever had been in their lives. Most of their money was going back to the company for their rent and groceries but they were able to keep their heads above water and were quite happy with their new life albeit quiet and meager. The town consisted of 180 families and everyone was very friendly. John, like everyone else, worked 6 days a week. On the 7th day, as prescribed by the Lord, the mines rested except for the maintenance crew who took the day to repair machinery so that come midnight Sunday night all would be ready for the first shift of the new week.

When John was working, Meta was busy tending to her daily chores as well as getting the house ready for their little one. Three months to the day after John and Meta arrived in

Sagamore, Meta went into labor and John called for the local mid-wife to help with the delivery.

Meta gave birth to a healthy baby boy but complications developed during the delivery. Meta experienced severe hemorrhaging and the mid wife suggested that she be taken to the closest hospital which was located about 30 miles away in the town of Connellsville, PA.

Meta never made it to Connellsville alive. John's hopes and dreams had been replaced by despair and nightmare. Mr. Wiggins allowed John one day off of work for the funeral. Just a mere 72 hours after the birth of his son (John, Jr.) and the demise of his beloved Meta, John was lost in his work in a dark cavern in the Allegheny Mountains deep under the surface of the small mining town of Sagamore.

Over the years as John Sr. rotated through his never ending shifts in the mine; John Jr. was raised by the families living in the community of Sagamore. He was a bright boy, articulate and possessed a good mind. He did well in school and had the potential to secure an occupation outside of mining but breaking that cycle of life was more easily said than done. The day after he graduated from high school John Jr. packed two lunch boxes for the second shift, one for his dad and one for himself. He was now a full-fledged second generation miner.

John Sr. and John Jr., Big John and Little Johnny as they were known in the community, worked in tandem the next five years as mine pumpers. As new underground caverns were carved out of the earth, below-surface seepage sometimes caused these new caverns to fill with water and it was the job of the pumpers to descend to the flooded area, run a pipeline (fire hose) from the flooded cavern back to the surface and pump the water out of the cavern so that the area could be bolstered and made secure.

A Cruel Twist of Fate

It was Christmas Eve and Big John and Little Johnny were sitting in the pump house feasting on their Christmas dinner.

"Who made these stuffed cabbages Johnny? Jesus are they ever good. Damn it to hell, best I ever tasted. You get these from old lady Kovach? Had to be her because nobody else around here can make pigs in the blanket like her."

"No pop, this here batch was made by Lucy Bahleda, my one and only true love."

"Lucy Bahleda? She comes from a good family. I know her dad, Frank. Good man. Plays the organ at church every Sunday. Now I knew that the two of you have been carrying on a bit lately, but true love? That sounds serious boy. But if that girl can make stuffed cabbages like this then you got every reason in the world to be serious."

"I am very serious pop. In fact I've been saving a little bit from each paycheck for awhile and last week I bought an engagement ring. After we get off of our shift, I'm going to get all cleaned up and pop the question."

"Well, congratulations son. You have my blessing as long as you promise that whenever you have stuffed cabbage for dinner you'll set another place for your old dad."

"I don't know, pop. They way you've been attacking this bunch I don't know if there would be enough left over for me."

"I know Lucy but I really don't know her. If she stole your heart she must be a nice gal. I need you to tell me all about her and all about the plans the two of you have for your life together."

Before Johnny could begin to tell Big John about Lucy the phone rang.

"Sagamore Brothel," answered Big John. "We got rooms by the day or the hour, or in your case Stan, by the minute."

"At least I can still get mine up for a minute, Big John. Now I was wondering if you could take time out from looking at dirty magazines and filing your nails and get your lazy ass down to shaft 13 and check out our situation as we have water in the hole."

"Stan, is this a leaker a squirter or gusher?"

"What in the hell's the difference John? Water is water and you need to get your ass down here and start pumping pronto. I want to finish off this hole so we can get out of here on time at the end of the shift. You know old man Wiggins ain't paying no overtime and I don't want to spend my Christmas not seeing the light of day."

"Ok Stan. I'll be down for a look see right away."

"What's going on, pop?"

"Stan says that he and his boys have run into a little water and we need to take care of it."

"Ok, pop. Listen, you stay here and finish your dinner and I'll go down and take a look."

"No way, boy. You're gonna need all the strength you can muster up to pop that question. You stay here; continue feasting on these cabbages and I'll go down. When I get there and check out the situation I'll get on the call box and let you know what needs to be done."

Big John put on his miner's cap and jacket and his hip-high boots, left the pump house, jumped onto the hand car and disappeared into the earth below.

About 10 minutes later the phone rang in the pump house and Little Johnny picked up the receiver.

"Johnny, we had a squirter when I arrived but the wall around the leak feels pretty soft so this one might turn into a gusher. Probably best to run the large hose down here so that we are prepared for the worst."

"Ok pop, I'm on my way."

As Big John was inspecting the wall the earth rumbled mightily. The next sound he heard was a loud popping noise

A Cruel Twist of Fate

and all of a sudden the ground underneath Big John gave away and he was sucked into depths of the earth and followed by a river of gushing water.

Stan and his crew heard the rumbling sound and the loud pop as the wall exploded. As a massive wave of water cascaded into the hole they all ran for their lives to avoid being swallowed up by the giant underground sink hole that had materialized. They jumped into their car and started heading to ground level when they spotted the light on Little Johnny's hat. They shouted for Little Johnny to stop. They told him about the sink hole that had materialized and said they all needed to get back to ground level to get help for Big John. Little Johnny's first reaction was to rush to his father's aide but he knew there was nothing he could do by himself so he reversed his path and followed Stan's team back to surface level.

The following day the rescue team found Big John floating in a pool of water in a sinkhole that was about 75 feet deep. It was a Christmas day in Sagamore that everyone in town would remember until the day they died. Little Johnny would never have the opportunity to tell Big John his story about Lucy and the plans they had for their life together.

Mining people are hardy folks who live with the knowledge of the dangers of their profession. More than most people, they fully understand the meaning of the biblical phrase, "the Lord giveth and the Lord taketh away." They understand how tenuous life can be and are keenly aware of the personal devastation that is caused by such a loss. But they also understand that no matter how great the loss, the hands of time cannot be turned back. Bread must be put on the table. Coal has to be mined and life has to go on.

Little Johnny, although devastated by the loss of his dad, got lost in the routine of his daily life in due time. He adjusted to living alone. What choice did he have? It felt strange to pack just one lunch and food didn't seem to taste as good any more. Over the years that they worked together the bond between them manifested itself in a number of different ways and their relationship took on more dimensions than that of a father and a son. Below the surface they were co workers and best friends who watched each other's back and worked in tandem to meet the challenges in a dangerous workplace. Above the surface they were family. After Meta's death, Little Johnny had become Big John's reason for living. He was all he had left in the world. He understood that and thanked God every day for the love of his son and for the relationship they shared.

On Valentines' Day Little Johnny proposed to Lucy, she accepted and they set a date for a May wedding.

Any wedding in Sagamore was a town event and the marriage of Little Johnny and Lucy was no different. For several days prior to the wedding the aroma of homemade soups and specialty foods from the old world lingered in the air all throughout the valley. Every household in the community was bringing a dish of some sort for the special occasion. The night before the wedding, tents were constructed on the grounds surrounding the church, long tables and chairs were placed in the tents and some of the men had fashioned a portable, wooden plank dance floor and situated it in the center of their tent city. On the wedding day Lucy looked stunning in her wedding gown which was the same gown that her mother Mary wore when she wed Lucy's father, Frank. Little Johnny, now called Johnny since the passing of his father, was a very handsome specimen in his suit, white shirt and tie. Johnny's best man turned out to be Johnny's best men as Stan and the crew he was with on the day of Big John's accident stood as one in memory and respect of their fallen friend. After the ceremony Johnny kissed the bride and as the new couple turned to face the congregation to begin their journey down the aisle the ushers covered the windows of the church and the room became very dark. At that time Father Mike was handed Big John's old miner's cap. He turned on the lamp on the hat and placed it on his head. He positioned himself in front of Johnny and Lucy and said to the crowd, "The pathway of life is not always a smooth and straight surface. It is a roadway that can be very rough and scored with twists and turns. Sometimes the road looks to be impassable and you feel that you cannot continue your journey. But fear not and have faith in the knowledge that you need not despair. The Lord is always with you on your journey and he will provide the light to guide you back to the straight and narrow. Let the light from Big John's hat and the inspiration of the Lord shine on your path and lead you to everlasting happiness. Johnny and Lucy, the Lord said to his flock, 'come follow me', so follow me as you begin your journey in life together. May God bless you and keep you and provide for you so that your life together is filled with love and happiness not just on this day but for all days to come." Johnny and Lucy followed the priest down the aisle and exited the church and were met by scores of well wishers.

On that special day Johnny made two vows. One was the vow of love and devotion to Lucy. The other was a vow to himself and God that if he were blessed to have a son, his son would not grow up to be a miner.

In the following February, approximately 9 months and 19 days after exchanging wedding vows, Lucy presented Johnny with their first child, a son whom they named Jake. As he held his son for the first time, Johnny looked down at Jake and said, "I don't know what you are going to grow up to be young man, but I know one thing, you aren't going to be a miner."

In Sagamore there was no mail delivery. The post office was run by old Cy Beck. Cy had fashioned old shoe boxes reinforced by tape for each home in the community and placed them on rudimentary shelves made from cement blocks and timbers. When the mail arrived he sorted it and placed it in the appropriate box ready for pickup by each household. Cy never locked the door to the building so that the men heading home after working their shift could stop by and pick up their box and take it home. As they headed to their next shift they dropped their box on the porch of the post office and Cy would retrieve the box and return it to its proper location in order to complete the cycle.

When Jake became of school age Lucy would allow him to go to the post office to retrieve their mail. Jake was a nice kid and had an entrepreneurial spirit so one day he asked Cy if he could be the mailman for Sagamore. "A young boy like yourself as a mailman?" Cy asked. "Now how do you plan on delivering all of these boxes? Sounds like a mighty big task for such a little man like yourself."

Jake replied that his dad had made a flat-bed wagon with rubber wheels and complete with wooden-slat sides on it for hauling wood and trash and that's what he would use as his mail truck.

"And what got you to thinking about this Jake?"

"Well my dad keeps telling me that when I grow up I'm not going to be a miner, so when I grow up maybe I'll be a mailman."

"Hmmmmm. Sounds to me like you're trying to put an old man out of his job. But I've got a ways to go and it would be easier on everyone if they didn't have to come traipsing here after their shift to get the mail. How much do you think you're going to get paid for this job?"

"I don't want any pay, Cy, it just seems to me like it is a good thing to do."

"Working for free doesn't put food on the table, but it is certainly nourishment for the soul. So you have my blessing boy. It will be good to work with a lad like you."

And that began the legend of Jake in the community of Sagamore. He delivered the mail and he took on other jobs as well. He helped Grandpap Frank clean the church and polished the organ every Saturday to get it shining for Sunday Mass. Sometimes during his mail delivery he would come across some women who were old and feeble and had no one to help them. For these women Jake would make runs to the store and during the winter he would shovel their walkways.

As Jake progressed in school he became a very good student and spent time tutoring younger kids in the community who had learning problems. He was very athletic and played all of the major sports. When Jake attended Connellsville Area High School he was the first four-letter athlete in the school's history. Academically, Jake was a national merit scholar. There was no doubt in Johnny's mind that Jake's lot in life would not be to follow his footsteps in the mines at Sagamore. Jake had progressed from a nice little boy to a caring and giving young adult who was gifted academically and athletically. If you asked Lucy to describe her son she wouldn't tell you about his academic achievements or his stellar athletic performances, with great pride she would simply say that Jake was a nice boy who grew into an even nicer young man. A nice guy, what more could you ask someone to become?

PUNXSUTAWNEY, PA

I graduated from Connellsville High School and based on my academic prowess I received a grant-in-aid from the University of Pittsburgh. The amount was minimal. Enough to pay for books and about 25% of the cost of tuition but certainly not enough to cover room and board at the main campus. Therefore I opted to exercise my good fortune at the Punxsutawney Branch Campus of the University which was within commuting distance to Sagamore. Another reason I decided on the Punxsutawney campus was that I had been editor of the high school year book and planned a career in journalism and I received an "honorary offer of internship" from The "Punxsutawney Pilot" newspaper. Basically this offer consisted of a weekend job working at the newspaper. The job didn't pay much but it was newspaper experience and upon graduation that experience might prove to be of some value. Since I had to commute, there was the issue of acquiring an automobile since my parents didn't own a car. Based on my economic scenario there

A Cruel Twist of Fate

were no two ways about it, before going off to college I had to take some time off to work to accumulate enough money to buy a car and get financially solvent.

During the year after my high school graduation I worked at a paper processing mill in Tyrone. I only worked there for three weeks as the continuous smell of the chemicals used in the paper-making process made me sick to my stomach. If you were ever around a paper mill you know what I'm talking about. If not, the only way I could describe the smell would be that it is the strong scent of the combination of boiling cabbage accentuated by a heavy dose of sulfur added to the mix. I have no idea how people can live or work in that area. I guess you get used to it after awhile, but in three weeks I never got used to it.

Luckily I landed a job with the BR & P railroad laying new track to the little burg of Enola. Enola was half the size of Sagamore and located at the base of one of the rolling hills in the Allegheny Mountains. When I asked one of the locals how come the town was named Enola he replied, "Son, we are in the middle of nowhere here. Hopefully this town will grow, but since nothing else is around here the founding fathers named this place Enola because Enola when spelled backwards is A L O N E, and we are all alone out here." I finished out the year with BR & P laying track in a number of places like Enola; Sparkle, Big Run, Anita, Canoe Ridge and Shinglehouse to name a few. By the fall term of the year after my high school graduation I had accumulated enough money to buy a decent second-hand car and fatten up my savings account. My dad's dream was that I would become a college graduate and I was now ready to begin that journey.

****

If you take state road 210 from Sagamore until it intersects with state road 436 and head west you'll arrive in Punxsutawney. The trip is a 23-mile journey, but a short trip can make a big difference. Compared to Sagamore, Punxsutawney is a big city. The population of "Punxy" is 8,000 versus that of 350 in Sagamore. In Sagamore the tallest building was the church if you included the steeple. It you didn't include the steeple then the 1-story post office was the tallest building in town. In "Punxy" they have a skyscraper. It is The Spirit Building which was constructed in 1905. This towering skyscraper is 8 stories in height! Imagine that. The folks at the Spirit Building run tours of the building for the local gentry and passersby. The high point of the tour, no pun intended, is to ascend to the top floor and peer out of one of the large windows at the scenic valley below. It is said that all participants on the tour receive a complimentary tissue in case they experience a nose bleed at such a staggering height. Even though there is much more diversification in commerce and industry in "Punxy" than in Sagamore, the coal mines are still the dominant industry in the area. The mines in the "Punxy" area are noted for being deep and long. You can walk underground to Reynoldsville from "Punxy" and that is a distance of 20 miles!

I got off to a good start, my classes were going OK and the job at "The Pilot" was boring. My job description was assistant to the copy editor in the obituary department. An absolute dead end job; again no pun intended. Since I worked Saturdays and since the biggest advertising day in the newspaper was Sunday, somehow my assistant to the copy editor of the obituary department job was revised to include bundling and stacking the advertising sections that were fed into the main section of the newspaper during the press run.

A Cruel Twist of Fate

This was not a hard job but the press run didn't occur until around mid night on Saturday which meant that I didn't begin my commute home until the wee hours of Sunday morning. Normally this wouldn't be a problem, but the road between Punxy and Sagamore was very dark, mountainous and peppered with hairpin curves and on a snowy night it could take well over an hour to traverse 23 miles and every mile was an adventure. Did I tell you that in the Allegheny Mountains it snowed almost every day during the winter? It could be a trace or it could be a full-blown blizzard, but no matter how you cut it, daily accumulation was a sure bet.

I was explaining one of my treacherous trips home to Eddie Wolfe, one of the guys in my Journalism 101 class, and he said, "Hey Jake, listen, my wife Patti and I are renting a double house on main street. Patti and I live on one side and the other side is occupied by Patti's best friend Aalexis. I'm not sure Patti would take to you bunking over with us on Saturday night, but maybe Aalexis wouldn't mind if you crashed on her couch."

"I don't know Eddie. It sounds awful good to me but this other girl might not like the idea."

"Tell you what, let me ask and if Aalexis is OK with it, then the two of you could meet and talk so that you get to know each other."

The next week after class Eddie tells me that Aalexis is OK with the idea and he invites me to his place for pizza on Friday night. You'd never think that going over to a friend's house for pizza on a Friday night would change your life, but it changed my life in a very big way.

****

Over pizza and beer I discovered that Aalexis Zorbadopolis was of Greek decent and because of the length of her name and because of her Greek decent she became known as Zorba the Greek to her friends and later in life that was reduced to Zorba and a further abbreviation resulted in just plain "Zorb". Zorb was not an attractive woman. Picture the famous painting by Grant Woods called "The American Gothic"…..OK….got that in your mind? Now concentrate on the woman in the picture and think about her when she was 20 years old and you have a good likeness of Zorb. She was pale, thin, wore glasses and basically homely looking. I found out that when Zorb was 15 she had been in a car accident in which her parents died. In the accident Zorb suffered a back injury. Not a major injury but one that left her with a chronic back problem. Zorb was an only child and she only had one living relative, an elderly aunt, who had taken her in after the accident. From a personality standpoint she seemed OK, but how much can you discover about someone's personality in one evening?

Before leaving, Zorb and I discussed the issue of me crashing at her place on the weekend and she seemed to be OK with it. One of my concerns was the fact that if she had a date, me showing up in the middle of the night was certain to create a problem. She snuffed out that concern with the answer, "I don't date." By the looks of her that didn't exactly shock me, but then beauty is in the eyes of the beholder. With that matter settled, I bid Eddie and Patti adieu and Zorb walked with me to the door to show me out. At the door she handed me the key to her apartment and said that I could use the key anytime I wanted. I told her that I didn't want the responsibility of having a key to her place and when I wanted to come in I would just knock. She wouldn't hear of it. "If you are going to stay here then I want you to have a key." I didn't want to argue so I took the key and was on my way.

The first night I stayed at Zorb's I didn't use the key. I knocked on the door and announced, "Zorb, it's me, Jake."

In a minute she answered the door. It was a cold night and I was surprised that she was wearing silk pajama bottoms a fairly sheer top and chiffon robe that was open. I'm thinking that flannel PJs and a cotton robe would have been more appropriate. She asked me if I wanted her to fix me a cup of hot chocolate or did I want something stronger like a beer or a shot of warm Rock and Rye. I refused on all counts and told her that I was tired and just wanted to hit the couch. She seemed disappointed but relented and bid me a good night. As she turned to go to her bedroom she asked me if I would come in and tuck her in the bed and give her a kiss on her forehead before I went to sleep. I didn't know how to respond to this request so I just stood there and said nothing. She broke the silence by telling me that her dad would always tuck her in and give her a kiss on her forehead every night and she missed that and it would really make her feel good if I would do that little favor for her. So I tucked her in, gave her a peck on the forehead and went to the couch for some much needed sleep.

The following Saturday, Mr. Gorman, my supervisor at "The Pilot", called me into his office and told me that his sports reporter was having major surgery and would be out for an indefinite period of time and that he needed someone to cover the Friday night football games in the area and provide writeups for their special Saturday morning High School Football Roundup. He said he noted on my application that I was an all-county football player at Connellsville and therefore I was well qualified for the task at hand. He pointed out that the copy writing required to perform the task wasn't all that demanding and it would be a good experience for me. How could I turn down that offer? The extra money would come in handy and I was thrilled at being given the opportunity to produce copy that would be published. I accepted on the spot.

The only problem now was that I needed a place to crash on Friday night as well as Saturday. I needed to check with Zorb to see if it she would extend her welcome mat for one more night. Not only did Zorb OK my request she also wanted to know if she could come along with me to the games and be my helper. Frankly I didn't know how she could help, but she was letting me stay at her place rent free and what harm could come if she accompanied me to the games? My only reservation was her health. It seemed to me that Zorb was always fighting a cold, or had a sore throat. Her resistance seemed to be very low to anything that was going around and then there was the issue of her back. I mean sitting on bleachers on a cold and/or snowy night certainly wasn't good for anyone's back let alone someone with a chronic back problem. I pointed out all of these drawbacks to her but she was adamant. She wanted to be Jake's little helper.

There were only three school districts in Jefferson County; Punxsutawney, Brockway and Brookville. Getting to all three sites in one evening was a real challenge. Watching all three high school football games in one evening was impossible. Before going out for my first assignment of the season I made a telephone call to each of the school's athletic directors and explained my logistical dilemma. Each AD told me that I could call them after the game and they would provide game highlight information, player's names and key game stats for my sports column. Once I had that avenue of information confirmed, my plan became to attend one game in total each week and rely on the AD's for information regarding the other two. I would rotate to another team each week and in that manner in 3 week's time I would see each team's game in person. The team I saw in person would be my highlight game of the week. It seemed like a good plan to me and my boss gave me a "thumbs' up" so I was all set.

A Cruel Twist of Fate

My first highlight game was an out-of-section game between Brookville and Apollo-Ridge and it was an away game for Brookville. Like most nights it was a cold night and sitting on metal bleachers for a couple of hours on a cold night put a chill up your spine. It really put a chill up Zorb's spine and the whole way back to Punxsutawney she was complaining about her back. She asked me if I would rub her back when we got back to her place. I told her that I needed to get back to the office to complete my game reports and submit them to the night editor but when I was finished and got back to her place, I would be happy to rub her back. And thus began the ritual that followed every game. We'd sit on the couch, she'd lie across my legs, and I would throw a blanket over her and give her a back rub. She liked it best when I massaged under her sweat shirt over her bare back. While performing the massage I'd crack a beer and watch TV.

To me, giving her a back rub was like petting a cat or scratching a dog behind its ears. I attached no special meaning to it, but for Zorb it had a much different meaning. I didn't know how much until several weeks later.

****

The sports reporter at "The Pilot" who I was subbing for was having one health problem after another and he wasn't ready to return after the end of football season. I had been getting a lot of kudos from Mr. Gorman regarding my football writeups and with basketball season already underway he asked if I could handle the high school basketball scene until the full-timer was healthy enough to return. It meant a few more bucks in my pocket, provided additional work experience and the time spent wouldn't adversely affect my prep time for my classes so I accepted. The only problem was since basketball games were played

Tuesday and Friday nights that meant facing a hairy late-night commute back to Sagamore after completing my game write ups for the Tuesday night games which meant that I needed to ask Zorb to grant me yet another night of staying over. I did ask her and she was thrilled to have me stay the extra night. She was also excited about the prospect of continuing her role in being Jake's little helper and attending the games with me. I guess I could have just told her NO I want to go to the games alone, but how could I?

It was a very cold and snowy Friday night and I had just returned to Zorb's place from submitting my copy to the night editor. Attending basketball games in a warm gymnasium was infinitely better than sitting on a metal bleacher braving the wind and the cold, but Zorb still complained about having a sore back from sitting so long. I grabbed a six pack of cold brew, turned on the TV and sat down on the couch and Zorb assumed her normal position of lying across my lap. That night she was wearing a short-sleeved flannel night top and matching flannel PJ bottoms. I used my left hand to use the TV remote and drink my beer and my right hand to rub her back. My hand slid under her top and I began to rub. When I got to her upper back I noticed she wasn't wearing a bra. I continued to massage. When my hand got to her lower back near the elastic on her PJ bottoms, Zorb clipped her right thumb around the elastic band in the material and pulled down on it clearing the way for me to continue my massage over the smooth contour of the right cheek of her buttocks. I wasn't sure what to do at that point in time. Her movement constituted a blatant invitation for me to explore her body. I had no romantic designs whatsoever on Zorb, but I was human, I had normal desires like any other college kid and I had drank a few beers, not anywhere near enough to have my judgment impaired, but enough to be relaxed.

I took her up on the invitation to see where it might lead. Where it led was the removal of her bottoms and an exploration of her entire backside. And when she turned over I touched her most private parts. I penetrated her with my finger, I removed her top and caressed her breasts and rubbed my fingertips around her hardened nipples. Zorb groaned in ecstasy while I disrobed. Very quickly I was on top of her. She spread her legs and beckoned me to enter her. She put her hands on my buttocks and pulled me to her; into her.

Afterwards as we lay there on the couch in an embrace I wondered what in the hell had just happened. I mean I knew WHAT had happened but WHY was the bigger question. During our moments of intimacy Zorb had whispered over and over again, "Jake, I love you." Meanwhile I had said nothing in return. I didn't love Zorb. I didn't even find her attractive. She wasn't ugly, but on my part there was absolutely NO romantic chemistry in my system regarding Zorb. She was a nice girl, a good friend and someone who kindly provided a place for me to crash a couple of nights a week. That was the extent of our relationship as far as I was concerned. But I had just made love with her. Whoops scratch that; had sex with her. What to do now? While I was absorbed in these thoughts, Zorb looked up at me and said, "Jake, when I told you I loved you, you didn't tell me that you loved me. Don't you love me, too?" I didn't want to hurt her, but I couldn't lie to her either just to make her feel good. And what would happen if I told her I loved her? Where would that lead? How long could I live that lie? I guess I could for awhile for the sake of convenience, but sooner than later I'd have to fess up and tell her the truth. I had to be straight with her now and not later.

"Zorb, I didn't tell you that I loved you because I don't. I can't say I'm sorry for what just happened because what happened was very special to me. Zorb, I've never been intimate with anybody else except you, and that's the God's honest truth, but that still doesn't mean I love you. To me, saying I love you to someone means the same thing as saying I'm fully committed to you in my heart, my mind and my spirit. I'm not ready to commit myself to anyone at this point in my life. I don't have an education. I don't have a job. I'm just someone who is wandering down a path in life hoping to secure a brighter future. What just happened between us felt very natural for me, but it wasn't love. I'm sorry. Do you want me to leave?"

"No, don't leave. I think I'll go to bed now. Maybe we'll talk more tomorrow."

With that statement she got dressed and walked into her bedroom. I got dressed, cracked open another beer and was sitting on the couch thinking about what just happened and what was said when I heard Zorb call out, "Jake, you forgot to tuck me in and give me a kiss goodnight on my forehead." Reluctantly I went to her bed room half expecting her to be spread eagled on the bed nude hoping to entice me into another episode, but she was in bed with the covers pulled up looking like a little girl lost. I tucked her in and gave her a peck on her forehead and said goodnight.

****

Tomorrow came and there was very little conversation between us. I didn't know what to say other than what I had said and I guess she felt the same way. I finally broke the ice by saying, "Look Zorb, I understand if you don't want me to bunk over anymore and maybe that would be a good thing because what happened last night could happen again and that would be playing with fire and would just lead to more hurt feelings and place us into a situation that neither one of us is prepared to handle at this point in our lives. Please understand that I like you Zorb and I don't want to hurt you. It's just that I don't love you."

After a sigh or two she replied, "I understand, but I don't want you to leave. I lost my mom and my dad. I don't have any brothers or sisters. I only have my aunt and she is sickly. I feel lonely and it would be good for me to have you around a couple of times during the week."

"Alright, I'll stay but no more back rubs. OK?"

"Alright, but will you still tuck me at night?"

"Ok, deal."

On the days and weeks that followed everything was good between us. We held to the no-back rub rule and I continued to tuck her in and give her a peck on her forehead each night. One night after tucking her in I turned to leave I thought I heard her say, "Goodnight daddy." Did I really hear that? Maybe she was dreaming?

Zorb continued to be sick all of the time. Any sniffle or cold she contracted seemed to linger. Most people got a cold and were able to shake it in a week or so, but not Zorb. I worried about her because I didn't like seeing her being uncomfortable but there wasn't much I could do.

School was going well. I made the dean's list and my mom and dad were really proud of me. My dad was especially happy because he understood how a college education was going to totally eliminate the possibility of me spending my life underground mining coal. At "The Pilot" I continued to receive good comments from Mr. Gorman. In fact, one day he hinted that upon my graduation he might be able to find a full-time spot for me on his payroll. Life just seemed like it couldn't get any better but that all changed the day Zorb returned from seeing her doctor.

During all of her various and sundry ailments Zorb never went to see a doctor. She experimented with over-the-counter remedies or sometimes she would ask the pharmacist for a suggestion. In recent weeks, in addition to her cold symptoms, she began to experience stomach problems as well so I encouraged her to go and see a doctor. She wouldn't consent to go. I told her if she didn't go I wasn't going to tuck her in a night anymore. So she went. The Saturday night following her visit to the doctor we were sharing a late-night pizza and she said, "Jake, I have something to tell you."

"What's that Zorb?"

She hesitated and with her eyes focused on the floor she said, "I'm going to have a baby."

I couldn't believe what I had just heard. "A baby? Whose baby?" I knew the answer before I even asked the question.

She replied, "Our baby."

Holy shit. I was stunned even though I shouldn't have been. My mind was swirling with questions to which I had no answers. I was angry with myself. I was depressed. I was bewildered. What could I do? What could we do? What about the baby? What about my life? What about her life? What about my dreams? What about my dad's dream for me? What in the hell were we going to do? In the midst of my reflections Zorb blurted out, "I could have an abortion."

"Abortion? Is that what you want?"

"No, but you don't love me so why have the baby?"

"Zorb, we are not talking about love, we are talking about a life? We are talking about responsibility."

"You mean you want me to have the baby?"

"I don't know exactly what I want right now because I have to think about it, but what I do know is that I do not want you to have an abortion just because I don't love you."

"So what do we do?"

"How far along are you?"

"Five weeks."

"And what does the doctor say about your health?"

"He thinks I'm OK. He feels that I'm just one of those people who has a weak immune system. He thinks I'm slightly anemic, but if I'm real careful and take supplements I should be OK and have a healthy pregnancy."

"Let me think about this Zorb and we'll talk more in a couple of days."

"Jake."

"What?"

"Can you hold me and give me a hug?"

So I gave her a hug and we sat there looking at the TV screen but not seeing anything.

****

On my trip back to Sagamore on Sunday I kept thinking about how I was going to break this news to my parents. If Zorb had an abortion this situation could be swept under the rug and no one except Zorb and I would be the wiser. But I didn't think that was the right way to handle this situation and that meant Zorb having the baby and that meant an incredible change is our lives and a change that would affect my parent's lives as well. So this matter had to be discussed with them.

We had any early dinner on Sunday because dad was working the midnight shift and he wanted to get some sleep before heading to the mine. At the end of dinner I told mom and dad that I needed to talk to them about something so we sat down and I began to tell them my story. After my story my parents sat in silence. They had the look of concern on their faces; not the look of anger. They didn't jump on me with criticism or blurt out questions like, "What were you thinking?" or "How could you make such a mistake?" They just sat there. Finally dad broke the silence.

"Jake, this is a lot to think about in a few minutes. But, before I give you my thoughts, what's your thinking about how to handle this situation. Let me hear your solution."

"Well, first of all I don't think that abortion is the solution. To me that would be like compounding our mistake. It would be the easy way out and I think Zorb would do it, but I don't think it's the right thing to do. So that brings us to what do Zorb and I do about raising the child. Do we raise the child separately or together? I don't think it would be fair to the child to have separate parents. I know in this day and age with divorce being so commonplace that separated families is a common occurrence, but that doesn't mean it is right or make it the right thing for Zorb and I to do. I think Zorb and I need to get married and once the child is born then I'll quit school and get a job. Maybe you can talk to Mr. Wiggins and see if there is a place for me working in the mines. I know you don't want me to be a mine worker but I really have no skill to offer a prospective employer."

"I think Mr. Gorman would find some low-level job for me at "The Pilot" but the pay wouldn't be enough to support a family. With no formal education and with no unique skill I'll have to turn to a labor job and I might as well labor in a coal mine as labor anywhere else."

After a minute of reflection on my dad's part, he looked at me and said, "First thing is that the three of us can't decide on the solution because the most important person involved in this solution is not here. Second thing is that you are NOT coming back here to work in the mines. If the two of you decide to get married, you and your wife can come back here to live and we'll take care of the baby while the two of you continue your education. Once you have your education then you'll have to find a job and a place of your own to live. Even if the two of you decide not to get married we'll take care of the child so that both of you are free to continue with your education. Come hell or high water Jake, you ARE going to get your degree. Do you understand me?"

"Yes pop."

"Now, you say that you will marry this girl but you also say that you don't love her. What kind of marriage is that going to be?"

"I don't know, pop, but it's the right thing to do. Maybe the child will create enough of a bond between us that it will override the absence of love. Maybe over time I'll grow to love her in some way so that it will work out. But I can't abandon her. She is all alone in this world. She has no one but an elderly aunt who is sickly and the fact of the matter is that she does love me."

"Not that I am in favor of such an arrangement, but why couldn't you just live together without getting married?"

"I guess we could, but to me that would be like living in a house divided. There would be no commitment in that kind of life. No, if we are going to live together and raise the child then we need to do it the right way. The three of us need to be one, not two and one."

The next day after the end of classes I stopped over to see Zorb and discuss our dilemma. I reviewed the conversation I had with my parents and the offer they made about helping to take care of the baby so that we could continue with our education. Zorb listened very carefully to every word I spoke and was visibly touched by the generosity of my parent's offer. When I was through she looked at me and said, "So you want to marry me and stay with me?"

"Zorb, I think it is the right thing to do so yes, I want to marry you and stay with you."

"Jake, does that mean you can give me a back rub again?"

"Back rubs are part of the deal Zorb."

It was February and the baby was not due until September so we decided to wait until the end of classes in May and have a June wedding. Since Zorb had no living relatives except her aunt, we thought it would be best to have the wedding in Sagamore. My folks were OK with that and it would be a great setting since Sagamore was a very close knit community and the people living there were all basically extended family members. It would give Zorb the opportunity to meet everybody and get to know the community where our child would be spending some of his/her formal years. In addition, we would be living there as well so it would be a nice way to transition into our new life together.

Over the next couple of months Zorb got to know my parents and they seemed to like her. Mom was all excited about the prospect of having a little one to take care of and dad had already begun to make plans to build a crib and a new rocker. There wouldn't be a separate nursery because there were only two bedrooms in the house but that didn't stop mom and Zorb in their plans to turn our bedroom into a baby's room. As long as I didn't have to sleep in a crib it was fine with me.

Zorb continued to be somewhat sickly even after getting over the morning sickness phase of her pregnancy. Not exactly sickly but just not healthy. She wasn't putting on the weight that you would expect with a pregnancy. She was frail to begin with so you would think that any weight she put on would be very noticeable. But after four months Zorb had only gained about six pounds and she didn't have that "glow" that is normally associated with a woman expecting a child.

In early May, Zorb's OBGYN, Dr. Conway, was a bit concerned about Zorb's inability to gain weight and her general state of health. In her May exam Dr. Conway noticed that the baby's heart beat was "irregular" and growth was "abnormal." He didn't think his exam results were enough to generate a panic but certainly enough concern was created to justify drawing blood and conducting a battery of tests. The blood was drawn and the samples were sent to the lab at the University of Pittsburgh Medical Center. Two days after Mother's Day the results were faxed back to Dr. Conway's office. Dr. Conway reviewed the results and called the lab in Pittsburgh to confirm their findings. The attendant at the lab reviewed the results with Dr. Conway and explained that after receiving certain types of results from their lab work their policy dictates that blood or tissue samples be sent on to the Cleveland Clinic for an independent test battery. The attendant reported that both testing procedures produced the same results. The results faxed to Dr. Conway were certain; there could be no mistake in the test results. Dr. Conway thanked the attendant for his time and explanation.

After hanging up the phone Dr. Conway dialed the Stalk residence.

"Hello Jake?"

"Hi Dr. Conway, need to speak to Zorb?"

"Jake I need to speak to both of you. Could you come into my office at your earliest convenience, I need to go over Zorb's recent test results with you."

"Any problem Dr. Conway?"

"I make it my policy not to review test results with any of my patients over the phone so I'd appreciate it if the two of you could come over today."

"No problem. How does four o'clock sound?"

The trip over to Dr. Conway's office was very quick, but the return trip back was the longest ride I ever spent in my life.

****

As the three of us sat down in Dr. Conway's office it was apparent by the look on his face and his quiet demeanor that something was radically wrong.

Dr. Conway began, "There is no way to put a positive spin on what I am about to tell you so I'm going to give it to you straight. The results from your blood test, Zorb, indicate a very rare condition. So rare that I had the lab at the University of Pittsburgh Medical Center run the tests again. The second run of test results didn't change. So I had the UPMC send your blood samples to the Cleveland Clinic to run independent tests as a check and their results only served to confirm the original test results. I'm sorry to tell you this, but you have a condition called T-Cell Prolymphocytic Leukemia. This form of leukemia is the most aggressive form of leukemia known to the medical world. In your case the disease is very pronounced and the test results indicate leukemic cells are present in the peripheral blood in your lymph nodes and your bone marrow. This type of leukemia does not respond to chemotherapeutic drugs. There is an experimental drug named Alemtuzmab which aggressively attacks the white blood cells. But even in cases of those who used this experimental drug the median survival rate was only 6 months. Bottom line is that your condition is so advanced that it precludes using Alemtuzmab. I'm so sorry to tell you that your condition is not treatable."

After a long silence I asked Dr. Conway, "Are you sure of these results? There is no other test to run? There can't be a mistake here?"

"Jake, the results of the tests are conclusive and irrefutable."

"So how long are we talking before..."

"My guess would be maximum 2 months, maybe a little more, maybe a little less."

"And what about the baby?"

"Mother and baby will not survive."

With the finality of those words Zorb began to weep uncontrollably. I was trying to be stoic but once she broke down I just fell to pieces as well. Dr. Conway sat there staring at the floor and I saw a big tear drop splash off of the top of his shoe.

After a few minutes Dr. Conway expressed his sorrow once more and excused himself so that we could be alone together. There was nothing either one of us could say. We just held on to each other and the tears flowed until our tear ducts ran dry.

When I told mom and dad the news when we got back home it set off an episode of group crying. I'd never seen my dad cry in my life until that moment. He tried to be strong but his lips were quivering and I could see a line of teardrops slowly accumulating at the bridge of his nose and falling gently to the floor.

Shortly after the diagnosis, Zorb seemed to go into a tailspin. In less than a month she was so weak that she became bed ridden. We did the best to keep her comfortable and nourished. Dr. Conway said that there wouldn't be pain associated with her condition; just a constant decline until her system was overwhelmed and could not fight the fight any longer.

Every night I held her hand, tucked in her covers and gave her a peck on her forehead. Each time she would look into my eyes and smile and gently squeeze my hand.

One evening while feeding Zorb I said, "Zorb, I have an important question to ask you. You don't have to give me your answer right now if you don't want to."

"OK. What do you want to ask me?"

"Will you marry me?"

"Jake, I'm dying. You don't have to marry me because you feel sorry for me."

"I'm not asking you because I feel sorry for you. I'm asking because I love you. Before you leave this earth I want us to be a family."

"Jake I don't know what to say."

"Say what's in your heart."

"If I say yes does that mean you'll tuck me in every night and give me a kiss?"

"You bet."

"If I say yes does that mean you'll never leave me?"

"Never."

"Then you leave me no choice. I accept. Yes, I will marry you."

When I told my folks they were a bit surprised. I thought I'd get a lot of questions and reasons why it was a bad idea but I only got one question…..Why?

I told them that I couldn't let her leave this world not knowing that someone wanted and loved her. I couldn't let her leave this world alone. She had to leave this world knowing that the child inside her had a dad; not somebody who created him/her by mistake. If there was ever a time in her life that she needed someone by her side it was now and that person was going to be me.

"Jake," my father said, "you mentioned the word love. I thought you said you didn't love her?"

"Through Zorb I have discovered that you can grow to love someone even though it may not be the kind of love that is generated by physical attraction and sets off all of the bells and whistles associated with that kind of chemistry. I feel connected to Zorb and that might not be the textbook definition of love but it is enough for me."

Plans were made to have the wedding in our house. We would wheel Zorb's bed into the middle of the living room for the occasion. The kitchen table would be moved into the living room as a makeshift altar and everyone in Sagamore would be invited just like any normal wedding. I called

A Cruel Twist of Fate

Grand Pap Bahleda and asked him if he could open all of the doors and windows of the church and play the organ for the ceremony. It wouldn't be like sitting in church but the sound would travel well in the valley and would help to provide a church like atmosphere for our union. Mom and dad would get the word out to the community and there would be no shortage of food as everyone would be bringing their own special dish to the house.

Mom went over all of the details with Zorb and she asked her if she would wear her wedding dress. "This was my mom's dress and it's been a lucky dress. Both of us ended up with a good man and I think you are getting a good man in my Jake as well." Zorb was overwhelmed with the gesture and the both of them hugged each other.

The date was set two weeks hence. During that time Zorb's condition seemed to worsen and I began to think that we waited too long. But the big day came and all seemed well. Father Mike showed up early to get the altar prepared. Mom helped Zorb get dressed and when finished we wheeled her into the living room. Dad and I moved the furniture to the ends of the house as best we could so that there would be room for people to attend. We opened all of the windows in the house so that folks who couldn't stand inside could stand by the windows and look in. People in the community set up the tents and the tables in our front yard and the food started rolling in. Grand Pap Bahleda went down to the church and made his preparations there. He turned up the organ to its highest level and played a piece as a test to see if we could hear it at the house. It worked! Everything was a go.

When Father Mike indicated that he was ready to begin the ceremony someone outside whistled loudly. That was Grand Pap Bahleda's signal to begin playing Richard Wagner's "Bridal Chorus" from Lohengrin, the traditional "Here Comes The Bride" wedding song. As the music gently graced our ears we gathered around the bed and Father began the ceremony. As I looked at Zorb she seemed to be energized by the events of the day. She had a little color in her cheeks and a twinkle in her eyes which I hadn't seen in a number of weeks. At the end of the ceremony after we had exchanged our vows, Father Mike asked that all of the blinds be drawn in the house to darken the room. He then pulled out Big John's miner's cap, switched on the light and placed it on his head just as he had done at my mom and dad's ceremony.

"He is the way, the truth and the light and may the light from this miner's cap serve to remind us that whatever path we travel in life it is HE who shines the light on our road providing guidance and comfort during our journey. Aalexis, we know that your journey in this life will be a short one and that Jake will be holding your hand along the way. But take faith in the knowledge that HIS hand will be there as well and HIS hand will be entwined with yours and your child's for all eternity. May God bless and keep both of you and may your both find everlasting happiness in this life and the next."

The celebration began and we were overwhelmed with good wishes from all in our Sagamore family. Zorb began to tire early into the evening so we moved her bed back to our bedroom.

By 9:00 P.M. all well wishers had vacated the premises except for a few good souls who where helping my mom and dad to clean up. Zorb was fast asleep and I was sitting next to her holding her hand. I'm not sure when, but I dozed off and awoke about mid night. The house was very quiet but I could hear the sounds of my dad snoring through his bedroom door. I wondered how my mom managed to get any sleep at all through all of that noise.

All of a sudden Zorb's eyes opened and she smiled at me.

A Cruel Twist of Fate

"Hi Mrs. Stalk, do you want anything?"

"A little bit of water Mr. Stalk. Jake I'm really tired."

"Well, you're in the right place to be tired. Go back to sleep if you feel that tired."

"Not yet. I need to tell you how wonderful today was. I can't believe the people in this town and how great your mom and dad are. I've never felt so loved in my whole life."

"Don't you know; you ARE loved?"

"I do now and I never thought I'd feel that way after losing my mom and dad. You are the best thing that ever happened to me, Jake. Wow, I really am feeling very tired."

"Ok, let me tuck you in real good so you can go back to sleep. I'm not going anywhere. I'm staying right here beside you. You know I'll always be here for you."

"I know that Jake."

I tucked her in and gave her a kiss on her forehead just like I had done so many other nights. She smiled and a very peaceful look came over her face. Just before she drifted off to sleep she squeezed my hand. As she drifted off to sleep I heard her whisper, "Good night daddy."

That was the last time I ever tucked Zorb into bed.

The condition Zorb had was so rare that UPMC, through Dr. Conway, asked if an autopsy could be conducted for research purposes. Although I didn't need to, out of respect I called Zorb's aunt to get her permission. Together we agreed that maybe the autopsy findings might help others afflicted with this condition. After the autopsy was conducted, Dr. Conway called me and told me that it was determined that the child Zorb was bearing was a girl.

We had a quiet ceremony for Zorb at our house and then had her body transported to Coudersport which is where her aunt lived and where her folks were buried. Zorb was buried next to her dad. The headstone was inscribed to read Aalexis Zorbadopolis Stalk and daughter.

****

I didn't know it until Zorb passed but her parents had taken out a life insurance policy on her for $5,000 and made Zorb's Aunt Elsie the beneficiary. At the funeral Aunt Elsie told me about the policy and that she wanted to give me the proceeds to help finance my education. How nice was that?

I had decided not to go back to Punxsutawney as there were too many memories there and the money from the insurance policy enabled me to consider continuing my education at the main campus of the University in Pittsburgh. I had the Punxsutawney Campus send a copy of my transcript to the Dean of Admissions at Pitt for review. Several weeks later I received a letter from Dean Mack and he told me that my GPA combined with economic status would qualify me for several scholarships and grants-in-aid that would cover most of my tuition costs and the cost of my books. He set up a time to-meet with him to take care of all of the necessary paperwork to complete my transfer from the Punxy campus to the main campus. The anticipated scholarship money added to the insurance money was more than adequate for me to make the transfer to the main campus. I would still have to get some kind of a part time job to keep my funds from dwindling but I would worry about that when I got to Pittsburgh.

PITTSBURGH

The dorms opened up about 10 days before the start of the semester for early arrivals and for freshman orientation. I wasn't a freshman but since I was new to the campus I had to go through that process. It wasn't a problem because the orientation sessions didn't take all day and that left me time to look for a part time job. I tried the Pittsburgh Press but they weren't hiring part-time staffers. Most of the service jobs were for waiters or bartenders with experience and the bus boy and dishwasher jobs paid next to nothing. I had a valid driver's license so I took a chance and tried the Yellow Cab Company and hit pay dirt.

The pay wasn't great but the hours were very flexible so I filled out the application and was told that before I began I had to attend a couple of orientation sessions in order to understand how they operated; clocking in and out, safety regulations, how to effectively interact with the dispatcher, etc. No problem there.

I was informed that part timers were assigned to the "old" cabs. Apparently they were outfitting all of their cabs with new bullet-proof Plexiglas safety-shield dividers to keep their full-time drivers out of harm's way. The old vehicles that were assigned to the part time drivers had no safety shields. As I was leaving the office the guy who handled my paperwork yelled, "Welcome. You are now officially a Yellow Duck."

"I get the yellow part because of the Yellow cab, but why the Duck?" I asked.

"Because pal, you are a sitting duck out there in case there is ever any problem."

I responded with a "quack, quack" and left the office. We both laughed as I closed the door. Little did I know at that point in time that what he had said to me was no laughing matter.

The city of Pittsburgh is no picnic when it comes to driving a cab. The place is full of hills and valleys and there is no rhyme or reason to the road patterns. Throw in 446 bridges and numerous tunnels and you have the recipe for disaster for a newcomer to the city trying to drive a cab. The runs from the hotels in the downtown area to the airport were pretty much straight shots and it was a fairly easy route to remember after a couple of trips but all other trips were challenging to say the least. I was constantly on the horn with the dispatcher for directions and even though I had road maps they didn't seem to provide immediate help. In fact, the dispatcher got so fed up with my requests for directional assistance he told me if I continued to bug him he was going to have to write me up on his weekly report. He didn't understand that I came from a town that had one main street, one stop sign and no traffic signals. But, I took the job and he was right, it was my responsibility and not his to find out how to get from point A to point B.

It was a clear, warm and sunny Saturday afternoon. It was the cusp of summer and fall and probably the nicest weather time of the year in the Pittsburgh area. It was great weather to be driving a cab because you could drive with your windows down, didn't have to be concerned about snow and ice and because it was Saturday, the major arteries were not clogged with traffic. I had just pulled out of the McDonalds, turned off the light to indicate that I was out of service and was looking for a place to pull over and eat my lunch when I received to a call to pick up a passenger at Mercy Hospital. I told dispatch that I was ready for lunch but I would be happy to make this pickup, but after this pickup I would be off for an hour. It didn't take me that long to eat lunch but I used my lunch hour for study time as well as grabbing a bite to eat.

As I entered the driveway in front of Mercy Hospital I saw a young lady dressed in a green hospital smock standing off to the side of the hospital by the curb smoking a cigarette. I couldn't tell if she was just taking a smoke break or waiting for cab, but as I got closer I saw her flick her cigarette to the ground, stomp on the butt and begin to walk toward the driveway. I pulled up and said, "Miss, did you call a cab?" She nodded in the affirmative and got into the back seat. "Where to?"

"Point Breeze," she replied. So we were off and just before I pulled out onto the boulevard I looked in the rearview mirror and saw that she had her eyes closed. I'm figuring that she must have had a long shift at the hospital and was really tired so I did not attempt to strike up a conversation. In about 5 minutes we were closing in on her destination and as the cab began to slow down I heard her say with a bit of panic in her voice, "Where are you taking me? This is not Point Breeze."

"I'm sorry; I thought you said, "The Point".
"No, Point BREEZE!"

Now I had a problem because I had never had a run to Point Breeze. I lived in Oakland at the University and I thought Point Breeze was somewhere that way but I really had no clue as to exactly where to go. I told her that I was a college student and new to the city and was having trouble finding my way around and that I didn't know the route to Point Breeze. I told her that I could call the dispatcher for help but that I was on his "list" and if I bugged him for directions he might get me fired.

"I know this is an imposition and I apologize, but do you think you could help me to get to your destination?"

"No problem, I can give you directions as you drive."

"I appreciate that, but can I ask you a big favor?"

"What's that?"

"Well, if I drive while you are giving me directions we'll get to your destination but it doesn't help me get a feel for exactly where I am going in relation to this area. I have a map of the streets and roads in the city and county on the front seat. If you could show me the route on the map, it would really help me to get a better sense of direction so that the next time I get a call to go that way I'll have a mental map of where to go."

"OK. Let me see the map."

She reached over the seat to get the map and spotted my bag from McDonalds. When she went to grab the map she bumped the bag and it opened a bit and the smell of the burger and onions escaped into the air in the cab.

"Were you just planning to eat lunch?"

"Yes. In fact I was planning to go to lunch when I got the call to pick you up. After this trip I'm on lunch for an hour."

"God that burger smells sooooooooo good. I've just come off of a 16-hour shift and I really need something to eat. Tell you what; I'll make you a deal. Let's drive to McDonalds and get me a burger, some fries and a cup of coffee and then drive to Point Breeze, find a place to stop and eat and while we are eating I'll go over the map with you. What do you say?"

"Sounds like a plan to me. But only on one condition."

"What's that?"

"I buy your lunch for you?"

"Deal."

We got her lunch and headed to Point Breeze. She rattled off the streets as we headed that way and told me that she would retrace our path on the map once we stopped to eat. On our journey we introduced ourselves to each other. I found out that her name was Jill Bodino, that she was an LPN and that she had just received her 2-year nursing degree from Mercy Hospital School of Nursing this past summer. She told me that she was in the throes of an ugly separation from her husband and was planning to get a divorce once she had enough money saved to secure legal representation. She told me that her husband was a bad hombre and that she had to resort to securing a restraining order after their separation since he kept stalking her and wouldn't leave her alone. She told me that he had been "physical" during their short marriage. I felt very sorry for her. I couldn't understand how a man could hit a woman and especially a woman who was as attractive as Jill. I told her my story about Zorb and she got very silent and somber. I hadn't told the story of Zorb to anyone else and telling it for the first time to a stranger I found myself getting a bit emotional. It was kind of amazing that an hour beforehand I never met this person and in such a short interval of time we both seemed to be very at ease with each other's company; so at ease that we could speak of very personal matters without the slightest bit of hesitation.

Like a quilt, the city of Pittsburgh has a number of neighborhoods woven into its fabric and Point Breeze is one of those neighborhoods. The area is in a very nice setting; quiet tree-lined streets and a mixture of homes from the rich to the lower middle class. The area was complete with its own public and private elementary schools as well as a baseball field and a basketball court. It was boarded by a cemetery and one of Pittsburgh's largest public parks, Frick Park, and there were a number of dead end streets which provided safe havens for young children to play. Jill told me that if you would have sat down at one of the streets in the neighborhood and fell asleep 50 years ago and awakened today that you will be hard pressed to know that time had passed. In a way Point Breeze reminded me of a residential Sagamore.

We came to a stop sign at the intersection of Willard Street and Lang Avenue and Jill pointed out to me that she lived in a 3rd floor apartment in the big red-brick house on the corner. She told me to keep going and after a few quick turns we pulled over to the curb on a tree-lined residential street a block up from the entrance to the park. I was so intent on following streets, listening to Jill and observing the neighborhood that I didn't notice the black Cadillac Escalade that slowly passed by us, almost stopping next to us, continue to the end of the street, turn around, slowly go past us again, turn around and slither up to the curb about 5 car lengths behind us.

After we pulled up to the curb Jill got out and got into the front seat next to me. The windows were down, the warm fall air was infiltrating the car and there was enough of a cross breeze to make it very comfortable. We both opened our bags and began to munch on our burgers. About three bites into my burger I felt something cool and hard against my left temple. Whatever it was, it was being held there with enough force behind it that I couldn't turn my head to see what it was. The cool sensation was followed by the sound of a voice that said,

"Don't move a muscle or I'll blow your fucking brains away." I was paralyzed with fear.

Jill turned her head in my direction and as she started to let out a scream, a hand wearing a black leather glove smothered her mouth and nose effectively converting her scream into an indistinguishable muffle.

"Ok you two love birds, we are going to get into the back seat and while we do that keep looking straight ahead and don't make a sound or the next sound you hear will be a bullet whizzing through your skull."

After the two men got in the back seat the lead guy says,

"Hi boys and girls we are Tom and Jerry. You know, just like the cartoon cats, but this is real life and no cartoon. Hey Tom, looks like we caught us two mice at play."

"Yeah, Jerry; just like Minnie and Mickey. Hey Jerry did you know on what grounds Mickey tried to divorce Minnie?"

"I heard it before, Tom, but tell it again for the benefit of our audience."

"Mickey told the judge his grounds for divorce was that Minnie was crazy."

"So the judge says to Mickey, 'You mean to tell me that your only reason for wanting to divorce Minnie is because she is crazy?'"

"And Mickey says, 'Not just crazy, judge. I mean she is fucking Goofy.'"

"Get it; fucking Goofy."

Tom laughs and says, "It's funnier every time I hear it Jerry, but our audience didn't laugh."

"Jerry, maybe Jill is trying to fuck Mr. Goofy here? Hey Mr. Goofy, what's your name?"

I reply, "Jake."

"Jake. Hmmm. That rhymes with mistake and it looks like you made a BIG mistake today. Jake's mistake. I like it Jerry."

Jerry says, "Jill, you've been a bad girl just like Dominic said you'd be. Dominic told us to keep an eye on you to see if you were cheating on him and guess what; it looks like Dominic was right."

"I'm not cheating on him. How could I be cheating on him when we aren't even married anymore?"

"Is that so? When did the divorce become final?"

"Well it's not final, but what is final is that we are not a couple living together and we are never going to be a couple again."

"I'm not a lawyer, but it seems to me that without the paper you ARE still a married woman and married women don't go to have a lunch in the park with another man. In Dominic's book that's cheating. It appears to me like you haven't taken your vows very seriously, Jill. What happened to love, honor and obey?"

"That all changed when Dominic cheated on me and beat me and treated me like a pile of shit."

"Hey Jerry," Tom said. "When you were going over those marriage vows you left out the best part."

"What part was that, Tom?"

"The part that says…. until death do us part…… or in Jill's case, until someone kills you, whichever comes first."

"Tom is right, Jill. Your bad attitude about your marriage could be injurious to your health. And as far as the divorce petition goes, remember that Dominic is a very religious man and that he abides by the premise what God has joined together, let no man put asunder. So in Dominic's eyes, divorce is not a binding option for you."

"So what am I, Dominic's slave forever? Am I his piece of property that is to be used until he decides that I have no more value to him?"

"Hear that Tom? Dominic was right, Jill needs some counseling. And counseling is our forte, right Tom?"

"Hey Jerry I like it when you use the word forte. Do you want me to use the word forte in a sentence?"

"Go ahead Tom."

"Ok. If I crack Jill's skull 39 times and you crack it one time, that means that Jill's skull has been cracked forte times."

"You are such a clever cat, Tom."

"Ok Jill, maybe we are jumping to conclusions here. After all, everyone is innocent until proven guilty. So let's start with Jake's explanation. We'll conduct a little court session right here and evaluate the absence of guilt or innocence. Sound fair to you Tom?"

"All is fair in love and war Jerry. Can I be the lawyer first?"

"OK Tom, call your first witness."

"I call Jake what's his name. Jake, state your full name."

"Jake Stalk."

"Jake Stalk? Are you kidding me? You mean like Jake in the Beanstalk?"

"Jerry, this here is Jake the Giant Killer. I like nursery rhymes. Do you like nursery rhymes Jerry?"

"Some nursery rhymes can have real-life meaning Tom."

"Jerry, I'll bet that the Beanstalk will like this one."

> "Little Jill Bodino sat on her bucket
> eating her burger and fries
> along came Jake in the Beanstalk
> and tried to fuck her between the eyes."

"Is that what was on your mind, Beanstalk; fucking this little girl between the eyes?"

"No! You guys have this all wrong. I didn't even know Jill until an hour ago. I picked her up in my cab. I didn't know how to get to her address so out of the kindness of her heart she told me that she would show me the route on my map so that I could get to know the roads in the city better. I was ready to go to lunch. She was hungry after coming off of a long shift at work. We decided to get a couple of burgers, go over the map and then I'd take her to her destination and that's all there is to it. I don't know this Dominic guy. I've never been to this location in my life. I have no idea what's going on. You guys are making a big mistake."

"You sound like an innocent man Mr. Beanstalk but do you know that every prison in this country is full of innocent men? Jerry do you have any questions for Mr. Beanstalk?"

"I'm getting tired of all of this bullshit, Tom, no more questions. I'm moving right to the closing argument phase. Ladies and gentlemen of the jury we have a man here who is a lost cab driver. Did you ever hear of a cab driver getting lost? Does this lost cab driver call his dispatcher for directions? No. Does he consult his map? No. What he does is to buy lunch for his customer, who happens to be a hot chick, and the two of them drive to a nice secluded spot next to a park for the purpose of map exploration. Happens every day in the life of a cab driver, right? Now this man claims he has never seen this woman in his life before she got into his cab and yet here they an hour later snuggled up in the front seat shooting the shit like old friends. This man had motive and opportunity and a smoking gun between his legs. The gun didn't go off but that was only because he was interrupted by yours truly and my good friend Tom. Give him five more minutes and he would have been exploring but it wouldn't have been any map. And what about a married woman who gets into a cab with someone she's never seen in her life, lets this person buy her lunch and then directs him to a nice spot to share lunch and talk about directions. How can anyone believe this crock of shit they are trying to feed you? My verdict is guilty for Jake and Jill."

Before either Jill or I could respond Tom said, "Jake and Jill? Jerry, that reminds me of another nursery rhyme. Jake and Jill ran up the hill to fetch a pail of water, Jake fell down and broke his crown and Jill came tumbling after."

"Like I said before, Tom, some nursery rhymes come true and I think this one is about to come true for our lying friend Jake right now. Tom, break Jake's fucking crown for him."

****

I awoke with an incredible head ache. My head was lying on the passenger side of the front seat on top of the maps and the maps were covered in blood and sticking to the hair on my head. I couldn't believe the terrible pounding that was going on inside my head and the ringing in my ears. My line of vision was focused on the floor mat and lying on the mat were the bags from McDonalds and there was a bunch of bees buzzing around and crawling in and out of the open bags. All of the sudden I felt nauseous and puked all over the seat and the bags. Some of the bees were drowned in the puke and the rest seemed to have lost their appetite as they flew past my face and out of the window. After that episode I felt a little better but I still didn't seem to have the energy to sit up so I just laid there. As I laid there looking up at the dashboard and the ceiling of the car I noticed evidence of blood splatters. My blood? Jill's blood? Where was Jill? What did those two goons do to her? All of a sudden I got really frightened because I wasn't sure that the goons had left. Were they still in the back seat? I managed to sit up very slowly and once erect I was overcome with a wave of nausea and puked again. It was then that I heard the voice of the dispatcher over the hand-held phone.

"Car 33, Stalk come in. Stalk come in. Stalk where in the fuck are you?"

It took me a minute to get my wits about me and I picked up the receiver and pushed the intercom button.

"Dispatch, this is Stalk."

"Stalk. What in the fuck is going on? Do you know how many times I've tried calling you without a response? Where in the hell are you?"

"I was beaten over the head and have been unconscious. I'm bleeding and I feel really sick."

"Where are you?"

"Point Breeze."

"Where in Point Breeze?"

"I don't know."

"Can you see a street sign anywhere?"

I looked around and saw a sign that said Reynolds/Lexington.

"Reynolds and Lexington."

"Are you alright to drive? Do I need to send anyone to get you? Do I need to notify the police?"

I really didn't want to get the police involved for fear of reprisal against me or Jill. In addition I really never got a good look at the two guy's faces. All I knew was the names Tom and Jerry and this guy Dominic Bodino and Bodino wasn't even there when all of this went down so he had an iron-clad alibi. So what good would it do to get the police involved?

"I really need to get some medical attention. I think I can drive but I'm not sure. Let me drive up a block and see how I feel and I'll get back to you."

I drove one block up Reynolds Street and I felt pretty shitty but I could see OK and drive OK. I still had this gigantic headache and there was a big patch of dried blood on my head about two inches up and behind my right ear.

"Dispatch. I think I can drive, but I really need to get to a hospital. What's the nearest hospital and I'll need directions."

"Stalk; you are in luck. Drive down Lexington. Lexington intersects with Penn. Make a right on Penn and Columbia Hospital is about a half mile down the road on your right."

Call me from the hospital when you get there and tell me what's going on. By the way Stalk, anything happen to the car?

"No damage to the car, just some blood spatters and a big puddle of puke."

"You puked in the car?"

"Sorry."

"Fuck."

"I'm heading to the hospital now. Call you later."

"Stalk; remember, as a part timer you don't have any medical coverage from the company."

"OK."

"Stalk, how big is the puddle of puke?"

"Really big."

"Fuck."

I got to Columbia Hospital and went to the emergency room entrance and checked in. I had student insurance at Pitt and everything regarding paper work was kosher. I was in the hospital for about 4 hours. Bottom line was that I had a large contusion on the back of right side of my head which was complemented by a nice gash that took 12 stitches to close and I was diagnosed with a mild concussion. They didn't want to release me but I told them that I was calling a friend and he was going to drive me home.

"Dispatch. Stalk here." I gave him a rundown of my medical condition.

"Ok. Bring the car back to the garage and then check in with me because you have to fill out a police report for insurance purposes."

"Insurance for what; the car wasn't damaged."

"Insurance to pay for someone to clean up the blood and puke you asshole unless you plan to clean it up yourself."

"I thought the dispatchers handled that job."

"Fuck you Stalk."

I turned in the car and went to the office and filled out the insurance paperwork regarding the incident. Just as I was finishing the paperwork a man in a dark suit approached me and introduced himself as Detective Thompson from the Robbery Detail/Pittsburgh City Police. I was a bit taken aback because I didn't expect the police to get involved. When he asked me what happened I told him that after I dropped off my fare I stopped to eat my lunch and while eating my lunch someone came up from behind me and smashed me over the head and that's all I remembered.

"Hmmmmm. Smashed you over the head but didn't take any of your money?"

"I guess not."

"Strange."

"Did you get a look at the perp?"

"No."

"Do you have any enemies who might want to hurt you?"

"No. I'm a student and new to the area and I hardly have any friends let alone any enemies."

"You haven't pissed anyone off by dating their girl friend or anything like that?"

"Nope. Don't have a girl friend and haven't dated anybody since I arrived on campus."

"Ok, Mr. Stalk. I guess that's it. Doesn't sound like much we can do in a case like this but chalk it up to back luck for you. But watch your ass out there and be careful of whom you are picking up and the neighborhoods you are traveling in and out of."

"Detective, I picked up my fare around noon on a beautiful day and went to a very nice neighborhood."

"Yeah, I know. That's what makes this incident even stranger."

****

For days after the incident I kept thinking about Jill and what happened to her. I understood it was only a chance meeting but a spark occurred for me during the short time we were together and I began to wonder if meeting her in such an odd fashion was a bit of destiny. I know that she was married, albeit very unhappily to a real asshole, and based on that fact alone, good sense should have told me to back off, forget about that day and move on. But I couldn't get her out of my head.

Even if nothing further developed between us romantically, I was still concerned about her welfare and curious as to what happened to her after I got slugged on the head. To that end I felt that I had to follow up in some way, shape or form. I looked up Jill Bodino in the phone book and nothing was listed. I found out that the dispatchers kept call logs so I went to the dispatcher to see if I could find out Jill's number.

"Well, if it ain't King Puke himself. If you are looking for a barf bag I don't have any. By the way, Stalk, how's the head?"

"Head's OK. Thanks for asking."

"So, what????"

"What do you mean so what?"

"So what; like in the phrase so what in the fuck are you doing in my office when you are supposed to be out driving a cab?"

"Don't you keep call logs?"

"Yeah. So what?"

"What do you mean so what?"

"Stalk. I don't have time to fuck around. Why are you here and what do you want?"

"OK. Remember that day I got mugged?"

"Yeah. So what? And if you say…. what do you mean so what…. I'm going to take this phone to your head and you'll wind up with dueling stitches on your little pin head."

"I need to find out the phone number of the passenger I picked up just before I got mugged."

"I'm not supposed to give out that information, but I'll do it for you if you promise not to puke in my cab again. Jesus, it took that company about 3 hours to clean that car after you turned it in. What was the date, time you received the request and your cab number?"

I give him the information, he pages through the log book and says, "232-8111."

"Great. Thanks."

"Stalk. I don't think that number is going to do you much good?"

"Why?"

"I know that number. That's the number for Mercy Hospital and we get tons of calls from that number. No way you can track a person from that number."

"Shit."

"Shit what?"

"Shit, I think I'm going to be sick again."

"Get the fuck out of my office NOW!"

With that avenue of contact reaching a dead end I was only left with two choices; go to the hospital or go to her apartment. Going to the hospital and asking for her wouldn't work because I didn't know where she worked or what shift and they'd never give out the phone number of an employee to a stranger. That meant going to her apartment but what if Tom and Jerry were lurking around somewhere?

During my travels in the city I decided to make a loop around Mercy Hospital whenever I could in the hope that maybe she would be out taking a smoke break. It was a long shot but I had nothing to lose. After a couple weeks of cruising by the hospital and not seeing her I decided that I only had one option and that was to go to her apartment. But could I take a chance of going there in the cab? What if she was being watched by the goons? Surely a yellow cab stopping near her building would set off all kinds of alarms and whistles as I'm positive they hadn't forgotten about our little incident near the park. The other issue to consider was I "think" they knew what I looked like but I had no idea what they looked like because I hadn't seen their faces. I remember seeing Tom, the guy who clamped his hand over Jill's mouth, for a brief second as he was turning to get into the back seat. But all I could remember was olive complexion, dark hair and slight build. I didn't see Jerry at all, but I knew he was a big guy because when he got into the back seat behind me the whole cab bounced and the balance of the car seemed to shift to my side of the cab.

Since the incident I had gotten to know the city streets better and realized that the Oakland section of the city where the University of Pittsburgh was located was only 5 miles from Point Breeze. I didn't have a car but I did have a bike and a 10-mile round trip on a bike ride was a piece of cake. I decided that I would make the trip on a Sunday afternoon. Sunday was a good choice because traffic would be minimal and maybe Jill wouldn't be working on the weekends. Additionally, the Steelers were playing on Sunday and everyone in Western Pennsylvania was Steeler crazy. Maybe Tom and Jerry would take time out to watch the game and not watch Jill between the hours of 1 and 4 o'clock.

 I left the dorm a little before 1:00 P.M. As a precaution I hadn't shaved in a week in hopes that a 7-day beard would alter my appearance. I wore a baseball cap pulled way down and a windbreaker. Luckily it was a nice, bright, sunny afternoon and that made it possible for me to wear sunglasses and look completely natural. It only took me about 20 minutes before I was closing in on Jill's apartment. As I was coasting down Willard Street about a block before Jill's apartment house I slowed down a bit and surveyed the area looking to see if one or two men were sitting in a car or standing on a corner. The coast looked clear to me. I pulled up in front of the big red-brick building, jumped off of my bike, put down the kick stand and walked up onto the porch. I remember Jill telling me that she lived in the third-floor apartment but there was no marquee with apartment listings. Even though I was standing outside on the porch I could hear that someone inside was watching the Steeler game. I rang the bell and waited a few seconds but no one came to the door.

 Someone had to be there. They must have had the sound up on the TV so loud that they didn't hear the bell. I pushed on the bell again and this time I kept my finger permanently in place so that it produced a constant ringing sound. After about 10 seconds I heard a voice behind the door say, "Alright I'm coming. I'm coming. Hold your horses. I'm coming."

****

 Located about a mile away from Jill's apartment house is the local Point Breeze watering hole; The Evergreen Café. It was Sunday afternoon and the bar was packed with Steeler fans. All eyes were glued on the huge screen that engulfed the entire wall behind the bar. Fritz, the owner of the Evergreen, was a huge Steeler fan himself, but his interest in the game today was business as well as personal. During pro football season 40% of his weekly income was generated on Sundays. Today was just like every other Sunday. The place was packed, everyone was wearing black and gold and waving Terrible Towels and each play of the game was met with wild cheers or groans. He and his two sons, David and Phillip couldn't get the beers out of the taps fast enough. Lena, his wife, was in the kitchen cooking hot wings and personal pan pizzas as fast as she could. It would be another very profitable Sunday for Fritz and the family. God bless those Steelers. All of his customers were locals but in the crowd that day were two guys he hadn't seen before. The one guy was huge. His hands were so big that they totally engulfed a bottle of beer. When he was drinking, it looked like he was sucking on his thumb. Fritz wondered how the little bar stool stood up to the weight of this man of Neanderthal proportions. His buddy had a wiry build and a mean look. He also had a tattoo on his neck that Fritz recognized as a prison tattoo. Fritz didn't want any trouble in his bar so he made sure that he gave these guys good service. He wanted to make sure he kept these hombres happy.

"Tom. How about them Steelers? 14 zip and the first quarter hasn't even ended. Looks like I'm going to have a nice pay day tomorrow after the game. Know what I'm going to do next week, Tom?"

"What's that Jerry?"

"I'm going to write a petition to the Federal Mint."

"Petition the Federal Mint? What for? Shit, I didn't even know you knew how to write?"

"Fuck you, Tom. I'm going to write a petition to the Federal Mint to have the signature on our coins changed."

"Changed to what?"

"Now it says....IN GOD WE TRUST......right?"

"Right."

"Well you can't trust God anymore, Tom. I mean look at all of the starving children in this world. Look at all of the people dying from cancer. Look at all of those crazy fucking terrorists in the world that we have to deal with. Pedophiles, drunk drivers; how can you trust God when he lets all of this shit happen?"

"So what do you want to change it to?"

"I want to change it to someone you CAN trust. Someone whom you can depend on; someone who comes through for you in the clutch; someone you KNOW is going to cover your ass week after week."

"And who's that Jerry?"

"He's right there in living color on the wall. I'm talking about the guy whom you can depend on to get the job done every time he steps on the field; the guy who makes me a C note or two every fucking week. The guy you can always trust. I'm talking about Big Ben Roethlisberger. That's right, every fucking coin should say IN BEN WE TRUST."

"I don't know Jerry, that sounds sacrilegious to me."

"Ah bullshit. How's this for sacrilegious Tom, what's the difference between God and Big Ben?"

"I give up."

"God didn't win two Super Bowls."

With that, the big fella laughed and then sucked down a bottle of Iron City in two quick swigs and slammed the bottle on the bar which was his way of getting Fritz's attention. In a flash Fritz popped the cap on an ice-cold Iron and exchanged the empty bottle with a full one. The big fella grabbed the bottle and gave Fritz a stare.

"What in the fuck is this barkeep?"

"It's an Iron City, mister."

"I know that, but this is a regular beer and I'm drinking IC Lite. Can't you tell I'm on a diet?"

"Sorry mister, I'll change that for you right away."

Fritz grabs an IC Lite and returns and says, "Here you go mister. This one's on the house."

All of a sudden a huge cheer erupted from the patrons. The Terrible Towels started waving and everyone starts banging beer mugs together.

"Look at that Tom, Big Ben just threw **another** TD pass. Twenty-one nothing Steelers and it ain't even halftime yet. Like I said, in Ben we trust. Better believe that shit Tom."

"Jerry, this game is turning into a rout and I'm hungry. Whadda say we blow this joint, make our run for Dominic and hit the Italian American Club for a big bowl of Spaghetti."

"OK and by the time we get to the club it will be halftime and I can get all of the scores and see how much more money I made today."

Jerry throws a $10 bill on the bar, which was more than enough to cover their bill and they turn to leave. Fritz watches them leave and notices that the big fella has to turn a little sideways just to make it out of the door.

Outside, Tom pulls out his cell phone and dials a number. On the third ring a connection is made.

"What's new pussy cat?"

(silence)

"Aw c'mon Jill baby; how about some afternoon delight?"

"Fuck you."

"Now see that's what Dominic means when he says that you have an attitude. That attitude is what turns Mr. Hand into Mr. Fist if you know what I mean?"

"What do you want?"

"Nothing darling. Me and Jerry were in the neighborhood and Dominic wants us to make sure that when the cat's away the mouse doesn't play; especially when it's your day off. No telling how much trouble you could get yourself into. Taking any cab rides lately?"

"Fuck you."

"There's that attitude again. You are a cruising for a bruising my love. Don't forget we are always around even though you don't see us. Remember Harvey the Rabbit? That's me and Jerry, invisible, just like Harvey. We are going to take a spin up your way just to make Dominic happy and we'll beep the horn when we pass buy. I'll expect you to be at the window to throw us a big kiss."

"Fuck you."

"See you in a few my beauty."

Jerry and Tom get into their shiny Escalade and head to Jill's apartment building.

****

The curtain on the door parts and the cherub face of an old woman appears behind the window. After a quick look at him the woman unlocks the door but keeps the door chain in place. The door opens a crack and she says,

"What do you want?"

"Is Jill there?"

"Who is asking?"

"I'm a friend of hers from hospital. She left work yesterday feeling ill and I was just out for a bike ride and thought I'd check with her to see if she is OK."

"What kind of work do you do at the hospital?"

"I work in the cafeteria."

"How do you know Jill?"

"She generally eats in the cafeteria and then goes outside for a cigarette."

"She's still smoking? She's going to get an earful from me later. She told me that she was quitting that dirty, filthy, disgusting habit. OK. You wait here and I'll go and tell her that she has a visitor."

The old woman climbs the stairs to the third floor and knocks on Jill's door and announces that she has a visitor waiting downstairs. Jill, thinking that it is Jerry or Tom tells the old women to tell her visitor that she'll be down in a minute. Jill is in no rush to get downstairs and decides to take her time just to piss them off.

Jake is standing on the front porch as the Escalade creeps up Lang Avenue toward Jill's building. He is passing the time away by looking around the neighborhood watching some kids on the street playing football. He sees the car but doesn't think much about it. But the more he concentrates on the car he begins to think that it seems out of place because this part of Point Breeze is a mixture of middle to lower middle class families and not many of the residents living here would be driving a shiny, new Cadillac Escalade. But maybe the car is just passing by or maybe its occupants are just paying a visit on someone in the neighborhood.

With Tom at the wheel, he and Jerry are about a block away from Jill's building when Tom spots the bike in front of the steps to the house. He knows that no kids live in the building. So what's up with the bike?

Tom crosses the intersection and does a slow pass of the house. He and Jerry are focused on the man standing on the porch. What's he doing there? Is the mouse at play again? Tom proceeds up to an alley way, turns around and starts to coast very slowly down the street toward the front of the house to get a better look at the guy on the porch. The guy on the porch is not moving. Why is he just standing there? Is he waiting for Jill to come to the door?

Jake keeps his eyes on the car which is now moving very slowly past the house. It's hard to tell who is inside the car because of the tinted windows, but whoever is in that car is taking his/their good old time going past the house. To be going that slow they must be looking for a house number.

Tom comes to a stop across the street from the house and depresses the button to lower the window on Jerry's side of the car. Both Tom and Jerry are now staring at the guy on the porch.

Jake sees the car come to a stop and watches as the window slides down. He can now see into the car and notices that its occupants are two men. The man on the passenger side of the car is a big guy. He's so big that he almost blocks the other guy from his view. Jake continues to stare at the car as Tom and Jerry continue to stare at Jake. Finally the staring contest is broken when Jerry calls from the window of the car,

"Hey you; what are you doing there? Who are you waiting for?"

Jake doesn't recognize the face but he knows the sound of that voice and he knows that this is dejavu all over again with Tom and Jerry.

"Hey you; are you deaf? I asked you nice, what are you doing there?"

Jake doesn't want to answer because he is sure that those guys know his voice and once they make the connection there is going to be big trouble. So he slowly starts to descend the steps toward his bike. But as he makes his way toward the bike all of a sudden Tom yells out, "BEAN STALK! Jerry, it's the fucking Beanstalk!" Tom jumps out of the car and starts running toward Jake. Jerry is having trouble getting the seat belt detached and his big fat ass out of the seat. As Tom rounds the front of the car Jerry finally get detached from the seat belt and opens the passenger side door.

****

Once Tom yells out my name I go into a panic mode. I've got to get out of here and fast but it's too late as Tom is coming full bore around the front of the car and is now maybe 10 feet from the bike. I don't know what Jerry is doing because my full attention is on Tom as he closes the gap between us. I grab the handle bars on my bike and when Tom is about five feet away I shift my weight and with all of my might I shove the bike right into Tom's crotch. He yelps and goes down like a ton of bricks. I see Jerry emerging from the car as Tom writhes in pain on the sidewalk. I turn and begin to run up the street but as I do I see that it ends at a 20-foot high brick wall topped off by spiked iron bars separating the cemetery from the street. I have no choice but to run down the alley on my left. As I turn down the alley I look over my shoulder and see that Jerry is going back to the car and that Tom has shaken off his injury and will be after me on foot any second. As I tear down the alley I look ahead and see that the alley also ends at the cemetery. But this time the wall is only about 6 feet high but on top of the wall there is a spiked iron fence as well. About halfway down the alley there looks to be another alley to the right and there is a row of garages next to that entrance and the garages run all the way to the end of the alley stopping near the cemetery fence.

I get to the next alley and as I look to my right I see that it also ends at another section of the cemetery fence. Shit! I look behind me and see that Tom has turned the corner and is heading down the alley toward me and see that the Escalade is in the process of backing up and ready to turn and move forward in my direction. It seems as though I am in between the proverbial rock and a hard place until I notice that there is a big tree next to the first garage in the row. On the tree I see that someone has nailed a series of wooden planks into the trunk. Maybe some kids built a tree house? I don't know, but what I do know is that if I climb those wooden planks, from that tree I can gain access to the roof of that first garage and since the roofs of the garages are all flat, I should be able to run all the way down to the end of the garages and use the last garage roof as a launching pad to jump over the spiked fence and into the cemetery. Once in the cemetery I should be able to lose Tom. At this point I'm not too worried about Jerry chasing me because he'd never be able to get his fat ass up the tree ladder and with his weight he'd probably fall right through one of the garage roofs. Off I go up the ladder and onto the roof of the first garage. As I start to run down the roofs I notice that even though they are flat they are not even and there is about a 3-foot space between each garage but neither of these obstacles cause me a problem. I scoot down to the last garage in a flash. When I get there I am sickened because the distance between the last garage roof and the spiked fence is about ten feet. I'm a good athlete but no way can I jump ten feet from a standing start. I'm going to need some momentum to make that kind of distance and that means going back a couple of garages to get a running start. As I turn around I see that Tom is running my way down the garage roofs at a very good clip. In a matter of seconds he is going to be on top of me. I also notice that Tom is carrying a gun in his right hand and I before I can think he points and fires in my direction. I hear the crack of the gun but his shot must have been way off. I guess it is pretty hard for him to be accurate when he is trying to shoot while running on an uneven rooftop and leaping from one garage to another. But the closer he gets the better his accuracy is going to become so I have to make some kind of move and make it fast because the gap between us is closing at a rapid pace. Jerry is now only one garage away. Like a sprinter blasting out of the starting blocks I launch myself in Tom's direction. I can see by the look on his face that I have caught him by surprise and it only took a second of confusion on his part to give me the upper hand. I drive my shoulder hard into his stomach and Tom goes flying backwards. The impact of my blow dislodges the gun from his hand and takes the air out of his stomach.

As Tom struggles to get air in his lungs I jump up, turn around and go into a full sprint toward the end of the garages and as I get to the end of the last garage I leap in the air as far as I can. I clear the top of the spikes by inches, tuck in my shoulder and hit the ground in an athletic roll. Thank God I'm in good physical shape. I'm a little worse for the wear but I'm in the cemetery and out of harm's way for the present. I look back at the garages and see that Tom is going to attempt to duplicate my feat. The only problem for Tom is that he hasn't been to the last garage and is not aware of the distance that needs to be covered from where the last garage ends and where the cemetery spikes begin. Standing on the top of the garage you get the perspective that it is a short distance and that is very misleading; not only misleading but injurious to your health as well. As I back peddle into the cemetery I see Tom begin his run down the garage roofs in his attempt to clear the cemetery bars. Once he entered the air on his jump it was obvious to me that he was not going to clear the bars. He almost made it but as they say, almost only counts in horse shoes and with a sickening thud Tom landed on top of the spikes and one of the spikes impaled his throat. As Tom hung draped over the bars with a steady stream of blood pulsating out of his neck Jerry came to a skidding stop at the cemetery wall, jumped out of the car and ran to the fence. By that time I was safely up on a hill hiding behind a mausoleum observing Jerry's actions. Jerry pulled out his weapon and looked for me but I seemed to have vanished in thin air. He went over the wall but there was no way at his size that he could attempt to scale the wall in order to retrieve his partner. He had no recourse but to get back in the car and vacate the premises. But just before he got into the car he screamed out at the top of his lungs, "Beanstalk, someone is going to pay for this you filthy little fuck. Someone is going to pay big fucking time!"

While all of this was going on, Jill had come down to the front door and when she opened the door there was no evidence of the Escalade being there, only a bike laying in the sidewalk. Probably some kid left it there she thought. As she was climbing the stairs to her apartment, Jerry was just turning the corner from the alley and heading down Lang Avenue. He stopped, popped open the trunk of the car, deposited the bike and left the neighborhood. He was upset because he had just lost a friend but was more upset because once he told Dominic what happened Dominic was not going to be a happy camper and when Dominic was not a happy camper generally something bad happened.

****

I stayed in the cemetery until it was dark. I was worried that Jerry might team up with Dominic or another one of his demented friends and come back to look for me. When I was pretty sure that no one was coming back I followed the cemetery bars down from where Tom was hanging and came across a bar that was bent enough for me to exit the cemetery. I discovered that it dumped me out at the bottom of Willard Street, just a block down from Jill's apartment building. I carefully made my way up Willard Street looking for the Escalade. When I got to the corner of Lang and Willard I saw that my bike was gone. I had no recourse but to jog back to my dorm in Oakland. I'm not a fast runner but I made the 5-mile run back to the dorm in record setting time.

The next day as I was returning to the dorm room after my morning classes I passed by the TV room and the noon news on KDKA TV was playing. I was stunned when I heard the announcer say, "Our lead story today concerns a bizarre event that occurred sometime yesterday in the Point Breeze section of the city. Let's go to the scene and check in with our on-the-scene reporter Carol Scheib. Carol, tell our viewers what happened."

"Thanks Bill. I'm here at the bottom of Roy Street, an alley in Point Breeze that ends at this barred wall that separates Homewood Cemetery from the community. As you can see there is a row of garages in this alley that end near this wall. This morning at approximately 7:00 A.M. a resident by the name of Ernie Troy was out walking his dog in the alley before going to work when the dog began to bark and act strangely. The dog began to pull Mr. Troy in the direction of the space between the last garage in the row and the cemetery wall. As Mr. Troy and his dog rounded the corner behind the garage the dog started to yelp at a frantic pace. It was then that Mr. Troy looked up and saw a man impaled on the fence above the wall. Mr. Troy ran home and called the police. Pittsburgh City Police detectives and the medical examiner arrived on the scene shortly thereafter. I spoke to the detective in charge, Detective Larry Sullivan, and Detective Sullivan said that the dead body is that of one Tommy "Tire Track" Concilla. If you remember Bill, it was 10 years ago that Tommy and his brother Phil were foiled in their attempt to rob the Mellon Bank in downtown Pittsburgh. During the shoot out between police and the Concilla brothers following the attempted robbery, Phil was gunned down as he and Tommy were trying to get to their getaway vehicle. Rather than stop to help his brother, Tommy jumped in the car and ran over Phil in an attempt to escape the scene leaving tire tracks on his brother's chest. After a short chase Tommy was captured by police when his car skidded out of control and crashed into a telephone pole."

"Initially Tommy was charged with armed robbery, vehicular manslaughter and a laundry list of other charges.

Subsequently the county coroner confirmed that Phil was dead before Tommy ran over him so the vehicular manslaughter charge was dropped. Tommy was found guilty of all other charges and was sentenced to 15 years to be served at Western Penitentiary. After serving 10 years, Tommy was released on good behavior. He was released just 6 months ago. Tommy is known to be an associate of Dominic Bodino a local henchman associated with Louie "Top Banana" Lamana who has ties to the Marino family in the New York City area. Currently police are somewhat baffled as to how Tommy ended up impaled on a cemetery fence in a relatively crime free and quiet section of the city. Neighbors in the area are being canvassed by police to see if anyone can recall seeing or hearing anything out of the ordinary that may have occurred in the last 24 hours. So far the police have come up with nothing but a lot of questions and no answers. This is Carol Schieb reporting live from Point Breeze. Back to you Bill."

What should I do now I thought? Go to the police and tell them what I knew? That would solve the mystery of Tom's untimely death but it would open up a whole new can of worms as well. Certainly Jill would get involved and I didn't want that. And if I went to the police and told them my story, somehow that information would be made public and that would serve as a trail of bread crumbs for Jerry and his gangster friends to come looking for me to find out what I told the cops. I thought the best thing was to just lie low and let this thing blow over. The cops would probably come to the conclusion that Tommy pissed someone off in prison or in the ranks of his friendly gangster family and in those kinds of relationships paybacks can be hell. The only decision I made was to quit my cab driving job because Jerry knew I drove a cab and he might come looking for me at the cab barn and decide to even the score in honor of his dearly departed sidekick.

A Cruel Twist of Fate

It was only one week later that another news story out of Point Breeze was the lead story of the day. I was in the TV room watching the 6:00 local evening news on KDKA TV and eating some pizza when the evening news anchor said, "Just last week we reported the bizarre death of a local gangster in the Point Breeze section of the city and today we return to that same area for another blockbuster story. Once again Carol Scheib is on the scene. Carol, hearing a live report from you from Point Breeze is becoming a common occurrence these days. Tell us about this recent event."

"Bill, right now I am standing in the backyard of a 3-story apartment residence located at 601 South Lang Avenue. Immediately behind me is Roy Street. It was at the end of Roy Street that just 7 days ago local bad boy Tommy Concilla was found impaled on cemetery fence."

"This morning as Mary Fitzgerald, owner and first-floor resident in this building, came out to deposit her trash in her trash can, she came across the body of Jill Bodino sprawled on the cement walkway. Mrs. Bodino occupied the apartment on the 3rd floor of the building. Ms. Fitzgerald said that it was not uncommon for Mrs. Bodino to come down the fire escape on "trash night" to deposit her garbage in the trash can. The obvious theory is that Mrs. Bodino slipped on the staircase and fell to her death. But Ms. Fitzgerald reports that there was no bag of trash anywhere on the ground when she spotted Mrs. Bodino's broken body. So what was Mrs. Bodino doing out on the fire escape without a bag of garbage? What makes this situation even more bizarre is that Mrs. Bodino is the estranged wife of local mobster Dominic Bodino. Six months ago Mrs. Bodino filed for divorce from Mr. Bodino and obtained a restraining order as well. The body of Tommy Concilla, who was found murdered last week, was discovered just 200 yards from this very spot. Tommy was known to have close ties with Mr. Bodino. Although this death has not yet been designated as a homicide, homicide Detective Larry Sullivan has been placed in charge of this investigation. When I asked Detective Sullivan if he thought that Mrs. Bodino had been caught up in some kind of love triangle between Mr. Concilla and Mr. Bodino he replied 'No comment." I also asked Detective Sullivan if any progress has been made in the investigation of Tommy Concilla's death to wit he replied curtly, 'Some'. Bill, it is almost impossible to believe that two violent events could occur within one week of each other in one of Pittsburgh's most tranquil and serene neighborhoods. And because of the cast of characters involved in these situations it is almost impossible to believe that these two grizzly events are not related. Reporting live once more from Point Breeze, I'm Carol Scheib."

I was stunned beyond belief when I heard that news report. Not only stunned but scared shitless. Was I next on their list? When I got back to my room the phone was ringing.

"Hello."

"Is this Jake Stalk?" I didn't recognize the voice.

"No. This is his roommate. Can I take a message?"

"Bullshit, Stalk. This is Detective Thompson and I don't forget a voice and I know it's you. Now listen to me you little prick, I don't know what in the fuck is going on but this is what I do know. Some weeks ago you picked up a fare at Mercy Hospital and on that very day you get mugged in Point Breeze. We talk and you don't know anything. Nothing. So I did a little leg work and I found out by checking the call records kept by your cab company that the last fare you picked up before your mugging was at Mercy Hospital. I know that the recently departed Mrs. Bodino was employed by Mercy Hospital and I also know that in the last two weeks two people died suspiciously in Point Breeze.

A Cruel Twist of Fate

You know how many suspicious deaths have occurred in Point Breeze since the beginning of time? How about none? Now I'm going out on a limb here and am guessing that the fare you picked up at Mercy Hospital was one Jill Bodino. After that I don't know what happened except that you got a big fucking lump on your head. Then shortly after that event Tommy Tire Tracks ends up with a cemetery fence spike in his throat. Then Jill Bodino has a mysterious fall to her death just one week after Tommy gets impaled on a fence that is a stone's throw from where she lives. And all of this happens in quiet, little old Point Breeze, the same place you got mugged. Somehow all of this shit ties together and I think you are right in the middle of the mix. By the way, just for your information, Detective Sullivan tells me that Dominic Bodino was sitting in his regular seat at the Steeler game when Tommy Tire Tracks expired and that he was out of town the night that Jill Bodino fell to her death. On the surface that eliminates Bodino as a murder suspect and seemingly elevates you into the picture of being a person of interest in one or two homicides. If you murdered that low-life, scumbag Tommy it is no sweat off of my balls. In fact I might just buy you a pizza and a couple of Iron City beers and call it a day. But Mrs. Bodino is another story. If you had something, anything to do with her death I'll do everything I can in my power to see that you fry. In fact I might make a special request to attend your final blaze of glory and toast a marshmallow on your ass. I think we need to have a little chat about recent events. Let me check my calendar. Wow, look at that Mr. Stalk, I'm free all day long; how about you and how about now?"

"Look Detective I had nothing to do with either of those deaths. Well, maybe Tommy in a way, but definitely not Jill."

"What do you mean by maybe Tommy? Maybe is like saying I'm a little bit pregnant. You did or you didn't. And when did Mrs. Bodino become Jill to you?"

"I can explain all of this to you tomorrow but I have this huge paper due tomorrow and I have to go to the library tonight to finish it. If I don't turn this paper in I'll flunk the course."

"I have to give it to you Stalk. You have a lot of balls. I tell you that you are a double murder suspect and you are worried about a fucking term paper. Most people would have their ass in my office as soon as time would permit. Sounds to me like you trying to buy time and might even have an idea of running off somewhere."

"No. I'm not going to run anywhere. I turn my paper in at 9:00 A.M. I'll be in your office before 10:00 A.M. OK?"

"Listen up Stalk. I know where you are. I know the dorm you live in and which room in the dorm. As we speak there are uniformed officers standing at each exit of your dorm. If you go anywhere you are going to have company. Understand? Go to the library and one of them goes with you. Go to class and one of them goes with you. Tonight there will be an officer posted at each end of the hall way in your dorm. Got it?"

"Got it Detective. I understand fully. By the way can I ask a question?"

"Ask away."

"In the movies they always offer a suspect something to drink. Will you have hot coffee for me tomorrow? If you don't, I'll stop by Dunkin' Donuts and grab one for the road because I need coffee in the morning, especially if we are going to talk for awhile."

"Do you take cream or sugar?"

"No, black."

"Then don't worry your little head because black I can do. Anymore requests Stalk? Would you want me to fry up a couple of eggs? Maybe bacon and sausage on the side with a couple pieces of whole wheat toast?"

"That would be great. I like my eggs over easy."

"How about over my dead body?"

"I don't think so because then I'd be a person of interest in three homicides."

****

That night I went to the library with my escort. I was in the computer cubicle putting the finishing touches on my paper when the library assistant came down to me and said, "Are you Stalk?"

"Yeah. Why?"

"Here's the book you requested on line."

"What book?" He hands me the book and it is entitled "A Child's Book of Nursery Rhymes" and one of the pages has been bookmarked. I open the page and it is the nursery rhyme about Jack and Jill but someone had scratched out every reference to Jack and put in Jake. Furthermore these words had been highlighted in yellow:

Jake………….broke his crown……..
and Jill came tumbling after.

"Who gave you this book?"

"I don't know. All I know is that the librarian printed out the online requests and when she saw that you signed in for a computer tonight she recognized the name, put 2 and 2 together and asked me to deliver the book to you."

"Is there any way to find out who requested this book?"

"I thought you requested the book."

"No I didn't. Someone must have requested it in my name. My question to you is can you find out the location of the computer user who requested this book?"

"Are you kidding me? That request could have come from any computer in the world. All I can tell you is the date and the time of the request."

I finished up my paper and went to the librarian and checked out the book of nursery rhymes so that I could show it to Detective Thompson.

That night I was happy to have two policemen standing guard in my dorm. Without them I don't think I could have slept a wink.

****

The next morning I jumped into a police cruiser and my two new best friends on the Pittsburgh City Police Force drove me to headquarters. There I was met by Detective Thompson and another gentleman whom I'm guessing was another detective.

"Good morning Mr. Stalk. And how is our top student and double homicide person of interest on this bright and cheery morning in the city with a smile?"

"I'm OK and I didn't commit a double homicide."

"Forgive me. Slip of the tongue. That's right. You didn't commit a double homicide but you MIGHT be responsible for just one homicide. Allow me to introduce Detective Sullivan from homicide. He's the chief inspector in charge of the investigations related to the two recent mishaps in lovely Pt. Breeze. I know you are a hungry boy, Mr. Stalk, and were looking forward to a 3-course breakfast but silly me forgot my apron when I left for work this morning so all I have to offer you is coffee, black."

"Thanks, coffee's great. It is hot?"

"Should be hot, but if it's not don't be disappointed because we are here to light a fire under your ass and in just a few minutes that coffee is going to be boiling. Ok, enough banter, let's get down to business. I want you to go back to the day you picked up Mrs. Bodino at Mercy Hospital and fill us in on everything and I mean EVERYTHING that occurred in your life since that moment that is related in any way to Mrs. Bodino and the dearly departed Tommy Concilla."

I tell my story in full answering a few questions along the way. In addition I show them the book I got from the library with the passage highlighted. After completing my dissertation Detective Thompson tells me to "cool my heels" while he and Detective Sullivan review their notes together. I'm feeling very much relieved about getting my entire ordeal out in the open and off my chest, and once the tension of telling my story has been removed I am beginning to feel hungry.

"Detective Thompson, while you guys are talking is there any chance that I can shoot out and get something to eat? I'm starved. The only thing I've had to eat all day is that coffee that you gave me, plus I have to go to the bathroom. By the way, I should have stopped at Dunkin Donuts on the way here. No offense but that coffee was the worst. How do you drink that stuff?"

"You didn't like my coffee, Mr. Stalk? Wow, how ungrateful. I'll have you know that I personally turned on the coffeemaker to satisfy your request for black coffee. And now you have the audacity to criticize my culinary efforts? Are you now adding to your list of offenses criticism of an officer of the law and denigration of the police department of the City of Pittsburgh?"

"No. I'm sure you did your job to the best of your ability, but no matter how good you are at brewing coffee it all comes down to the beans. Obviously, unbeknownst to you, somebody slipped you bad beans. So I'm not criticizing. It's just that my bladder is full and my stomach is empty and I need some relief on both counts."

"OK mister bullshitter, the can is down the hall, first room on the left. The door is unmarked but there is a singular smell in that area of the hall that will lead you to your destination. As far as food goes, I'm going to steal a line from Brother Patrick who taught me Latin at Central Catholic. We weren't permitted to chew gum or eat candy in class but one day Brother caught me eating a candy bar. He promptly assigned me to detention that night and the next day when I came into class the good Brother asked me if I wanted a piece of candy. I thought he was being a nice guy and letting bygones be bygones so I told him that I'd love to have a piece of candy. You know what his response to me was?"

"No. I give up. What did Brother Patrick say when you told him that you'd love to have a piece of candy?"

"Are you ready for this Mr. Stalk?"

"Ready."

"Brother Patrick said to me that same thing I'm going to say to you right now and that is open your mouth and let your gumdrop. Get it Stalk? Gumdrop."

"Yeah, I get it. You know what else I get?"

"Enlighten me."

"You're a better coffeemaker than you are a comedian."

"Ouch Mr. Stalk that hurt. Now go take your piss and come right back here and wait for Detective Sullivan and myself to return."

After the detectives returned, Detective Sullivan tells me, "I need you to complete a report for the Concilla file so that I can put that case to rest. After canvassing neighbors in the area, Mrs. Fitzgerald, owner/occupant of the apartment house when Mrs. Bodino lived, said she recalled seeing a very large man in a black car stop and put a bike in the trunk and drive off the day of Tommy Concilla's death. She didn't know the make or model of the car, didn't think to look for the license number and couldn't provide and description of the man other than he was unusually large. Her story jibes with your description of the events. From your and Mrs. Fitzgerald's description we are positive that the unusually large man she saw was Jerry "Moose" Milano. Milano and Concilla were long-time pals who are closely associated with Dominic Bodino. They've been known to do a lot of dirty work for Bodino. Attempts to locate Moose Milano have been unsuccessful at this time. For all we know he could be back in Italy eating a pizza by now. I don't think you are directly involved with Mrs. Bodino's death, but if you would have been upfront with Detective Thompson the day of your mugging maybe she wouldn't be dead today. Mr. Stalk, let me be very clear with you, if you look up bad luck in the dictionary your face might be part of the definition because it has been very bad luck for you to have become involved with Mrs. Bodino and those two creeps that were shadowing her. Dominic Bodino is a bad man and people who associate with him are bad men.

Tommy Tire Tracks is dead because of you and your association with Mrs. Bodino. It doesn't matter that the dumb fuck accidently killed himself. What matters is that Dominic thinks that there was something going on between his estranged wife and you. I know and you know that the relationship between you and Mrs. Bodino was innocent and that you were just trying to be a nice guy. But apparently Dominic and his crew interpreted that relationship differently and now Mrs. Bodino is dead. These people know what you look like and where to find you as evidenced by the little book trick they played on you last night. Right now they are just playing with you like a cat pawing at an injured mouse. They might dick around with you for awhile but sooner or later they are going to get tired of the game and that's when your bad luck turns really bad. Bad like in a severe beating, a dismemberment or maybe even murder. I wish I could tell you that we could protect you but there is no way on a college campus that we can post a sentry or have someone hold your hand 24/7. We can move in immediately after your death but that isn't going to do you much good. So, my suggestion to you is that get out of Dodge. Maybe if you get out of the picture they will feel that it's not worth tracking you down because they have already satisfied their revenge by taking out Mrs. Bodino. Now that Mrs. Bodino is out of the way, Dominic won't have the hassle and personal embarrassment of going through a divorce and maybe that will calm him down. Maybe they'll think that your punishment will be living a life of fear not knowing when someone might come around the corner and stick a knife in your back. Maybe, just maybe they'll write you off as dumb-ass college kid; a harmless fly on a horse's ass that landed and went away."

After completing the report for Detective Sullivan I went into Detective Thompson's office to say goodbye. "Thanks for looking out for me last night and I guess thanks for everything Detective."

"No problem Mr. Stalk. I wish you luck, I really do. I wish we could provide protection but we can't and I hope you understand that. We'll do our best to locate Milano and will do our best to keep tabs on Bodino, but those people are like roaches. You see a bunch of them at night and by morning they disappear like they were never there. All I can say is that the advice Detective Sullivan gave you is solid. I know leaving is going to totally disrupt your life but better that your life is disrupted versus having your life snuffed out some night when you are on your way back to your dorm after visiting the library."

"Gotcha."

As I turn to leave Detective Thompson says, "One more thing Jake."

"What's that?"

"Watch your ass out there. We hate to see the good die young."

"Don't worry, Detective. If I can survive your coffee and your jokes I'll probably be able to survive anything."

****

I got a ride back to the dorm in the police cruiser and when I got to my room I packed all of my belongings and drafted a letter to my advisor telling him that I had a family emergency and I was going to have to drop out of school. I thanked him for providing guidance to me as I scheduled classes and told him once I was ready to return that I would contact him, but I knew that I was never going to return to Pitt.

I caught a cab to the Greyhound Bus Station and purchased a ticket to Indiana, PA. From there I would buy a bus ticket to Punxsutawney and from there I would find a way to get to Sagamore. I didn't want to risk calling my parents; I'd explain everything when I got home.

It's not that far from Pittsburgh to Sagamore but it took me most of the day to get there and when I got home my mom was shocked to see me. I'd told her that I needed to talk to her and dad and what I was about to tell them would change our lives radically. Mom told me that dad was sleeping but he was about ready to get up for dinner because he was scheduled to work the 8 to 8 shift.

During dinner I told mom and dad every detail of my entire saga. There was complete silence when I finished until my dad said, "And what do you plan to do? Run away? Running never solves anything son."

"It may not solve everything, dad, but it eliminates a lot of possibilities, mainly you, mom or someone in our community getting hurt. I can't risk these goons coming here. Coming after me is one thing but I will not put anyone else in harm's way because of me. Yes, I have to run for now. Maybe I'm exaggerating and these people won't come looking for me, but I can't take that chance. Maybe after some time passes they'll lose interest and life will return to a sense of normalcy. I HAVE to go and I can't tell you where I am going, at least for the time being." At this point mom started to cry.

"I can't jeopardize your well being. The less you know the better. At the bus station in Pittsburgh I bought two of these disposable cell phones. I have memorized the number of the phone I am going to give you. I can't risk calling our home phone. Who knows what these people can do. Maybe somehow they can tap into our line and listen to phone calls and trace the origination of the caller and if it's me it will lead them right to my location. I'm not going to give you the number on my disposable phone. It's not that I don't want you to call me, but again, the less you know the better. I want to travel at night when I leave here so I'm going to pack my bags now and you can drop me off at the bus station in Punxsutawney. If we leave soon, dad, you'll be able to get to Punxy and back so that you don't miss the start of your shift. Missing the start of your shift would not be normal and we need to keep everything as normal as possible. When we get to the bus station I don't want you to get out of the car. Just drop me off and leave as I don't want you to know my destination. When I get to where I'm going and I feel safe, I'll call you."

On the way to Punxsutawney mom held on to me for dear life. We both cried a lot, even dad shed some tears. We pulled up in front of the station and I got out of the car. Dad got my bags out of the trunk while mom and I shared a last tearful embrace. Dad set the bags down and hugged me so hard that it almost hurt. After the hug he handed me an envelope. "What's this dad?"

"Money your mother and I were saving up to buy a new car. There's $8,500 in that envelope. That should be enough to get you where you are going and ensure that you have a good roof over your head and a safe environment in which to live."

I didn't know what to say except, "Thanks dad, I love you." We were all crying now. The last thing in this world that I wanted to do was to leave them but I knew I had to. I climbed the steps of the bus station and took a last look back. Mom mouthed I love you. I mouthed back I love you, too. I watched as dad pulled away from the curb and began the journey back to Sagamore. I watched until they were a speck of light in the distance. My God how I missed them. How was I ever going to get through this alone? I entered the bus station to see what buses were running that night, when and to where. I needed to get to a place where I could get lost; a big city; a place where I could find a job and maybe get back to school and most importantly, just blend into the fabric of the city. I had to become just one of many; a needle in the proverbial haystack. There were four buses leaving that night. One was to Barnesboro, PA; another to Pittsburgh, PA; another to Bradford, PA and another to West Chester, PA. Barnesboro was a little dink town and Bradford was a very small city. Pittsburgh was a no brainer; no way I could consider going back there. By a process of elimination, West Chester became my choice. West Chester was a small community and not one that I could settle in, but it was a location that was much closer than the other three destinations to a place where I could get lost in the maddening crowd. I purchased my ticket and boarded the bus to West Chester.

NEW YORK CITY

The bus pulled into West Chester about 3:00 A.M. At 6:00 A.M. there was a bus scheduled to leave for Philadelphia. I stored my bags in a couple of lockers in the bus station and walked across the street to an all-night diner for some breakfast. After breakfast I took a stroll around the area of the bus station to clear my head and to stretch a bit before boarding the bus to Philly. Most bus stations and areas around bus stations are filthy and frequented by pan handlers and a variety of low-life people, but West Chester was different. The station was bright and clean; even the bathrooms. Generally speaking, at 3:00 A.M. it wouldn't be unusual to find some scumbag is in the restroom taking a bath with a roll of paper towels or asleep on a toilet, but not the men's room in the bus station in West Chester. That men's room looked like Mr. Clean just passed through. It even smelled fresh! I think the air quality in that men's room was better than that of the Greyhound bus. Inside the terminal a West Chester County Policeman was making his rounds and outside there was another policeman on a bike gently peddling around the perimeter of the building. These folks in West Chester surely had their act together.

West Chester is only 25 miles from Philadelphia and the 6:00 A.M. bus from West Chester pulled in at the bus station at Filbert Street about 6:45 A.M. I flagged down a cab for a very short ride to 30th street train station. Once at the 30th street train station I looked at the leader board and saw that the next Amtrak Express train from Philadelphia to NYC was scheduled to leave in 10 minutes. Too much rushing I thought, so I decided to wait for the next express train which was scheduled to leave at 8:00 A.M. Probably better to wait for that train anyway since the 7:00 A.M. was going to be packed to the gills with NYC commuters. Traffic should lighten up in the next hour. I found the kiosk where the automated ticket machine was located, bought my train ticket, went to Hudson News shop and bought a guidebook to NYC and one of those city pocket maps. I took a look at the leader board around 7:45 A.M. and it was flapping away updating the status of departing and arriving trains. My train; the Amtrak Silver Streak Express to NYC was on time and scheduled to leave on track #7 East. I grabbed my stuff and followed the mass of humanity to the platform. As promised, the train arrived on time; I climbed aboard, found an empty seat and threw my stuff into the overhead rack. Scheduled run time to Penn Station in NYC was 1 hour and 10 minutes, plenty of time to look at my map and figure out the next leg of my journey when I arrived in NYC. So far my journey had been painted with a broad brush, but now I really had to zero in on a specific location as I had some big decisions to make in a very small amount of time; like where to start life over again? I knew that somehow, some way, some day I needed to continue my education. I also felt that living near a college campus would help me blend into the woodwork. IF someone did choose to pursue me they'd have a harder time finding me in a community full of college students and the bigger the campus the better. I also had to find a neighborhood that might offer affordable housing; a pretty tough assignment in NYC. I looked in my city guide to the university and college section and came across New York University. The guide stated that NYU's population consisted of 50,917 students situated in 16 schools, colleges and institutes around the world. With 12,500 students at the main campus in Greenwich Village, the housing system was the 7th largest in the United States. I looked at some other schools but NYU was the largest and the fact that it was located in the heart of one of the largest cities in the world made it a perfect location. Thus, the Greenwich Village section of NYC was going to be my ground zero.

Upon arriving at Penn Station I found a couple of lockers and deposited my bags with the exception of my backpack. I felt a little uneasy leaving eight grand in a locker but better there than to be carrying it on my person. I took a cab to NYU. I asked a student where the Student Union was located and headed in that direction.

Normally at Student Unions you can find a bulletin board with all kinds of post-it notes offering items for sale as well as solicitations for off-campus rooms to rent. It was mid-semester so there weren't many ads for rooms but I did find one stuck under another note that read:

Studio. Reasonable rate.
Must be willing to help clean bakery.
SWM only. No phone calls.
Come in person to Sorrento's Bakery, 157 Grand St.

I looked at my pocket map and found Grand Street. It was in the heart of Little Italy; about a 15-block walk from NYU.

Sorrento's Bakery was a 3-story sliver of a building sandwiched in between the SoLita So Ho Hotel and Beto's Pizza Parlor. There were no lights on inside and it appeared that Sorrento's was either closed or not in business anymore. As I cupped my eyes and placed my nose against the window I saw a couple of counter cases but nothing was in the cases but empty racks. There were a few small tables draped with red and white checkered table cloths; three chairs to a table and there was also a stand-up refrigerated cooler in the back of the room. There was a light on in the cooler and you could see that it was stocked with various soft drinks. Thus, Sorrento's must be in business, but for some reason no one was there. I banged on the door and yelled out, "Anybody home!" I did this a few more times and then a guy came out of the pizza parlor and asked me what I wanted. I told him why I was there and asked him if he knew if the studio apartment had been rented.

He wasn't sure but he told me that Mrs. Sorrento went to 10:00 A.M. Mass and that she'd be back at any moment. "Hey, howa bouta somea pizza until she comesa back?"

Sounded good to me so I ordered a couple of slices and sat by the window awaiting the arrival of Mrs. Sorento. While I waited I found out that Mr. Sorento had recently passed and Mrs. Sorento was struggling along trying to keep the business alive. The Sorento's had two girls, both married. One lived in Seattle and the other in Boston and other than holidays, they might stop by once or twice a year.

I was putting the finishing touches on my second piece when I saw an elderly woman wearing a babushka and sporting a cane hobbling up the street toward the bakery. As she began struggling to get her keys out of her purse I paid my bill and went next door to introduce myself. I showed her the note I took from the bulletin board and expressed my interest in looking at the apartment. She asked me to sit down and I spent the next half of an hour answering her questions and giving her information about my family and my background. I conveniently left out the part about being on the run from some Mafia associates in Pittsburgh.

She gave me the key to the apartment which was located on the 3rd floor. She said she'd like to accompany me but the steps were too much for her; it was enough for her just to get to her apartment on the second floor. The apartment was small and basic. It consisted of a living room/kitchen combo, a small bedroom and a bath. It was a bit dusty and smelled like donuts but it was furnished and in general was neat and clean. I told Mrs. Sorrento that it looked fine to me and I was ready to move on to the next step and discuss rent and what was meant in the note by "willing to help clean bakery". She told me that she was up at 4:30 A.M. every day to begin the baking process and that she was on her feet all day long. By 6:00 P.M. when she closed she was very tired and needed someone to sweep the floors and wash the equipment and get the place cleaned and ready for the next day's business. I told her I could do that. She said, "No drugs and no parties."

I told her I didn't do drugs and I wasn't a party animal.
"What about women?" she said.
"What do you mean, what about woman?"
"Do you like woman or men?"
"Ok, I understand. I like women and **only** women."
"When would you like to move in?"
"Is today OK?"

"Today is not good. Two days from now would be good."

"Why two days from now?"

"Tomorrow you come and clean and if you do a good job you can move in the next day."

By the end of the week I was settled in my new place, established an account at a local bank, deposited my money, visited the NY Motor Vehicle Bureau and got a NY Driver's license and was ready to look for a job and enroll in a night class at NYU.

I called home and talked to my parents. I didn't tell them where I was but I told them that all was going well and that they need not worry about me. I asked them if anyone strange had been snooping around Sagamore looking for me or if they had received any telephone calls requesting information about my whereabouts. Nothing there seemed to be out of the ordinary and for that I was thankful. They asked me when I was coming back home. I told them I didn't know but I would when I felt that it was safe for them and me. It was hard to end that call, but I felt like they were safe and I could always call again and for now I had to accept the fact that my only link to my parents was going to be via the phone. After I ended that call I disposed of my phone as I was afraid that if someone got a hold of the phone I gave to my parents they might be able to track me down because the manufacturer's ID numbers on the back of their phone and my phone were sequential. Maybe their phone could be used as a link to my phone and subsequently as a link to the origination of my calls to them? I know that sounds like some convoluted paranoia but let's face it I WAS paranoid. I could always buy another disposable phone, so better to be safe than sorry.

After spending a couple of days getting to know the neighborhood and getting a flavor of the subway system I decided it was time to get myself established at NYU. It was mid November and the new semester didn't start until January but many of the administrative offices shut down for Thanksgiving and Christmas break so I needed to get myself registered so that I would be listed on a class roster come the start of the second semester. During my registering process I decided that I needed to switch my major. At Punxy and Pitt I majored in Journalism and I figured if someone came looking for me at NYU they'd probably hang out around the School of Journalism. I decided to declare a major in hotel management because there seemed to be a hotel on every block no matter where you went. My NYC Guide stated that there were 218 hotels just in Mid-Town Manhattan! The opportunities in that industry for part time work or full time work seemed to be very plentiful. In addition, NYU offered a co-op program in hotel management which meant you could go to school and gain valuable work experience at the same time. And the bonus was that you got paid for your co-op work and I was going to need all of the money I could get with the prices that NYU was charging per credit hour. I registered as a part-time student and selected two courses. There was no way I could afford to be a full-time student as the cost per credit hour was $450.

The holiday season was in full swing and I got very homesick. But I couldn't go home. I told Mrs. Sorrento about my plans at NYU. I commented on how expensive it was and she told me she and her husband had been very good friends with the owner of the Solita So Ho Hotel next door and she would talk to him and see if he could find a part time job for me.

December was a hard month for me as I had never been away from my parents during the holiday season. Christmas in Sagamore was one big family gathering and I was going to miss out on all of those festivities. The consolation for me was that the more time I spent around Mrs. Sorrento the closer we became. This was her first Christmas season without her husband so both of us were in a similar emotional state and because of that we bonded very quickly. Christmas was a busy season for her, so in addition to cleaning I found myself spending most of my day helping her in whatever way I could. After the store closed and we finished cleaning up she'd make dinner and we'd eat together. She became my surrogate mother and I became her surrogate husband.

Her daughters and their husbands came to visit for Christmas and Mrs. Sorrento invited me to have meals with them. They were very nice people. I liked them and they seemed to like me; it was almost like spending time with family. On Christmas day I was surprised and emotionally overwhelmed during the gift exchange when Mrs. Sorrento picked up a gift and said, "This one's for Jake." It was an apron with my name on it. "Now, you have your own apron and you no wear my apron anymore. OK?" We all laughed. The best thing that happened to me in a long time was finding that note on the bulletin board that brought me into touch with the Sorrento family. Someone was definitely looking out for me.

NEW YEAR'S EVE

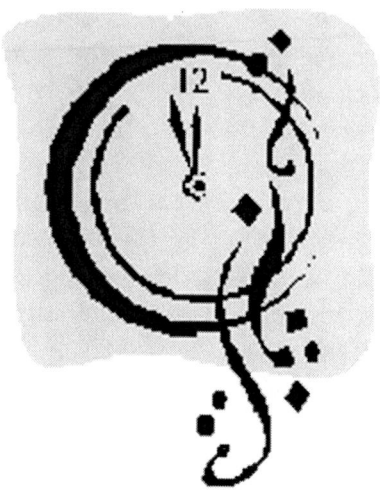

It was a brutally cold New Year's eve in Pittsburgh but Mickey Della Stritto and Louie Calgaro; AKA Mickey D and Louie C, were warm and toasty inside the posh Italian American Club on the city's South Side. Both were dressed in expensive silk tuxedos and putting the finishing touches on a bottle of Montepulciano d'Abruzzo Colline Teramane Reserve.

"Hey Louie, slow down on the wine. You think you're drinking a bottle of Peroni beer? This shit is over $200 a bottle. Fine wine is to be savored and treated like you are making slow foreplay with a lover. Where's you class and sophistication?"

Louie grabs his groin and replies, "My class and sophistication is a right here. You want some?"

"What a fucking Goomba you are Louie. Dress you up in an expensive suit, take you to a classy place, provide you with a fine bottle of wine and you're still a low-life bastard. You are living proof of what they say about putting lipstick on a pig."

"Lipstick on a pig? Is that like putting lip gloss on your mother?"

"Fuck you, Louie."

"What time is it Mickey?"

"Ten O'clock. For you that's when the big hand is on 12 and the little hand is on 10."

"Oh yeah? Well I don't have a watch with hands. I have a digital watch. See, I'm more sophisticated than you think."

"What's the drive time to Sagamore, Mickey?"

"Hour and a half or so unless we run into snow. I think we'd better leave now just to give ourselves some slack time. I don't want to fuck this up and get Dominic or Mr. Lamana pissed. Last thing I want to do it start the new year off in the fucking dog house."

"You know, Mickey, I don't get this whole deal at all. Why do we have to go out on a night when the weather is colder than a witch's tit, drive to some fucking no-name town just to put a bullet into some college's kids head while everyone else is drinking them up and starting off the new year in as you might put it, a sophisticated style? Tell me the story one more time so that I have this shit straight in my head."

"Actually I don't have to tell you shit other than the fact that Dominic says I have a job for you to do, now go do it. But, I'll humor you and give you the story in a nutshell. Some time back, Dominic slaps his wife, Jill, around a little bit and she goes ballistic, moves out, files for divorce and gets a restraining order. This pisses off Dominic to no end because in his mind he owns her no matter what the law says; owns her like she's a piece of property. In addition

Dominic thinks there's more to it than that and he accuses her of cheating on him. She denies it so he slaps her around some more and decides to watch her ass in the hope that he catches her with someone else; in which case he'll have justification to do more than just slap her around. He puts Jerry and Tommy on her case. Jerry and Tommy catch her being all friendly with this college kid cab driver, Jake Stalk, whom they refer to as "Beanstalk". To scare the kid away, Jerry opens up the Beanstalk's skull with the blunt end of his revolver and Tommy give's Jill a right cross and takes out a couple of teeth. A few weeks later, while checking in on Jill, Jerry and Tommy spot the Beanstalk standing on the front porch of Jill's apartment building obviously waiting to have another rendezvous. Jerry and Tommy chase the little fucker and during the chase Tommy tries to jump over a spiked fence, jumps short and ends up like a shiskabob on top of the fence. The Beanstalk gets away and Dominic is so pissed that he has Jerry pay a visit to Jill during which Jill happened to fall 3 stories to her death. Dominic sends Jerry to Italy for a 2-year all-expense-paid vacation and begins to hunt for the Beanstalk. Dominic can't find the kid; somehow he seems to have vanished into thin air. Dominic feels strongly that this kid will somehow make it home for the holidays to spend time with his family and that's where we come in. It's New Year's Eve, everyone will be glued to their TV screen waiting for the ball to drop which means that there will be no witnesses around. At midnight everyone will be hooting and hollering and blowing horns and shit and that will be the perfect time to make some noise of our own, only our noise will be the phhhhhhhhhhht sound that a bullet makes as it leaves the silencer of my gun and passes through the Beanstalk's brain."

"Sounds like a lot of bullshit to me Louie. Jill is dead, Jerry is safe and sound and out of the country, Dominic doesn't have any legal shit to deal with or any cops on his ass and the kid's life is all fucked up as he is on the run wondering if every day is his last day on earth."

"Why stir up any crap now? Once this kid is eliminated the cops are going to put two and two together and connect the Beanstalk to Jill and the heat comes on once again. Why not just let bygones be bygones? It's not like this kid owes money to the family or is a bad ass who deserves to die. Personally I think a nice beat down would be sufficient. You know, like put him in a cast for a couple of months and then move on. To me this is just petty shit."

"I hear you Louie, but you and me ain't boss and the boss says wrap up this loose end and you too, like Jerry, can have an all-expense paid vacation to the Mediterranean."

"Mickey, you didn't tell me that part. We get to go on vacation when this job is done?"

"That's right."

"Well, shit, let's go pop the little bastard and get the hell out of this cold weather."

In less than ten minutes Mickey and Louie were in the comfy interior of their sleek, black Escalade heading East on the Pennsylvania Turnpike. A light snow was falling and snaked across the roadway but visibility was good and it was so cold outside that there was no real threat of any accumulation.

"What exit are we looking for Mickey?"

"It is the exit for route 711."

"711, now that's a lucky number."

"Ain't going to be a lucky number for one Mr. Beanstalk. It's about 11:00 P.M., Louie, when we get to the exit we head south and it should only take us about another 20 minutes to get to Sagamore. From here to there, I'd say we'll be at ground zero about 11:30 P.M. There's only about five streets in the whole fucking town so it should be real easy to find Zemko Road where Beanstalk's parents live. On the map it looks like you take Church Street which is the main drag and hang a right onto Zemko. Once we do a drive by I want you to pull over so that we can go over the plan one more time so there aren't any mistakes. This operation needs to go a smooth as a baby's ass."

Mickey's ETA was right on. At exactly 11:37 P.M. the Escalade was slowly approaching the outskirts of Sagamore and after a minute or so they cruised passed by the post office and headed down Church Street. The little town represented a holiday season picture post card. The outside of every house was strung with blinking colored lights and as you looked at the front of each house you saw a Christmas tree framed in each window. Some of the houses had fireplaces and the smell of crisply burning pinewood was heavy in the air.

"Just like we thought, Louie, no one here is stirring outside, not even a fucking mouse."

There might not have been a mouse stirring but old Cy Beck was stirring. Since Jake's departure, the residents of Sagamore took turns sitting in the darkened post office each night on the lookout out for any "strange" vehicles coming into town. Tonight Cy was the sentry. As the Escalade passed, Cy phoned the Stalk residence.

"Johnny, we have a stranger in town. A shiny Cadillac Escalade just passed by and is heading down Church Street."

"Ok Cy. Thanks. Looks like tonight's the night our plan goes into action. You call the rest of the folks and I'll take care of the situation here."

"Will do, Johnny. Be careful now, OK?"

"You bet, Cy. Thanks a lot and make those calls right now. The only chance we have is the element of surprise."

Mickey and Louie found Zemko Road and the Stalk residence very easily. They did a drive by and then found a nice dark spot to pull over about ½ a block away. They made sure that they were pointed in the right direction so that they could exit easily without having to turn around.

"This is it Louie. We leave the car engine idling and proceed to the front door just like we are guests for the party. No need to go sneaking around back or breaking any windows. This has to be a very natural scene. The people in little towns like this are close knit. Shit, probably a lot of incest going on. One of those deals in which you sister and your mother are the same person. So they'll answer the door willingly. Won't be any of this looking through a peephole to see who's there or opening a chained door.

We knock, they open. If the Beanstalk opens the door I put a bullet in his head and you take out anyone else who tries to make trouble. When I say "take out" I don't mean killing them. Shoot for a kneecap or a shoulder. We want them down but not out. We are not the Manson family on some mission to take out everyone in the house. We're sophisticated, right? Our job is to get the Beanstalk and get out. That's it. Whether Beanstalk does or does not open the door, you hold your gun on whoever is in the room and I rip out the phone line. We tell everyone to disrobe to their underwear, throw their shoes into the fireplace, put their hands behind their backs and get into a nice close-knit circle. We select the biggest, strongest looking person in the group hand him a roll of duct tape and tell him to play ring around the rosey and tape everyone into a nice, big, tight communal ball. We make sure he exhausts all three rolls of tape and we make sure he pulls the tape nice and tight. If this guy gives us any shit at all we shoot him in the foot. This accomplishes two things: First, the biggest potential physical threat to us is rendered helpless and second, it will get everyone else's attention real fast and the next person we pick to continue the taping will have that tape around the group so fucking fast he'll look like the road runner on crack. If Beanstalk doesn't open the door and is not in the crowd you handle the taping chore and I'll go and search the house. If I find him, I'll shoot him. When I return, we'll wish everyone a happy New Year and calmly leave the house. We have to be careful to maintain all speed limits and be careful not to make any kind of moving violations as we leave this town. We don't want some local cop who is bored out of his skull to stop us just so he feels like he is doing something to earn his paycheck. When we get to the PA Turnpike we will head EAST to Philadelphia NOT WEST back to Pittsburgh. Even though these folks are tied up, eventually they'll find a way to get lose and they will assume we came from Pittsburgh and the initial search will be directed in that direction. We will be at the Philly airport in about four hours. A couple of our boys will meet us at the Philly airport and take the car. We get our bags and get on the 6 A.M. flight from Philly to Miami. From Miami we take a flight to the Dominican Republic and hang out there for a week and then head to Rome for a glorious year-long vacation. Capisci?"

"Capisci."

"OK, put on your ski mask and let the games begin."

****

Inside the Stalk house Johnny alerted everyone that trouble was on the way and would be there very soon. He turned off all of the lights except for one small table lamp. Thus most of the light in the room emanated from the tree lights, the decorative window lights and the fireplace. Everyone assumed their position in front of the door. One group assumed a kneeling position, the next group stood behind them and a third group composed of the tallest people stood behind them. Big Red O'Reilly, the strapping six-foot, eight-inch, three-hundred and eighty-pound behemoth went out the back door and snuck around to the front porch and positioned himself under a tarp about eight feet to the left and behind the doorway. If anyone casually looked at the tarp he would think that it was being used to cover a pile of firewood. If anyone looked very closely at the tarp one would see that two eye holes had been cut in it so that big Red would have a bird's eye view of anyone standing in front of the door jam.

After receiving Cy's call, Stan and his 6-man crew had come up from the mine and were strategically positioned on the other side of street behind Johnny Masterson's house. Mac's house provided a clear view of the Stalk's residence and an area a half a block in both directions from the Stalk property.

Mickey and Louie left the gear shift in "park" and the engine idling and walked across the grass to the front steps of the Stalk residence. Little did they know that seven sets of eyes were following their every step. As they made their way to the house they noticed that the house was a bit dark but they picked up silhouettes of a group of people from the reflections generated by the Christmas tree lights and the fireplace. They could hear the muffled voice of Dick Clark's voice emanating from a TV. Obviously they were all poised and ready for the countdown of the drop of the big ball in Times Square. Mickey checked his watch; 11:57 P.M. and all was well. He swiveled his head and could see no evidence of anyone else in the vicinity of the house. The coast was clear. In five minutes this deal would be done and he and Louie would be off to the land of sun and white sandy beaches. As they stood at the entrance to the house Mickey couldn't find a door bell so he politely knocked on the wood frame of the door.

Johnny opened the door and before Mickey and Louie could react, three rows of people armed with the old-style-screw-in-the-bulb flash cameras simultaneously pushed the buttons on their cameras and created a blazing ball of white light. The flash momentarily paralyzed Mickey and Louie with blindness. In that moment of their paralysis Big Red flipped off his canvas cover and in 2 gigantic steps he was standing directly behind Mickey and Louie. Red spread his massive arms so that one was next to the right side of Louie's head and the other on the left side of Mickey's head.

With tremendous power, Red snapped his arms together and as he did Mickey and Louie's heads smashed into each other and both crumpled to the floor. In a flash Stan's crew was on top of them and within 15 seconds both Mickey and Louie had been hogged tied with bull rope, had a Christmas stocking stuffed in their mouth and had a strip of duct tape over their eyes. Stan's crew carried Mickey and Louie to the Escalade and deposited them in the back seat. Stan took the wheel and the rest of the crew jumped into the vehicle. Big Red wanted to get into the car as well but he was too big to fit so he jumped in the back of Johnny's truck and he and Johnny followed Stan as they headed to the mine entrance. Once they arrived at the mine entrance Stan and his crew pulled Mickey and Louie out of the Cadillac and placed them on separate hand cars. By this time, Mickey and Louie were both conscious and struggling to move around but with the thick rope around them about all they could do was to twitch a little bit. Down they went until they reached the bottom of the mine shaft almost 2000 feet below ground level. When they arrived at their destination they removed Mickey and Louie from the hand car and dragged them over to an area were two freshly-dug 15-foot holes had been dug. At this point Johnny said to Mickey and Louie, "When I'm done talking to you we are going to untie you, remove the duct tape, the gags, your shoes, your socks and all of your clothes, but before we do that listen up. Right now you are about a half a mile under the surface of the earth. You could set off a bomb here and at ground level the sound would be that of a muffled firecracker. You can yell and scream as loud as you want and no one is going to hear you. I know why you came here and I want to tell you that Jake Stalk had NOTHING to do with that girl who was killed. Yes, he knew her but he only talked to her one time. There was no love affair going on. The only reason he went back to see her a second time was to find out how she was because he knew all of the blood on the seat of his cab didn't come from him. He was just trying to be a nice guy when your two friends came along. The fact that one of your friends died in the pursuit of Jake had nothing to do with Jake and everything to do with the stupidity of your friend. Because of you bastards, Jake is gone and I don't even know where he is. You have taken my son away from me and ruined our lives and now they send you two messengers of death to hunt him down like he is a criminal. Tonight you are going to stay here and have a long time to think about what will happen if you or any of your demented friends come back here looking for Jake. We have a brigade of miners here who are pissed off and pissed off miners aren't people to fuck with. IF you or your people decide to come back here you'd better bring an army because if you don't you'll all end up in a hole like the hole you two will be in tonight. The only difference is that you two are going to get out of this hole and they won't. How do they say it in your language... Capisci? Shake your heads up and down if you capisci." Mickey and Louie shook their heads indicating that they understood.

"Ok, good boys. Now, like I said we are going to remove the rope, the gags, the tape and your clothing. You're 2000 feet under the surface of the earth and there are no lights here. It will be pitch black. When we remove the tape you will see little spot lights. Those lights are the lights on our miner's caps. If we turned off the lights on our miner's caps you would see nothing. Don't try to fight us as you are outnumbered. Remember you have no weapons and won't be able to see the hand in front of your face anyway, so any resistance on your part would be foolhardy. Even though it is about zero degrees at ground level, at this depth under the ground the temperature is pretty much a constant 60 degrees so it will be moderately cold but not cold enough that you'll suffer from hypothermia."

Stan and his crew removed the bull rope, gags, and duct tape and Mickey and Louie removed their clothing. "For your own protection we've dug a hole for you boys to stay in tonight. If we don't confine you, you could possibly get lost as there are miles of underground tunnels in this area. Left to your own devices, you might fall into some cavern and kill yourself. So we are going to put a rope around your torso and lower you into your sleeping quarters. Capisci? We'll give you some water so that you can raise a toast to the New Year and we are also going to provide you with a midnight snack just in case you get hungry through the night."

At that point Stan and his crew secured the ropes around Mickey and Louie and just before they started to lower them into the hole Johnny says, "Stan, lather up our men."

At that point Stan and his men opened up this 5-gallon container and began to apply the contents over Mickey and Louie.

"What in the fuck is this shit?" asked Mickey.

"Peanut butter," replied Johnny.

"Peanut butter? Why in the fuck are you putting peanut butter all over us?"

"I told you that we were giving you a snack and the snack is peanut butter. It's very nutritious."

"And how do you expect us to eat it?"

"You can lick it off your body or each other's body."

A Cruel Twist of Fate

"Fuck you. I ain't licking any peanut butter off of my body and I certainly ain't going to lick ANYTHING off of Louie's body."

"Maybe so, maybe not; but I will tell you this, there are rats in these holes and they like to eat peanut butter, so what you don't eat, the rats might try to. And while they are eating the peanut butter they might not be able to distinguish the difference between peanut butter and your flesh. Capisci?"

Stan and his men lowered Mickey and Louie into the hole and cut the ropes. Once into the hole Johnny said, "Happy New Year. Think about what I said to you and we'll see you in the morning."

As they were about to leave Johnny picked up a cloth bag and dropped its contents into the hole. Immediately you could hear Mickey saying to Louie, "What in the fuck is that? Jesus fucking Christ Louie, it's rats! Get em off me. Get em the fuck off me!"

As they were walking back to the hand cars Stan said to Johnny, "Were there rats in that bag?"

"No, just a dozen harmless field mice, but they don't know that," replied Johnny.

"Mice don't like peanut butter, Johnny."

"I know that, but they don't. This will be a New Year's Eve those assholes will never forget."

Johnny, Stan and the rest of the guys climbed aboard the hand cars and began their journey to the surface. In the meantime, Mickey and Louie were freaking out in their hole. It would be a long night for the two of them. Their dreams of sitting on a sandy beach in the Dominican Republic had been replaced by the reality of licking peanut butter off of their bodies to save themselves from being eaten by a pack of hungry rats.

At 8:00 A.M. the next morning Johnny, Stan and Big Red returned to the hole. "Good morning boys. How was the night? Enjoy the peanut butter?"

"Fuck you. We're freezing! Get us out of here before the rats attack us again."

"Listen up boys. Here is how this is going to go down this morning. We will pull you out of the hole and then put a piece of duct tape over your eyes. Your hands will be free. If you attempt to remove the duct tape you'll find yourself back in the hole for another night. After we tape your eyes we are going to take you to the shower room so that you can take a hot shower and get all squeaky clean. You will shower with the tape on your eyes. Again, you attempt to remove the tape and bang, back in the hole you go. The good women of Sagamore have cleaned and pressed your clothes and even polished your shoes. After your shower you will dress yourselves keeping the tape on your eyes. After you are dressed, we'll take you to your car. Once in the car, we will lightly bind your hands in front of you. Then we'll drive your car to a drop-off location. Once at the drop-off location I'll put a box cutter in one of your hands, we'll leave and you'll be free to go. It will be easy for the two of you to figure out how to cut the binding around your hands and once that's done you are home free. And finally, to show our gratitude to Mr. Bodino for sending you here to break in the New Year, there will be a nice gift-wrapped box on the front seat of the car. It's not a bomb so he doesn't have to worry about something exploding in his face. Let's call it a souvenir from Sagamore. Something to remember us by, if you will. You must promise to not open this package as this is a special gift for Mr. Bodino and is to be opened only by him. Do you understand the procedure? Are you straight on everything?"

Mickey replies, "We got it. Let's go. Like I said, we are freezing and these rats are driving us fucking crazy."

"OK. One last order of business; I told you last night that I don't know where Jake is and that's the truth. I wish to God that I did know where he was. I also told you that he and that poor girl, Jill Bodino, never had relations together and that's the truth. In fact, they never established a relationship of any sort. You need to relay this information to Mr. Bodino because this whole scenario about Jake and Jill is simply a figment of his imagination."

Mickey and Louie were pulled out of the hole and the procedure outlined by Johnny went off without a hitch. At 10:30 A.M. with Stan at the wheel of the Cadillac, Big Red riding shot gun and with Johnny tailgating the Escalade in his truck, they pulled into a roadside rest about five miles West of Somerset, PA. By 11:15 A.M. Stan, Big Red and Johnny we're back in Sagamore having a beer and getting ready for a New Year's Day lunch.

It took Mickey and Louie less than 10 minutes to cut the bindings on their hands and to remove the tape from their eyes. After spending a few minutes getting used to the daylight, they went to the restroom to take a piss, got a cup of hot coffee from the vending machine, returned to their car and headed back to Pittsburgh. Neither one of them spoke a word during the entire trip.

At 1:00 P.M. Mickey and Louie entered the Italian American Club. They were informed that Dominic was at home sleeping as the New Year's Eve party at the club hadn't ended until about 5:00 A.M. that morning.

"Mickey, are you going to call him?"

"Louie I HAVE to; he's gotta know what went down."

"Yeah, but Mick, we fucked up big time. He's going to be really pissed and when Dominic gets pissed very bad things happen."

"Yeah, I know, but we have no choice. What else can we do?"

"Well, I don't know about you but I'm so fucking hungry that my stomach hurts. Why don't we eat something before we call. If I'm going to get worked over or shot I'd like to do it on a full stomach. How about you?"

"I'm not that hungry, but I have to eat something to get the taste of peanut butter out of my mouth, so let's eat."

"Hey Mickey, now I know how THE MAN felt."

"What man?"

"THE MAN; you know, JC, Jesus Christ."

"What in the fuck are you talking about?"

"I'm talking about THE MAN and how he felt at the Last Supper. Mickey, this could be our last supper."

By 2:30 P.M. Mickey and Louie's tummies were full and their courage to call Dominic had been bolstered by the consumption of a half a dozen "boiler makers" a piece. After misdialing twice, Mickey finally got the numbers right and Dominic answered on the third ring.

"Who's this?"

"Dominic, Happy New Year this is Mickey?"

"Oh yeah, Mickey; are you in Miami or the Dominican Republic?"

"Neither, Dominic."

"Listen, my head is about to explode and I have no time to play twenty questions. So where are you and why are you calling? If you woke me up just to say Happy New Year the next time I see you I'm going to break your fucking skull."

"We're at the club."

"What club?"

"Our club."

"You fuck, there you go again. Our club where?"

"The Italian American Club in Pittsburgh."

"WHAT? Didn't you and Louie pop that little fucker last night and go on to Miami as planned?"

"No Dominic. It's kind of a long story."

"Listen you asshole. This could be a story that ends up with a bullet between your fucking eyes. Don't go anywhere. I'm going to call Mr. Lamana and he and I are coming to the club and you and Louie are going to tell us your long story. I'm bringing Mr. Lamana along so that he knows why I'm going to kill you. This family has protocol about eliminating members of the family and if it weren't for that protocol I'd come down there right now and waste the both of you. Now, stay put and one more thing Mickey."

"What's that Dominic?"

"Stop drinking. You're slurring your words. You need to be sober when you tell your long story and besides I hate shooting a drunk."

Mickey and Louie spent the next hour drinking coffee and running back and forth to the men's room. At 4:00 P.M. Dominic Bodino and THE MAN, Louie "the banana" Lamana entered the Italian American Club and headed straight for the bar where they found Mickey and Louie smoking heavily and sipping cups of coffee. Mr. Lamana walked up to Mickey and clipped him a good one across the back of the head. "You, fuck you, don't you know that this is a non-smoking club?" Both Mickey and Louie immediately dropped their butts into the coffee cups.

"Upstairs, to the back office with the both of you!" screamed Mr. Lamana.

"Wait a minute Mr. Lamana, I have to get something."

"Get what you dimwit? You've been sitting here for hours and now you have to get something?"

"I'm sorry Mr. Lamana, it will only take a second."

Mickey ran to the other end of the bar and got the package that was left on the front seat of the car by Johnny.

"What's this; a fucking gift for me? Don't think a gift is going to do anything to save you sorry ass."

"Actually this is for Dominic and not you."

Mr. Lamana led the group and was followed by Mickey. Louie and Dominic brought up the read and Dominic was pushing Louie along all the way to the office.

Once in the office, Mr. Lamana took his place behind a huge mahogany desk. He quickly ran his hand through his hair a couple of times, adjusted the collar on his shirt, repositioned his tie and cleared his throat. Dominic took the seat to his immediate right, unbuttoned his jacket and smiled a demented smile as he stared at Mickey and Louie. Mickey and Louie sat in chairs on the opposite side of the desk. The first thing Mickey did was to give the gift to Dominic.

"You dickheads give me a gift when I came here to blow your fucking brains out? I gotta tell you Mickey, you have balls, but those balls may be splattered all over this room in a few minutes."

"Aren't you going to open it before we talk?"

"Ok, I'll humor you." Dominic looked at the card on the gift and it read:

Happy New Year Mr. Bodino
from Local #33 of the UMW in Sagamore.
If you like this you can always stop by for a refill.

Dominic opened the gift and inside was a 6 quart jar of peanut butter.

"Peanut butter? What in the fuck is this, some kind of joke? Are these people morons?"

Louie replied, "They are not morons and it's no joke, believe me."

Mr. Lamana said, "Ok boys, you've had your fun, now it's time to tell your story and it had better be the best story you ever told in your life. In fact, your life depends on it if you know what I mean."

Over the next 30 minutes Mickey reviewed the events of the previous evening. Louie didn't participate in the flow

A Cruel Twist of Fate

of the story but he did interject a few comments here and there in order to drive home a point. When Mickey mentioned the big guy with the red hair, Louie said, "You know how big Jerry is? Well this guy made Jerry look like a fucking lightweight! Never saw a guy that big. And strong? Jesus, he pulled me up out of that hole with one hand!" When Mickey mentioned "the rats", Louie said, "And Mr. Lamana, there must have been a hundred of them squealing and nipping at our balls all night long. And every one of them was as big as a cat. We're lucky they didn't eat us alive."

Dominic didn't seem to be impressed with of these comments as he kept repeating under his breath, "Fucking liars."

After Mickey concluded, Dominic said, "Mr. L, this is the most cockamamie fucking story I ever heard. The only thing missing was that Mighty Mouse didn't show up to save the day or that Snow White and the Seven Dwarfs didn't suddenly appear and a sex orgy broke out in the hole with the rats. In fact, I'll bet Louie tried to fuck one of them rats but his dick was too small."

All of a sudden Mr. Lamana slammed his hand down of the desk with a deafening blow. The blow was so hard that the pitcher of water on the desk toppled over. It was so loud that Dominic got wide-eyed, Mickey's mouth opened wide and his jaw dropped and Louie almost pissed his pants. "ENOUGH DOMINIC! E FUCKING NOUGH! Shut up and let me think about this for a minute."

During the next few minutes of silence Dominic, Mickey and Louie sat there with their eyes downcast. Mr. Lamana went through his ritual again; ran his hands through his hair, adjusted his shirt collar and repositioned his tie. He pulled out a big cigar from his coat pocket, lighted it and took a slow, long drag and then he pulled out a flask from another pocket and took a quick swig. He opened the desk drawer and pulled out a 357 Magnum and placed it in front of him. He was now ready to speak. "Mickey and Louie I believe your story. It's disappointing to know that you got outsmarted by a bunch of people who don't have a full set of teeth and couldn't spell **C A T** if you spotted them the C and the A. But it happened. In fact it was an ingenious plan they engineered, so I have to give credit where credit is due. Maybe we should see if that Johnny guy would like to join the family. That still doesn't eliminate the fact that you two are morons. Let me revise that statement, you two are not just normal morons, you are stupid morons. How can you be trusted in the future to carry out any assignments? Dominic, you have used members of the family to carry out your personal vendettas. We lost Tommy because of your arrogance. We had to send Jerry away because of your temper and your brashness. And last night we could have lost two more of our soldiers because of your stupid fucking pettiness. You beat up this college kid, you kill your ex wife and then because of your wild jealously you use company resources to carry out a personal grudge. And all of this was going on without my knowing, without my consent? Who in the fuck do you think you are? Where in the fuck do you think that you got the authority to act out on your own in these matters? Why didn't you come to me for advice? No, you didn't because you think you are smarter than everyone else. You think you are THE MAN when I'm still THE MAN. People like you in the family represent a danger to all of us. You're a fucking loose cannon Dominic. Mickey, come here, I have a job for you before you leave."

Mickey got up and stood in front of the desk. Mr. Lamana slid the 357 Magnum across the desk and said, "Do us all a favor and remove this cancerous growth from our family. Put Dominic to sleep."

Dominic's eyes went wide with fright. He was aghast and began to plead for his life, but the plea was a very short one as Mickey pulled the trigger and Dominic went to sleep... for good.

As Dominic lay on the floor with a puddle of blood seeping out of his head, Mr. Lamana said to Mickey and Louie, "This shit with this college kid is over, you hear?"

"Yes, sir," Mickey and Louie repeated in harmony.

"Now, clean up this mess. After you clean up the mess follow our normal procedure in cases like this. Take the body down to the steel mill, see our crew down there and have them dispose of body. Call ahead so they're ready when you arrive."

"Yes sir, Mr. L."

As Mr. Lamana was leaving the room, Louie said, "Mr. L what about the peanut butter?"

"You boys flip for it." On his way out of the door Mr. Lamana uttered to himself, "What morons. What stupid fucking morons."

BACK TO NEW YORK

On New Year's Day I called my parents to wish them well and to reassure them that I was doing well. I told them about the time with the Sorrento family over Christmas and they seemed very happy that I was not all alone during the holidays and that I had met such nice people. When I asked my dad if there was any news about "those" people he told me about the incident that had occurred and how they handled it. If it wasn't such a serious topic, I think I would have been very amused at how a small group of backward miners had outsmarted members of a sophisticated family operation. I did laugh out loud during my dad's description of the part when he threw the mice into the hole. But it was no laughing matter because it meant that those guys were still on my trail. The good news was that even though they had been looking for me it was obvious that they had no clue as to my whereabouts. I hoped to keep it that way. We ended the call with sentiments of love and with my mom asking when I might be coming home. "When it's safe, mom and not before. I'm doing fine and I'm living in a good environment. Maybe yesterday's incident will make them think twice and they'll back off of their pursuit. But, for now let's be safe and not sorry."

In January the semester started and I was back to being a college kid. Somehow Mrs. Sorrento worked out a deal with Saul Waxler, manager of the Solita So Ho Hotel next door and Mr. Waxler hired me as a part-timer for 20 hours a week. In addition, Mrs. Sorrento told me that I could continue to live with her rent free. "No way you can pay me and those bandits at the college at the same time. You need to get that education to have a future. Me? I'm an old lady and my future ended when I lost my Tony but somehow I'll continue the journey. But you? You're young and have your whole life ahead of you. You are a good boy and you have been a big help to me. You have become part of my family and part of this business. Right now you need that money more than I do. When you graduate and make big money then you can repay me. Maybe then you can buy me a new apron?" How could I have gone from being so unlucky to being so lucky in such a short period of time?

The weeks turned into months and before you know it I had been away for almost a year. I called home once a month and there had been no evidence of any strangers visiting Sagamore looking for me. Maybe the hunt was off? I was doing great in school. In fact, I qualified for a Pell Grant which greatly reduced my tuition costs. The money I was making from my part time job at the hotel was keeping me in spending money and I was even able to sock away a little each month as well. I got along very well with Mr. Waxler and he was more than willing to teach me everything he could about how to manage a hotel operation. Mrs. Sorrento and I had formed a bond that went well beyond that of tenant and landlord. I grew to love her and saw her as my second mother. In like fashion, I became her adopted son. I was very tempted to go home during the holidays but I thought that maybe, just like last year, the goons from Pittsburgh might be hiding in the bushes waiting to ambush me. I decided to give it more time. My parents still did not know of my whereabouts. During the past summer, my uncle Albert who lived in Westfied, MA died and my folks drove up to the funeral. When they told me about his death and their plans to attend the funeral they mentioned that they were going to spend a night in New York City to break up the drive. I was so tempted to tell them I was in the City and I could meet them, but I was afraid that maybe somebody might be shadowing them on their trip thinking that they were coming to visit me. I just couldn't chance it and it broke my heart to know that they would be so close and I wouldn't see them.

The following year my studies called for entering a co-op program and I was assigned to work at the Washington Square Hotel which was right next to the NYU campus. The location couldn't have been more convenient for me. Obviously I had to quit my position at the Solita and I hated leaving Mr. Waxler, but he understood and told me that he would continue to help me in any way he could.

Sometimes my shift interfered with my ability to help Mrs. Sorrento, but ninety per cent of the time I was there to help her. Life was actually very, very good except for the fact that I was still disconnected physically from my family. Approaching the end of my second year away from home there had been no further instances in Sagamore of anyone looking for me. In all of my time in New York City not once did I ever see any suspicious characters or feel threatened in any way. There comes a time when you have to throw caution to the wind and that time was now for me. I decided that I was going home for the holidays. Mrs. Sorrento and I celebrated Chanukah with Mr. Waxler and, as usual, her daughters came to visit and I celebrated Christmas with my new family. I was bound and determined to get home before the holiday season ended so my plan was to go home for New Year's Eve. I asked Mrs. Sorrento to come along with me but she said that if she went then Mr. Waxler would be all alone so she was going to stay and keep him company.

I didn't tell my parents I was coming because if I did they'd be all worked up in anticipation of my arriving. I rented a car and arrived home in the afternoon of New Year's Eve day and when I saw my mom we both melted in each other's arms. Dad was coming off of a shift at 4:00 P.M. and when he arrived it was another emotional scene. School was starting up the second week of January so I had about week to renew old acquaintances. During that time I filled my parents in on everything that had happened since the night I left for destinations unknown. They were a bit upset that I didn't attempt to meet them when they visited New York, but they understood. It seemed like I had only been there a minute and it was time to return to the city. On the way back to New York City I stopped by to see Zorb's aunt Elsie and the two of us visited Zorb's grave. It was still hard to believe that she was gone.

When I got back to my bakery loft apartment I felt like a gigantic weight had been lifted from my shoulders. I felt that I could now lead a life without fear. I felt free for the first time in over two years. I felt that it was time to venture out socially as well since I had been living much like a hermit since arriving in New York. To that end I met and dated around, but the day Rose Feltzer came into my life was the day my life and my destiny changed forever.

THE FELTZER CONNECTION

David and Abraham Feltzer were twin brothers. They were also Polish Jews who grew up in the Baltic Sea Port town of Danzig, Poland. Their father, Mort, was a shoemaker but Mort's skills far surpassed the general ability to stitch, repair and replace soles and heels on shoes. Mort could size someone and create a perfectly fitting pair of new shoes from fine leather and he had the ability to make custom purses, vests, jackets, boots and sea caps as well. He was an absolute master craftsman when it came to working with leather. Mort began to prepare his sons to take over the family business as soon as they were able to walk unattended in his shop. And it was obvious from their very first attempts at working with leather that both boys had inherited their father's God-given gift.

All was wonderful for the Feltzer family in this quaint village located on the Bay of Danzig until the Nazi's invaded and took possession of the city. At that time the boys had just turned 20 years of age and were looking forward to finding a mate, starting a family, carrying on the family's name and maintaining the family business. But all of those hopes and dreams came crashing down the day Nazi storm troopers burst into their house and took their parents away. They would never see them again.

The boys were sent to Stutthof which was the first concentration camp built by the Nazis outside of Germany. Stutthof was located very near Danzig.

During their processing at the camp it was discovered that David and Abraham were skilled in leather craft and they were assigned to a shoe repair shop. Within a very short time it became obvious to their handlers that their talent for working with leather far exceeded the mundane task of replacing sole and heels on German soldier's boots. In a very short time the boys had their own shop in the camp where they made leather boots for the camp commandant and his staff. When visiting military dignitaries would visit the camp, the camp commandant would find out beforehand the boot size or their distinguished guests and the Feltzer brothers would create a new pair of boots from fine Corinthian leather for these camp visitors. It was a win, win, win situation as the visitor received a new pair of comfortable, perfectly-fitted boots made by fine craftsmen, the camp commander received acknowledgement for his forward thinking and hospitality and the Feltzer brothers got to live another day.

The Feltzer brothers were very gifted and they were very lucky as well as they survived their interment until the end of the war. After the war Abe couldn't wait to get out of

Danzig as Danzig was very near the German boarder and the camp where he and David were held prisoner was only a few miles from the heart of town. "David, I love you and I love this city, but I can't stay here with the vile memories I have of momma and poppa being dragged from our home and of all of the atrocities we witnessed during our years in captivity. I hate the Germans and I need to begin my life over again in another country." David understood his brother as he harbored many of the same emotions, but he felt that he owed it to his parents, especially his father, to stay in Danzig, restore the family business and pick up life where they had left off before the invasion.

It was a sad day for each when Abe left Danzig. As they stood on the train platform David said to Abe, "Go and find yourself a good eesh (wife) and begin anew. Don't ever forget me, mamma, poppa and don't let the shoah (holocaust) fill you with so much hate that you cannot live with a clear mind. If you allow those thoughts to poison your heart and soul it won't make any difference where you go as you will remain the same man; only the location will have changed and all of your good efforts, your hopes and your dreams of a new life will never blossom and bear fruit. Shalom aci hakatan (Good bye my little brother)."

Abe smiled and said, "Aci hakatan? You call me little brother because you were born 7 minutes prior to my birth? Ah, I guess you are right, I am your aci hakatan. I love you David, more than life itself. How could you think for a second that I could ever forget you or momma or poppa? You will be in my heart and my soul and my mind for all days to come. I will contact you when I am settled wherever that may be. Shalom."

As the train neared the station the brothers embraced each other until the whistle sounded and the conductor called for all passengers to board. They brushed away their tears and David watched as Abe climbed the steps and entered the car as the train began to pull slowly out of the station. As the train rounded the bend and out of sight, David was not aware that he would never see his brother again.

In a little over a year David's life changed dramatically for the better. He was able to resurrect his father's shop on its original site and for a very good price he bought a dilapidated old house which was located next to the bay. It was a sow's ear, so to speak, but with hard work and determination David turned the little bungalow into a silk purse. It wasn't a large home and was absent of any adjoining land, but it was a well-kept and comfortable residence.

One day a young woman with long, jet black hair, a beautiful face and striking eyes entered David's shop and inquired about securing work. David was smitten with this young girl and although he didn't need assistance he hired her to a part-time position helping keep the workshop clean and attending to the mundane paperwork associated with running his business. Truth be known, David just didn't want to let this woman out of his sight and he felt the only way to do so was to hire her. Her name was Soshana which is Yiddish for Rose and what a beautiful Rose she was. Although she was 10 years his junior, Soshana didn't seem to mind the age difference and found David to be a somewhat handsome man. He had an established business, had long-time roots in the community and he owned his own home. In her estimation, David was a very good catch.

As David got to know Soshana he discovered that she had undergone a similar experience as he when the Nazis invaded Poland. Soshana and her mother were separated from her father whom they never saw again and she and her mother were sent to Ravensbruck which was a camp for women that Herr Himmler had established north of Munich in the town of Furstenberg. During her time in Ravensbruck she and her mother worked in the shoe factory. Of the 132,000 women who were imprisoned at Ravensbruck, 92,000 died of starvation, illness or execution. Soshana's mother was one of those victims. Since the only work she had ever done in her life was at the shoe factory she felt that she might be able to find work in a shoe shop and destiny lead her to make the inquiry at David's shop.

Once David discovered that Soshana could work with shoes a grand business partnership was molded. Soshana handled the everyday business of repairing soles and heels and that freed up David to solicit the more profitable jobs of personalized boot making and other unique leather craft projects.

In a short time the grand business partnership gave way to a romantic relationship and David and Soshana became man and wife almost a year to the day after Soshana entered the shop looking for work. Not long after their marriage Soshana gave birth to a bouncing little girl and they named her Rose after her mother.

Soshana had a very difficult pregnancy and with the fear that future pregnancies might pose a grave danger to Soshana's health or to the health of an unborn child, the doctors suggested that she undergo a tubal ligation after the birth of Rose. Thus, Rose would be an only child and that fact served to deepen the bond that Soshana and David had for their child.

For the next 15 years David, Soshana and Rose led a good life. The business was decent but it didn't prosper as David thought it would because as Danzig, now Gdansk, was primarily a seaport town and its population was very blue collar. His clientele never transitioned much from those having soles and heels repaired to those desiring high quality leather products or custom-made shoes.

Although David never received a visit from his brother, Abe did manage to write an occasional letter. It turned out that Abe's path in life took him to Naples, Italy where, like David, he met a woman, got married and opened up a shoe repair shop. And like David his clientele was composed of low to middle income folks who wanted nothing more than replacement soles and heels on their shoes in order to extend their original investment. Business was not bad but it was not good. You could make a living wage but Abe wanted more than a living wage from his work. After not hearing from Abe for several years David received a letter in which Abe told David how excited he was about his recent move from Naples to Licola, a province of Naples which is located on the coast of the Mediterranean Sea. It seems as though the first suburban railway linking the coastal area of Licola-Cuma with the center of Naples had been constructed and with the completion of that railway the Licola-Cuma area had become fertile ground for developers to construct fine hotels and casinos. These hotels and casinos drew people of great wealth to the pristine beaches of Licola to relax and gamble. Abe had secured a location near a large casino-hotel complex and his business was booming.

He had hired 6 young boys and had trained them in the art of spit polishing shoes and these boys walked the streets near the hotels offering shoe shines for free. They existed on tips. This didn't put any money in Abe's pocket but it didn't cost him any money either except for the polish he furnished the boys. But upon completion of the shoe shine the boys would be sure to hand each patron Abe's business card and a brochure which advertised custom-made men's and women's shoes and a fine array of leather products that would be hand-made and personalized. In a very short time, people of wealth were visiting Abe's shop requesting a fitting for custom-made shoes and/or boots and/or a fancy gift for a friend a wife or a lover. Business was good; VERY GOOD. It would be no time before Abe would be a wealthy man himself.

Back in Gdansk the relationship between Soshana and David began to change. When Soshana left the concentration camp in Ravensbruck she was bitter and was sickened by the fact that she had lost her family, had been humiliated, violated and forced to live like an animal. She was young, she was pretty and she wanted nothing but the finer things in life to compensate for the years she lost in the camp. Many left the camps thankful for having their life spared and to them the simplest things in life became luxuries. Freedom, family and lack of persecution became their most valued assets. But Soshana wanted more; much more. When she first met David she thought he would be the person who would be her great provider; the one who would change her life and shower her with riches. After all, in a very short time after he left the camp he had become an established man with a home and an ongoing business. If all that occurred so quickly, surely a life with this man would provide the gateway to the riches of which she dreamed. But she and David had entered their second decade together and the riches had not come and the future was not looking bright. She felt that they were stuck in a limbo-type existence; two steps removed from hell but one very long step from heaven.

Soshana's heart and mind began wander as did her feelings for David. The age difference that seemed not to have been an issue when they got married became a major concern for her. What was she doing with this old man when she was still full of youth and vitality?

One day when David had gone to the bank to inquire about a loan, Soshana was minding the shop when a dashing young man appeared behind the counter asking if she could replace the heel on his shoes as he had caught it on a cobble stones in the street and it had become dislodged. "Not a problem," Soshana replied. "Take off your shoe and I'll have it replaced in no time." Soshana noticed that the young man was wearing a beautiful fur-lined coat and when he removed the coat he revealed a very fine silk suit that was perfectly tailored.

After introductions, Soshana discovered that this dashing and well-spoken man, Thomas Checkov, was a Russian importer/ exporter who was expanding his business and was visiting Gdansk checking on some of their shipping facilities. Thomas must have been a rich man as he owned residences in Greece, France, Belgium and Portugal as well as a several apartment buildings and a his main residence in Moscow.

"And what do you import and export Mr. Checkov?" Soshana inquired.

"Diamond, furs, original paintings and antiques; all things of beauty. I'm sure that you can associate with such beautiful things."

"And why do you say that Mr. Checkov?"

"Because you have such beauty yourself. How does such a beautiful woman as you repair shoes? You should be wearing precious stones, expensive furs and fine dresses, not hammering heels on broken shoes."

Soshana was turning red as she was embarrassed by the comments she was hearing. This man was not only handsome but he was obviously rich and he must have been attracted to her in some small way or he wouldn't have been so complimentary toward her. Soshana felt that this may be the day that her ship finally came in.

"The owner of the shop has gone to the bank and asked me to watch the shop in his absence."

"Then I consider it good my good fortune that my heel broke at the time the proprietor chose to go to the bank. Soshana, I am in town for only a few days and am not familiar with a good place to eat. With your local knowledge, might I be so forward as to ask you to accompany me to dinner tonight at the restaurant of your choice? Of course

I will understand if you refuse as you hardly know me and a woman of your natural gifts is likely to be pursued by all of the eligible men in Gdansk."

This question posed a problem for Soshana as she could not risk being seen for dinner with a strange man in Gdansk. Although Gdansk was a not a small town, you just never knew when someone might see you; especially since David's family had lived in this area for scores of years.

"I am free tonight Mr. Checkov and I know of a very nice restaurant but it is not Gdansk. It is in Sopot just 10 miles outside of the city. The restaurant is located at the Hotel Rezydent. I think you would find it quite suitable as The Rezydent has a 5-star rating; the kind of establishment l to which I'm sure you are accustomed."

"Hotel Rezydent it is. In fact, my next question was going to be a hotel recommendation. It looks like The Hotel Rezydent will satisfy both of my desires. How lucky I was to met you Soshana. What time is good for you for dinner?"

"Can you meet me at 6:00 across the street from this shop?"

"I can and I will and I look forward to being in your enchanting presence this evening."

Soshana handed Thomas his repaired shoe and as Thomas reached in his pocket to pay her Soshana said, "Since you are taking me to dinner, there will be no charge for this repair. It will be my way of thanking you in advance."

"Nonsense my lady; I am a man of means and I always pay my debts in full. Now open your hand and close your eyes and promise me you will not open your eyes until you hear the door close as I leave the shop."

"I promise." Soshana opened her hand and closed her eyes and when she opened them again, Thomas was gone but in her hand there was a large red ruby.

****

Soshana told David that she was going shopping in the city that night and she would see him later in the evening. And that began the first of many lies she told David during the next year and a half whenever Thomas came to Gdansk on business. Soshana forbade Thomas to come to the shop as she told him that the owner was very strict about socializing during business hours and that he was also very protective of her. It would be very awkward for her if Thomas would stop at the shop even if it was just to say hello. Thus, she would always travel to Sopot on her own and meet him at the Hotel Rezydent. During the time they were together they shared a good meal, fine wine, good conversation and it wasn't long before they shared a bed as well. Thomas had fallen madly in love with Soshana and Soshana was filled with the same emotion for Thomas. It wasn't hard to keep David in the dark because Thomas visited Gdansk only every several months or so, thus it was easy for Soshana to manufacture an excuse to leave the house alone for a short period of time. If Thomas had moved to Gdansk or visited weekly, well that would have been a different story altogether and matters would have been much more complicated.

Every time Soshana was leaving to go home Thomas would always ask her to close her eyes and open her hand and he would place a ruby or a diamond in her hand and tell her, "Every time you look at this stone think about me and how much I love you and how much I can't wait until you are in my arms again." One day as Soshana was about to leave, Thomas began his goodbye ritual and Soshana was expecting him to place another raw stone in her hand. But this time the stone felt different and when Soshana opened her hand she saw the most beautiful diamond ring imaginable. She looked at the ring and then she looked at

Thomas and then her eyes rested on the ring once more. She was so taken aback that she was speechless. Thomas broke the silence by telling her that his business in Gdansk was coming to a close and that he would only be making one more trip and on his return to Russia he wanted to take her with him to become his wife. "So this is an engagement ring, Thomas? You want to marry me? Is that what you are saying?"

"Yes, my love. Come with me and be my bride and let me shower you with love and riches until the day you die. As my wife you will have a life of nobility and will experience nothing but the finest things money can buy. You will be my love and my queen. Say yes and make me the happiest man on this earth."

Soshana thought about Rose and David. Could she leave them? She knew if she left that she would never see them again. David she could live without, but could she live without Rose? If she told Thomas the truth and said she wanted to go with him but only on the condition that her daughter could join her what would he say? Of course, she thought, he would be dumbfounded upon the revelation that she had a daughter AND a husband and that she had deceived him during the entire length of their relationship. He would be angry and leave and she would never see him again and she would have to go back to a future without promise living with David. A future with David would be a future without the slightest possibility of attaining a life accentuated with wealth or a touch of class. A future with David would be merely a never ending series of days that repeated themselves. Slowly and painfully time would pass, she would grow old, Rose would get married and move away and she would spend her remaining days with David in the shop replacing soles and heels. It would be like a life at Ravensbruck without guards and fences. "My love, you seem lost in deep thought. What is your answer?"

"Thomas I love you dearly. My answer is... YES!"

Thomas and Soshana made plans for his final trip to Gdansk. Thomas told Soshana to pack nothing as he would buy her a whole new wardrobe when they arrived in Russia.

The time had finally arrived and Soshana was about to leave to meet Thomas. Soshana told David that she needed to go to the market before they closed in order to buy eggs and milk for the next day's breakfast. Rose was already fast asleep in her bed. Soshana brushed her hair back with her finger tips and kissed her tenderly on the forehead. "Shalom my libin." (Goodbye my love.) She placed a locket in Rose's hand. The locket was in the form of a heart and when you opened it on one side was a picture of Soshana and on the other side was an inscription that read... "Always follow your heart." Soshana quietly tip toed out of the room, bade David adieu and went off in the night never to be seen again by her husband or her daughter.

****

Life after Soshana left was very difficult for David and Rose. David spent over a year making inquiries about Soshana's disappearance and had discovered nothing. Even police investigations turned up no facts. It was as though Soshana vanished into thin air.

At first Rose was frantic and upset and thought that her mother's leaving was her fault. Then she became angry and blamed David. It HAD to be something HE had done to make her so unhappy that she would run away. She didn't want to leave the house for fear that she wouldn't be home if her mother returned. It was very difficult to get Rose to go back to school. And when she did return to school, she was inclined to become confrontational with teachers and her fellow students. She threw tantrums and became a great distraction to the learning process. So much so that the school administrator strongly suggested to David that Rose not return to school until she received psychiatric help. Rose was now almost 17 years of age and normal 17-year old girls were a challenge for even the most able parents. The understanding and guidance of a mother during those years for an adolescent girls was of paramount importance and David was severely handicapped when it came to the matters of a helping a young girl turn into a woman. To make matters worse the business was not doing well. Much of his trade revolved around replacing heels and soles and repairing leather products; enough to pay the bills but hardly enough to consider paying for psychiatric help for Rose and/or any other extras in life. And furthermore, people in the community began to give David strange looks and rumors were abound that maybe David had killed his wife and dumped her in the bay or buried her in a bog somewhere out of town. Because of these rumors, some of his most loyal customers took their business elsewhere. It was clear to David that he and Rose had to move away from Gdansk and start life anew. But where?

    As David lay sleepless in bed one night thinking about where he and Rose could go to start a new life together, he remembered the letter he received from Abe and how Abe's life changed dramatically when he moved his shop near a casino where foot traffic was abound with people of wealth; people who were looking for the finer things in life; people who appreciated excellent craftsmen and were more than willing to pay for their services; people who wouldn't even consider having shoes repaired; why repair them when you can buy a new, customized pair made from soft, fine leather? Yes, that was the answer. He would follow the lead of his brother and move to a similar location. But the next question that entered his mind was, where would that be? After some thought; the answer came to him. It was so obvious. Why hadn't he thought of it before? So many others had chosen the same location, began their life anew and had successfully taken advantage of the opportunities available. After all didn't they call it the land of opportunity? Yes, he and Rose would go to America! America would offer a fresh start for both of them and a better future for Rose. Gdansk was a dead end road that had led him to despair while America was a highway of hope. It was a place that would offer Rose a new surrounding and an environment that would be free of the demons present in Gdansk.

During any free time David had in the weeks that followed his decision to move to America he went to the library to study the country and it's cities. Obviously they would land in New York City but New York City didn't have casinos. What city near New York had casinos? It didn't take him long to discover the location of Atlantic City. Atlantic City would be a perfect location. It was short trip from New York City and was the gambling capitol of the East Coast of America. Multiple casinos dotted the boardwalk area of Atlantic City and his research revealed that rental properties in the Atlantic City area were very reasonable and just a stone's throw from the world of the rich and famous.

That evening when he returned from the library he sat down with Rose to present to her his new plan for their lives. He was very concerned about how Rose would react to his proposal. What would he do if she didn't want to go? Was Rose still intent on staying in Gdansk to wait for Soshana's return? It was almost three years since Soshana had left and not a word from her. Not a letter, not a phone call, nothing. Surely Rose didn't think the possibility existed that Soshana would just walk through the door one day like nothing happened. Or did she? After a thorough explanation of his plan and all of the whys and wherefores David said to Rose, "We will go only if you want to go. I am never going to leave your side. If you think staying in Gdansk is the best for your future, we will stay."

Rose remained pensive for a few minutes with her eyes cast downward at the table. She raised her eyes and looked up at her father and said, "Can we leave tomorrow?"

"I wish we could leave tomorrow, Rose, but we will need money to start our new life and that money will come from selling the business and this house. Those things don't happen overnight and besides you must complete your final year in high school. When we get to America you will have to find a job and you will need your graduation certificate and a transcript to verify that you are an educated young woman." Surprisingly, David's assessment of the situation was not met with resistance from Rose. She understood the situation and promised to behave and do her best in school while David was busy taking care of all of the necessary details associated with their plan to move.

The house sold early on in their timeline but the buyer was amenable to an arrangement in which David could stay in the house and pay rent until he was ready to move. The business took a little longer to sell but it occurred within the timeframe of their plan. David went to his banker and arranged for his funds to be held until they arrived in Atlantic City whereupon notification from David the banker would transfer the funds to his new institution. Rose became a new person. She was well behaved and conscientious about her school work and helped David with all of the details associated with housekeeping and even helped at the shop when needed. She finally came to grips that David was not responsible for her mother's abandonment of them. She continued to harbor mixed emotions about her mother; everything from hating her to loving her to missing her to not wanting to ever see her again. Through all of the waves of emotions that Rose experienced concerning her mother, there was one constant and that was the locket her mother had placed into her hand the night she left. From the day her mother left, Rose wore the locket 24/7. The inscription became her philosophy of life.

The day after Rose's graduation Rose and David were on a train headed to Warsaw. From there they had a flight on LOT Airlines, a Polish carrier, from Warsaw to a connection in Brussels, Belgium and then onto JFK Airport in NYC. Total travel time 11 hours and 45 minutes. In less than one half of a day their lives would change forever. As the inscription on her locket read, Rose and David were following their hearts.

ATLANTIC CITY

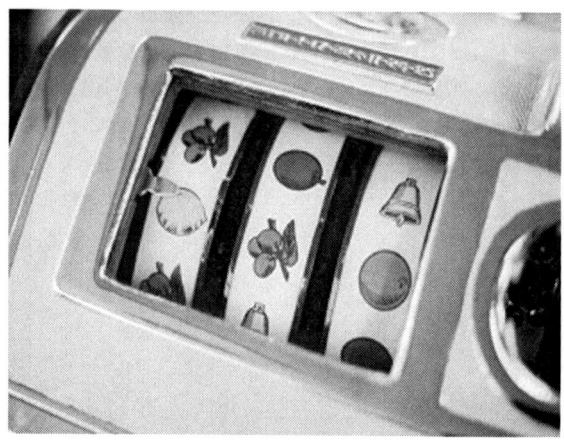

The trip from JFK to Atlantic City was quite an adventure for David and Rose. It involved a bus ride to Mid-town Manhattan, a cab ride to Penn Station, a train ride to 30th street station in Philadelphia and another train ride aboard the Atlantic City Express which ended up at the Atlantic City Convention Center. Right outside of the Convention Center was the Sheraton Atlantic City Hotel. The hotel was very expensive by Gdansk standards but David felt after such a long trip he could splurge a bit so that he and Rose could spend a few nights living in the lap of luxury. Rose never closed her eyes the entire trip as she didn't want to miss seeing anything in America. When they got settled in their room, David ordered room service but before the food arrived, Rose had descended into a deep sleep. In fact, David took just a few bites of his food and before long he fell asleep as well.

In the morning David and Rose took a walk to get familiar with the area. It was about a 10-minute walk from the Sheraton to the Boardwalk and the center of the Casino complexes. Along the way David noticed that once you were in the casino area the environment seemed to be safe and clean, but just several blocks away the store fronts were somewhat dilapidated and the apartment buildings and homes were run down. This area was not the vibrant metropolis that David had envisioned, but he didn't have a plan B; they were in Atlantic City so there was no turning back now. He and Rose took a walk through the Trump Taj Mahal Casino, Caesar's Atlantic City, Bally's and the Showboat Atlantic City. They were overwhelmed with the opulence and decadence and even at this early hour in the morning there were groups of people milling about gambling and playing the slot machines. Even though the neighborhood wasn't quite what he expected, David was sure of one thing and that was there was money in this town and he was going to get his share.

The next day David met with a realtor and of the properties she showed him, the ones he liked he couldn't afford and the ones he could afford he didn't much care for. As they were ready to part company the realtor said, "Mr. Feltzer, I have another property that I can show you but I must tell you up front that this property is not in good condition. The property is located at the corner of South New Jersey and Oriental Avenues which is very near the Showboat Casino. This location will be to your liking, but this building suffered some interior fire damage and the owner and the insurance company got into a squabble regarding coverage. The insurance company claimed that the owner torched the building just to collect on the insurance policy and wouldn't pay the claim. The owner sued the insurance company for breach of contract. For four years they argued in court, motions were filed and were met by counter motions; back and forth it went like that until a judge sided with the insurance company's position. When the owner didn't get his money he let the property go to hell. The city fathers have been on the owner's case charging him with a host of violations hoping to force the owner to repair the building as it has become an eye sore to the community. If you are willing to invest in making repairs to the building I'm sure that the owner would let you have the property for a very reasonable rate per square foot."

"What kind of business was operating at this property before the fire took place?" asked David.

"It was a small produce market and the owner lived in the apartment above the building. The property does not contain a lot of square footage, but with the kind of shop you are proposing to open, that shouldn't be a problem and the apartment upstairs will be plenty big enough to house you and your daughter."

As David walked through the building he looked at it in the eyes of seeing the glass half full rather than half empty. The major systems of the building and the core structure seemed to be in relatively good shape and he was sure that it wouldn't take much of an investment to bring them up to code. The interior walls and floors were going to need a major overhaul but that was work he could do himself with the help of another laborer. He asked the realtor to check with the owner about price and she left to make a phone call. When she returned with the price even David was surprised by how low it was. This place was a steal, but there would be a lot of hard work ahead. The next day David signed the contract and he felt very positive about his future; he was in America; he had his own shop; he and Rose had a roof over their heads and money would soon be in the bank once he had it wired from Gdansk. He was excited and anxious to begin the renovation of the building and lay the ground work for his new life.

David and Rose checked out of the Sheraton and found a small flat on N. Trenton Avenue near the Atlantic City Airport. It was a bus ride away from the site of his shop and the casino area, the neighborhood was run down and the apartment wasn't roomy, but it was a place to stay and the landlord was willing to give him a 6-month lease.

The next day David and Rose were waiting for the bus when a young man walked up to the bus stop. He was dressed in work clothes and was wearing steel-toed boots and carrying a lunch pail. Both David and Rose watched the young man approach them but each viewed him with a different set of eyes. David saw a young, strapping lad, wearing garb that indicated that he was on his way to some kind of construction job. Rose noticed his solid build, his thin waist line, his tight fitting jeans, his handsome face, his rugged jaw, his piercing blue eyes and his dark curly hair that was so thick that that the morning's ocean breeze hardly moved a hair. In David's eyes, the young man was nothing more than a common laborer. In Rose's eyes, this guy was an Adonis. As Rose starred at the young man their eyes met and locked and immediately she began to blush. The young man merely smiled, nodded his head and said, "Good morning." Rose remained speechless.

The bus arrived, and as fate would have it, there were only three empty seats on the bus. The young man took a seat, David sat down next to him and Rose sat next to David. David spoke first.

"Young man, this is our first ride on the bus. Could you tell us the stop closest to the Showboat Casino?"

"Just follow my lead as I'm working on a renovation job inside the Showboat."

"What is your specialty?"

"Mostly drywall and flooring, but I'm certified in electric and plumbing as well. I can do some carpentry, but

I'm not certified in that area yet. On this job they needed a drywall man and I fit the bill."

"Is this your own business?"

"No sir. I'm not that lucky. I'm just a union laborer in a pool. When a contractor gets a job, if he needs outside labor he calls the union hall and the union chief assigns men from the pool to handle the work."

"How long will you be on this job?"

"Probably another week or so and then I'll wait for a call from the union chief."

"By the way, I'm sorry, my name is David Feltzer and this is my daughter Rose. We just arrived from Poland and I'm starting my own business here in Atlantic City."

"Very glad to meet you sir and I'm especially honored to make the acquaintance of your daughter. My name is Tom McGraw. Most people call me Slim."

"Slim? You certainly don't look slim to me, Tom."

"Well sir, that's because you haven't met my brothers. Compared to them I am slim and my folks labeled me with that name when I was young and it kind of stuck with me my whole life."

"Slim it is. Slim, I just leased a small building adjacent to the Showboat and it is in need of some major interior repairs. I'm pretty handy myself, kind of a jack of all trades but master of none, and I will sorely need a good man to help me get this building in shape so that I can start my business and Rose and I can have a decent place to call home. I was wondering if you might know of a good man in need of work who would be willing to come and talk to me about helping me out. I'm willing to pay a fair wage for the right man."

"OK, Mr. Feltzer, I'll check around and let you know."

"Slim, my property is at the corner of S. Jersey and Oriental, just across from the casino. Stop by there and let me know when you have an answer. The sooner the better as

I need to get started as soon as possible. I can't afford to keep my future on hold."

"OK, Mr. Feltzer. I know the exact location of your building as I walk by there almost every day. I'll make my inquiries today. I work until 6:30 P.M. so I'll stop by around 7:00 P.M. if that's OK."

"That would be fine, Slim. And Slim, one more thing; you don't have to call me Mr. Feltzer; David would be just fine."

"Ok, Mr. Feltzer, I mean David. See you later. And Rose it was a real pleasure to meet you and I hope to see you again."

As Slim said, "I hope to meet you again," he and Rose locked eyes and you could tell that Slim's remark wasn't said just to be polite.

The first day at their new property, David and Rose spent time clearing out old junk and investigating their new surroundings. During her investigation Rose made a discovery. "Poppa," she called, "come and look at this." Rose was back in the far, right-hand corner of the first floor of the building. David approached her and Rose said, "What is this poppa?"

"What is what, Rose?" Rose pointed to the wooden floor and David still didn't see what she was pointing at. It was when he got down on his hands and knees that he noticed a small indention in the floor board about the size of a half-dollar. Surrounding the indention was a small metal ring. David pulled on the ring and to his surprise the ring was attached to a trap door and a section of the floor opened up revealing a pair of steps which led to the basement of the building. David retrieved the blueprint plans of the building and nowhere on the plans was there a reference to a basement in the building. Rose had discovered a secret room! With flashlight in hand, David descended the stairway and Rose followed after. He looked around for a switch plate and found a light switch on a pillar just to the right of the stairway. Rose flipped the switch and once illuminated, David and Rose found themselves in a long and narrow room about 30 feet long, 15 feet wide and about 8 feet high. The floor was made of pinewood just like rest of the floors in the building and the walls were cement block that had been whitewashed. The ceiling was made of cedar wood. One would think that the smell in the room would be musty but the cedar wood served to absorb any musty odor. The room was clean and absent of any furniture. At the far ends of each wall, at ceiling height, were two louvers which provided cross ventilation for the room. In addition there was a 6-foot by 6-foot cut out at the end of the room and in the cutout were a small sink and a commode. "What do you think this room was used for Poppa?"

"I'm not sure, Rose. The previous business was a produce shop. Maybe they used this room to store potatoes or grow mushrooms. Maybe they kept canned goods or jars of preserves down here."

"That makes sense, Poppa. But why go to the trouble of installing a sink and a toilet?"

"I don't know the answer to that question, but if we had had such a room in our home in Danzig maybe the Gestapo would never have found us. I don't know what this room was used for, but I know one thing and that is that room is to remain our secret. No one, absolutely no one is to know about this room but you and me. Understand?" Rose nodded in agreement and the two of them went up the stairs. David closed the trap door and they resumed their task of clearing out unwanted items.

It was about mid afternoon when David heard a knock at the front door and before he could get to the door two gentlemen walked into the building. Both were well dressed. One wore a top-of-the-line suit by Zanetti, complete with a crisply-starched white shirt with monogrammed cuffs, a silk tie and a pair of Antonio Zengar black cross designer shoes. The other man, by far the larger of the two, wore a grey, Steve Harvey suit with a black turtle-neck shirt and around his neck hung a large gold medallion inlaid with several diamonds. The fabric in the suit and the turtle neck was stretched to the limit by the muscular build of this man. The man of normal proportions introduced himself as Walter Bruno and he said, "This is Salvadore Pappano, my business associate who handles all of my personnel issues. You might say that Sal is in charge of enforcing company policies." David was very irritated that these two men had forced their way into his building. They didn't even have the courtesy to wait until he answered the door before they came barging in. But this was his first day in the neighborhood and he didn't want to start on a sour note so he kept his emotions in check and said, "And what can I do for you gentlemen?"

Walter replied, "It's not anything you can do for us, Mister... Mister..."

"David Feltzer, and this is my daughter Rose."

"Oh yes, Mr. Feltzer and may I say that your daughter is one very attractive woman." At this point Mr. Bruno stared at Rose and undressed her with his eyes. "But, back to why we are here. It's not anything you can do for us, Mr. Feltzer, it's what we can do for you. You see, we provide a much needed service for all of our clients."

"And what is it that you can do for me?"

"We can make your life easy or we can make your life difficult. Given the choice, most people choose easy and I'm sure you aren't any different than most people."

"Easy or difficult in what way Mr. Bruno?" David was fast losing his patience.

"First of all, Mr. Feltzer, you need to know that my father and members of his, ah family, own a controlling interest in a number of the casinos here in lovely Atlantic

City. He is also connected, you might say, to many of the other business establishments as well."

"Mr. Bruno, I find all of this information enlightening but my daughter and I have much work to do here and I really don't have any more time to listen to a dissertation about your father's involvement in the community. Now if you don't mind, we'd like to get back to our work."

Ignoring David's statement, Walter continued, "Mr. Feltzer I see that you are an impatient man and rude besides, so let me cut to the chase. By the end of this week Sal and I are going to return and you will hand me an envelope containing $5,000 in small bills."

"$5,000 for what? Are you crazy? Pay you for what!"

"Let's call it a contractor fee as I am going to help you as you renovate this property."

"You and I, Mr. Bruno, have no business together now and will not have any business together in the future. Now get the hell out of my building before I call the police."

"Call the police Mr. Feltzer? You don't even have a phone. Now, shut your little mouth and listen to me. If you interrupt me again I'm going to ask Sal to give you a lesson in manners that you won't forget. To get this place renovated you are going to have to have building inspectors sign off on any improvements to make sure that the work is up to code. If not up to code, this building will never open. The electric company will never turn the power on, the gas company will never turn the gas on and the water company will not permit you to draw one drop of water. It will be in your best interest to make sure that the various building inspectors inspect your work in a timely fashion. That's where I come in as your personal contractor. With my help, permits can be issued very quickly and inspectors will conduct their inspections in a very timely fashion. Without my help, it may take months to get a building permit issued and even longer to schedule an inspector. Without my help, by the time you get this place up and running your pretty little daughter will be an old woman. Look at it this way, Mr. Feltzer, you've invested a nice piece of change in this building and will be investing even more money in repairs and labor. Five thousand dollars to protect your investment is a very reasonable amount don't you think?"

"I think you are a god damn crook that's what I think. And as soon as you leave here I'm going to find the nearest policeman and report you. Now get the hell out of my sight!"

"Mr. Feltzer, you need to calm down. Remember the old saying about a policeman? To refresh your memory, a policeman is always your friend. That's so very true here in Atlantic City and I can vouch for that because all of the policemen are my very good friends. They are, you might say, part of the family. Whom do you think they are going to listen to, someone in the family or a loud-mouth little Jew like yourself. Maybe you think $5,000 is a little high. Well, maybe it is and I could reduce that by several thousand by spending a night with your daughter. How does this sound? Three thousand for my contractor fee and your daughter and I spent a night of gambling, fine dining and lovemaking? That's what I would call a win/win situation."

No sooner were those words out of Walter's mouth than David lunged for his throat. But Sal intercepted David, grabbed him by the skin of his neck and with one hand lifted him into the air, shook him around like a rag doll and dashed him to the ground. As David laid there in a heap, Rose stood by in a petrified state. Walter then said to David, "I take your reaction to my generous offer as a no which means the price is back up to the original $5,000. We will be back at the end of the week to collect payment in full. Now, if for some reason you don't have the money, my friend Sal will conduct a personal conference with you that won't be pleasant and on top of that you will be expected to pay a late fee of $100 a day until your debt has been paid in full. Good luck with your renovations and I wish you much success in your new business and your new home. Rose, it was nice seeing you. Maybe someday I will see a lot more of you if you know what I mean."

When David returned to his chores at hand, his mind was racing and filled with fear and concern and a lot of unanswered questions. His fear was not for himself, but for Rose. He saw how that scumbag Bruno looked at his daughter and it was a look that scared him. His concern centered on his decision to come to America and start life anew. And many questions kept racing through his mind. Was it a mistake to choose Atlantic City? Were there people like Bruno in other cities? Was Bruno correct about the police being his friend? If he paid the $5,000 would that be the last he would see of Bruno or would he keep coming back for more? If he paid the $5,000 would that guarantee that permits and inspections would be made in a timely fashion or was that all myth and the $5,000 paid out would be for nothing?

About 7:00 P.M. David and Rose were finishing up for day when there was another knock at the door. David thought it was Bruno and Sal returning to provide another dose of their fear tactics so he ignored the knocking. But the knocking continued followed by a shout, "Are you in there Mr. Feltzer?" the voice cried out. It was Slim. David rushed to the door and apologized for taking so much time to react to his knock, asked him to come in and then recited to Slim what had occurred earlier in the day when Bruno and Sal had paid a visit. Slim became visibly upset as he listened to David tell his story, especially during the part about Bruno offering a discount as a trade off in order to spend time with Rose. When David was finished he asked Slim how much truth there was to Bruno's threats.

"Mr. Feltzer, I mean David, I hate to tell you this but the Bruno family and some others of his kind control this town. I have been working in this town long enough to tell you that everything Bruno said about inspections and permits is true. All of these people, including most law enforcement officers are on the take from the Bruno family and those who are not keep their mouths shut for fear of reprisal."

"So what do I do, Slim?"

"In any given situation, David, you only have three choices. One, you accept it. Two, you change it. Three, you leave it. In this case you can't change it, so you are down to accepting or leaving."

"What would you do?"

"David, I would accept and pay the $5,000 if you can afford it. If you can't afford it I would walk away from this building tonight, go back to your apartment, pack your belongings and leave Atlantic City before the sun rises."

"And go where? To some other city and risk having the same thing occur again? No, for my business and my dream Atlantic City is the perfect place to start. This building is in a perfect location. I spent years in a death camp in Poland and survived. I am not going to be bullied and forced to change my life because some big dog barks at me."

"I understand what you are saying David, but be aware that these dogs bite as well."

"Slim, you know about these things and yet you still stay here. Why did you come to Atlantic City and why do you stay here?"

"Kind of a long story, David; tell you what, if you are about finished up here today, why don't you close up and you, Rose and I go out for a bite to eat, my treat, and I'll tell you my story."

About a half of an hour later David, Rose and Slim were seated in Angelo's Fairmount Tavern and Slim began to tell his story. "My family is from Carrick-on-Suir, Ireland a small town of about 6,000 people that is located in the southeastern part of Ireland not far from the city of Waterford. Originally named Carrick MacGriffin, many of the original townspeople have names like Mac Griffin, or Mc Griffin or Mac Graw or in my case, McGraw. For years my family has owned and attended to a 500-acre farm on the outskirts of the town as well as operating a local tavern/eatery in the town itself. Running the farm and the tavern became a family affair. The family consisted of my mom and dad and my four brothers as well as my dad's two older brothers; Uncle Tim and Uncle Shamus, both confirmed bachelors. Financially we did OK; never rich but never poor, but my dad heard from friends of his who migrated to America and did very well for themselves. He always dreamed of going to America but my mother wouldn't hear of it, so to keep the family together he stayed. When I was sixteen years old I had just graduated from formal school when my mother died. After mom passed, my dad's dream of going to America resurfaced. It took him two years to finally make the decision to leave. His plan was that he, his brother Tim and myself would come to America and my older brothers and uncle Shamus would stay in Carrick-on-Suir and continue to farm and run the tavern. That was three years ago. When we arrived in New York, it was a rude awakening for my dad and my uncle as they were hard working people but not educated and possessed no specific skills.

My uncle secured a job as a doorman at a hotel and my dad took common laborer jobs whenever, wherever he could. When my dad saw the need for specialized training and education he enrolled me in an apprentice program at a vocational/technical institute so that I could gain a marketable skill. He said he was too old to go back to school. For two years he worked basically to put me through school. After I graduated, he said that he was going back to Ireland and that I could return with him or stay in America. I decided to stay and live with Uncle Tim. Uncle Tim worked 6 days a week as a doorman and weekends as a security guard at a department store and was perfectly happy with his life in NYC. He said that farming was hard work combined with long hours and the work that he was doing in America was long hours but the work was easy. The technical school I attended had information on new construction projects all over the United States. In one of their job bulletins I saw that Atlantic City was undergoing a building boom in the Casino industry. Atlantic City wasn't far from New York and I like the smell of the ocean versus the smell of the city so I came and the rest is history. In terms of Bruno and his type; I know they exist and I have seen how they operate, but they don't mess with me personally so I just go to work and play by the rules and don't get involved. David, those people own this town and they can be cruel and vicious and are nobody to mess with. If you decide to stay here and I hope you do, it may be hard to accept, but you have to play the game by their rules. Compared to other businesses in this town you are very small potatoes to them, but they have to poke you and prod you because that's part of their game. They can't let you slide because they don't let anybody slide. Maybe this $5,000 they are trying to squeeze out of you will be enough to satisfy them and once paid they'll feel like they did their job and will concentrate on the bigger fish in the pond."

"Thank you, Slim for your comments and your advice. Even though it pains me and goes against my grain, I am going to stay and I'll pay those scoundrels their $5,000. But I still need a helper to get the work done on my building. Rose and I can only do so much and I am not familiar with the construction codes in this country, so working by myself I would be severely handicapped. Have you found anyone who might be willing to sign on with me to get my place remodeled and up to the required standards?"

"I have and it's me! David, I would me more than willing to help you and Rose in any way I can. I understand your financial situation, so whatever you think is a fair wage is fine with me. I must tell you that after I finish up my current job at the Showboat Casino and your job I am going to return to Ireland.

America is the land of opportunity, but the pace is too fast for me. I long for the slower-paced life style associated with Carrick on the Suir, the family atmosphere, the smell of the air and the quality of life there. I might not make the money I'm making here, but I'll enjoy life more and someday when I get married and have children I want them to know my family and live with my family. I don't want a relationship with my family that consists of letters, emails and/or phone calls. If you want me to help you, I'll need about two weeks to finish up my work at the Showboat and then I'm all yours."

David had taken a liking to Slim the first time they met on the bus and he was thrilled to have such clear-thinking, trustworthy and well-grounded young man help him in his work. It was hard to tell who was happier, David or Rose.

The following week Sal and Walter returned to collect their cash. David remained silent as he handed over the envelope. Walter counted the money and acknowledged that the amount was correct. He then informed David that once the building was remodeled, it would be good business to have a fire insurance policy taken out on the property, to wit David replied that he already had insurance. But Walter informed him that he may have fire insurance but he didn't have arson insurance and what Walter would provide was insurance against arson; another slimy squeeze play. On the way out, Walter inquired about the whereabouts of Rose and mentioned that he was looking forward to the day when he and Rose might spend some time together. David didn't say a word regarding Walter's inquiry about Rose, but he did muster up a good wad of saliva in his mouth and spat in Walter's direction. Walter smiled a sinister smile and he and Sal turned and walked away.

Two weeks later, Slim joined in earnest with David in remodeling the upstairs apartment. At this point Rose couldn't provide much help and she decided to seek out employment of her own and ended up with a position in the housekeeping department of the Showboat hotel. The job didn't pay much, but it was job experience and the casino/hotel complex was just across the street from her soon-to-be-home.

David and Slim worked well together and David discovered that Slim was not only a hard worker but a skilled one as well. In seemingly no time at all, the entire apartment was in move-in condition and they began work on the shop area downstairs. As promised by Walter, any and all permits and inspections were granted and carried out in an expeditious fashion. David despised Walter and hated to pay the $5,000, but with everything moving along as smoothly as it was, maybe the $5,000 was a good investment after all.

Walter was right; the inspectors could hold up progress months if they chose to do so. In fact, even the inspectors had their hands out for a few extra bucks during their inspections. They would pull stunts like coming at 4:30 P.M. and saying they weren't sure if they could get the inspection completed by 5:00 P.M. and that "maybe" they'd have to come back tomorrow. That would mean holding up progress for a day. The solution was to lay a $20 bill on the floor and walk away. In that fashion the inspector could never be charged with taking a bride. He just happened to find some money lying on the floor. The inspector would say, "Hey, is this your $20?" and the response would be, "No, I think I saw you drop it." And the inspection would be completed before the end of the day.

It wasn't long after Slim and David began working together that Slim and Rose began to get acquainted. It was plain to see that the stage was being set for a full-fledged romance. Slim ate all of his meals with David and Rose and he always accompanied her on her way home from the Showboat no matter what the hour. After being told about Walter's crush on Rose, he wanted to make sure that Rose was safe at all times.

The days quickly turned into weeks and remodeling work continued at a good pace. After almost 2 months of work the only remaining work to be done was finishing touches and painting. At that time David decided to leave the work at hand to Slim as it was time for him to start advertising his trade. Every day David would go out and set up a small stand on the boardwalk or at a location near a casino advertising a free shoe shine. He'd take along samples of his fine leather handiwork and distribute cards announcing the grand opening of **Feltzer's Fine Leather Products and Shoe Repair.** In less than a month he had orders for a number of custom-made shoes and boots and several purses. It was very evident that business was going to be good and that the decision to come to Atlantic City was a wise one. During all of this time he only saw Sal and Walter once and that was the day he set up his stand near the Knife and Fork restaurant. As the two exited the restaurant they stopped by for a free shoe shine and in the process reminded David that they would be stopping by his shop on his grand opening to collect his monthly fire insurance premium of $100 per week which he could pay weekly or monthly or six months in advance. As Walter was leaving he turned to David and said, "I see that my sweetheart-to-be-Rose, is working at my hotel in the housekeeping department. Maybe someday she can personally show me how to change the sheets on a bed; that would be after we used them."

David's face became flush with anger and he approached Walter with a shoe hammer and said, "If you ever get near my daughter I will crush your skull with this hammer and nail your penis to the wall; that would be if I could find it. I'll bet your penis is about as big as your brain which means I'd have to have a pair of tweezers to find it."

Walter merely smiled and said, "Sal, give David a tip for the free shoeshine." Sal reached into his pocket like he was going to pull out some money, but the only thing that came out of his pocket was a fist and he proceeded to sucker punch David below the belt and David crumpled to the ground in agony. Walter walked over to David, bent down and with his face inches away from David's he said, "You might have a hard time finding my penis, but it looks like Sal found yours pretty easily." And then Walter kicked David in the groin and he and Sal walked away. As David lay crumpled in a ball writhing in pain, several restaurant patrons came to his aid and one asked if he should call a policeman and David said no. He knew that it was useless to call the police as justice would not be done. For now he wouldn't make waves, but someday, someway, somehow he would make Walter pay.

On the lighter side of things, during the two months that Slim and Rose began to see each other, their infatuation turned into a relationship with serious overtones. During their tender moments together they talked about what they both wanted out of life and their views mirrored each other's. Rose was very happy that her father's dream seemed to be coming true and she hated the thought of leaving him alone, but during her brief time in America she had the feeling that she'd have a better life in a slower-paced atmosphere and she was very excited about the prospect of getting married and becoming a part of a close-knit family and living in a small town where she would have a lot of friends and neighbors. The idea of marrying Slim and starting a life in Ireland became her dream. They talked to David about their plans and he seemed very happy that Rose had met such a fine and upstanding young man. It would be hard for her to find a man who came from better stock or one who could make a better life for her. He felt that she was bit young and might be rushing things, but he knew that once someone began to fall in love the decent was a freefall that was impossible to stop. David made only one request of the couple and that was that they promise to wait one year before getting married. He knew that after the marriage Rose would be leaving the country and he wanted as much time with her before she left to make a life of her own. Both Slim and Rose agreed to David's request. Slim had gained a lot of respect for David in a short time and he understood the importance of family ties. If David needed more time with his daughter before they separated, then so be it. He and Rose would be together forever, so waiting a year wasn't a big deal in his eyes.

The grand opening of **Feltzer's Fine Leather Products and Shoe Repair** occurred just about 3 months to the day after David had signed the lease for the building. Business wasn't exactly brisk on opening day, but David was still very busy with all of the pre orders he had accumulated during the prior weeks when he had been out promoting the business.

During the next six months David's business continued to grow by leaps and bounds and the best thing about the growth was that it was coming from profitable, custom-made orders. The word was spreading amongst the affluent regulars who frequently came to Atlantic City that if you wanted fine, custom-made leather goods there was this little shop next to the Showboat Casino run by a man named David Feltzer who was a master craftsman. Forget going to Philadelphia or New York City, at Feltzer's you could get the finest in custom-make leather products at a fair price; a price that was much less than you'd have to pay in specialty boutiques in the big cities.

Many of the affluent people who came to Atlantic City to gamble arrived from cities all across the United States and from foreign countries as well. It was not uncommon, for example, for a couple from France to vacation in New York and have a driver take them to Atlantic City to gamble for the weekend. People like this who placed orders with David inquired about the possibility of having their products shipped to their home so they would not have to add their purchases to their already over-packed baggage and before long, David was offering free shipping to his customers. It wasn't free as the cost was imbedded in the price of the product, but the customer's didn't know this and even if they surmised that the shipping cost was buried in the cost of the product they didn't seem to care. Soon David was overwhelmed with work and he had to hire a man to handle the shoe repair end of the business so that he could concentrate all of his time on the custom-made orders. Slim also joined the employ of David on a part time basis. He continued with his construction jobs and on days in which he wasn't assigned to work or after work on days in which he was assigned, he was in the shop handling all of the packing and shipping of out-of-town or out-of-country orders.

Rose continued with her housekeeping job at the Showboat. She was doing very well in her job. So well, in fact, that she had received a promotion from attending to the general rooms to attending to the suites and penthouse rooms. The work was the same but the clientele was much different. The people who stayed in the suites and penthouses had serious money and thought nothing of providing the housekeeper with a $100 tip for keeping the room in order and it could be more if they had a big night at the tables.

Walter came by the shop to make his regular collection for the fire insurance. When he saw how David's business was growing and the quality of the products he was creating, he informed David that buying theft insurance from him would be a wise investment as well.

David could have refused, but he was fearful that if he didn't play Walter's game, one of Walter's cronies would torch his business some night or break in and destroy his equipment or steal his raw leather. Better to be safe than sorry even though he detested giving one cent to such a low-life weasel as Walter.

Another reason David was reluctant to give Walter any grief was because he was worried that if he upset Walter too much that Walter, to get back at David, would make an advance on Rose. David had never said anything to Slim about Walter's remarks regarding Rose as he feared that Slim would do something rash and then all hell would break lose. There was no telling what those people could do if any harm came to Walter and with the police in their back pocket there would be no legal repercussions for whatever actions they took.

For the better part of the next year, the dream David had of starting his own business and becoming a wealthy man in America was on track. The business continued to grow. In fact, it was going so well that David entertained the possibility in the near future of opening another location in Las Vegas or Reno. Slim and Rose were still very much in love and the longer David knew Slim the happier he was that he and Rose had the good fortune to meet such a good man. They had set a wedding date and it seemed like time was passing in a breakneck fashion. Soon Rose and Slim would be on their way to Ireland. For David, Rose and Slim a storybook ending seemed to be their destiny, but all of that changed in dramatic fashion in one 24-hour period.

****

ONCE UPON A CHRISTMAS PARTY

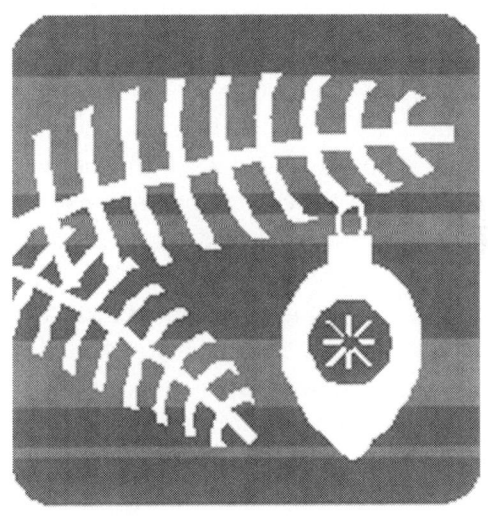

Every year old man Bruno would host a number of Christmas parties in the various hotels and restaurants in Atlantic City. People invited to these parties would be those on "the payroll" as well as select employees. As a family member, Walter was front and center at every party sniffing around any young girl he could find as well as rubbing elbows with the important people like the mayor of Atlantic City, the Chief of Police, etc. At every party Walter drank too much, ate too much and smoked a little pot on the side. And the more liquor or weed that Walter consumed the more obnoxious he became. Sometimes Walter would be "in the mood" even before the party began. This particular night the party was being hosted at the Show Boat hotel. Old man Bruno had rented the entire top floor of the Show Boat for the evening; six penthouses in all; this was going to be one hell of a night! In anticipation of a good time Walter decided to get "loosened up" before going to the party so he and Sal stopped at a few bars on the way to the Show Boat. As they exited their last stop before heading to the hotel, Walter was already half in the bag; maybe closer to three quarters.

The weather all day had been transitioning from a misty rain to snow flurries. As a result, the Boardwalk and the streets were slippery and wet and puddles of various sizes presented an obstacle course to those out and about on such a foul evening. About two blocks from the entrance to the casino Sal stepped off the curb into a mud puddle and cursed loudly as he felt the cold water seep into his sock just above the level of his right shoe. "Son of a bitch, Walter, I can't spend the evening wearing a fucking cold and wet sock and on top of that there's mud all over my shoe."

"Well, big fella, we're only a few blocks from that little Jew's shoe shop. He could clean up that shoe for you and the last time I was there I think I saw socks on display. Tell you what, why don't you go there while I go on to the hotel. I need a little tote to keep me going and I can't smoke pot at the party with all of those big officials there. So, if the service entry door is open around back I'm going to duck in there and mellow out a bit with some Columbian gold. If the door is open, I'll put something in the door jamb to keep it from locking. In that way, after you get your shoe taken care of you can just come in that entrance and take the service elevator up to the penthouse floor. I'll see you later at the party." With that Sal and Walter parted ways.

A few minutes after Sal had stepped into a mud puddle, Rose and Slim were on their way out for the evening. Before walking up to the front entrance of the Show Boat to grab a cab, Rose told Slim that she needed to make a quick stop at her locker in the employee's locker room to get a necklace she had left there the previous evening after leaving work.

She was off from work for the next few days and said that she felt uncomfortable leaving the necklace in her locker as locker theft in the employee's locker room was a common occurrence. Rather than go through the front entrance of the hotel and down to the basement level, Rose suggested that they try the service entry at the back of the hotel first as that would save some time. "Isn't that door always locked?" asked Slim.

"It automatically locks after it closes but since smoking is not permitted in the locker room, employees shove a small piece of wood at the base of the door to keep it open so that they can catch a smoke outside and return to the building without having to walk all the way around the block back to the front entrance of the building."

As they got closer to the service entry Rose saw that it was open a crack which meant that some employee had jimmied the door so that he/she could escape for a smoke. "We are in luck, Slim. The door is open." Rose opened the door and as she and Slim entered the building, Slim accidently kicked the small piece of wood that was at the base of the door. The door slammed behind them and locked.

"Rose, I accidentally kicked that piece of wood and I don't know where it went to. While you go and get your necklace I'll look for the piece of wood." Rose began her journey down the hallway leading to the locker room and Slim began his search for the piece of wood. When Slim didn't see the piece of wood in the immediate vicinity of the entrance he thought maybe the piece ricocheted off of the door jamb when he kicked it and it somehow bounced away from the building. Slim opened the door to take a look outside. As he stepped outside he held the door open with one hand as he looked around for the piece of wood. All of a sudden a heavy gust of wind hit the door, the door slipped out of Slim's hand and slammed shut. Slim was locked out of the building.

Walter was taking a deep drag on his Columbian Gold when he heard the door slam. He thought it was Sal, but as he turned and looked down the hallway he saw the image of someone coming toward him and it wasn't Sal. The person coming his way was a woman and this woman had a very nice set of legs connected to a very attractive figure. Walter started to get aroused and he became even more aroused when the light hit the woman's face and he saw that the woman was none other than Rose Feltzer. "Ahhhhhhhhhhh my little chickadee," said Walter under his breath mimicking the words of W.C. Fields.

Rose was unaware of Walter's presence and walked right by him as Walter was hiding between a couple of rows of lockers. Rose's locker was the second to the last one at the end of the row at the end of the aisle which dead ended at a wall. As Rose was working the combination on her lock she saw a shadow appear on the wall at the end of the lockers. She figured it was Slim, so the image didn't startle her but when she looked up and saw Walter the hair went up on the back of her neck. "Walter, what are you doing here?"

"I've come to ask you to be my date for the big party tonight. I think we'll make a handsome couple."

"Walter, please leave me alone. I just came to get something out of my locker and then I'm leaving and I'm not leaving with you to go to any party."

"Then we'll have our own little party right here and right now. And guess what my beauty, we are going to skip all of the introductions, the small talk and the romantic dinner by candlelight and we are going to move right ahead to the point where we are together in the bedroom and you disrobe for my pleasure. Now take your clothes off."

"Walter, you're either drunk or crazy or both. Now please get out of my way before you make a big mistake.

Just let me leave and I'll forget this ever happened. I won't tell my dad or go to the police."

"Tell your dad? That little fucking Jew midget of a man? What could he do? And the police? Darling, I am the police in Atlantic City. Take off your fucking clothes NOW!"

Cornered like a wild animal, Rose panicked and tried to run past Walter. The aisle between the lockers was only about three feet wide and Walter, even though he was high on liquor and drugs, had no trouble grabbing onto Rose as she tried to get by him and he roughly threw her into the bank of lockers. As Rose crashed to the floor, Walter ripped off her coat. As he started to grab for her blouse, Rose reached up and scratched Walter's face. Walter recoiled and screamed, "You little bitch, when I get a hold of you I'm going to fuck your eyes out!" The fraction of a second that occurred when Walter recoiled was just enough time for Rose to squirm by Walter and head down the aisle and out of the locker room.

Walter reacted very quickly and was only a few feet behind Rose when she reached the end of the row of lockers. Rose should have turned right toward the exit door, but in her panicked state she turned left and that path led to the men's shower room area. Rose ran as fast as she could thinking that she would be running into Slim at any second, but all of a sudden her path dead ended in the shower room. Walter, seeing that Rose had made the wrong turn felt no need to run any longer. He saw her ahead in the shower room and there was only one way out of the shower room and that was through him. By now the effects of the weed and the liquor had been dissipated by his adrenalin rush and he was now like a lion waiting to put the finishing touches on a wounded antelope. Rose was standing in the shower room frozen with horror as Walter approached her. Walter stopped, flipped off his shoes and took off his clothes. No need to get a $5,000 suit messed up for the party he thought. He neatly laid his clothes in a pile and walked toward Rose. "Get your clothes off, bitch; it will make this so much easier on both of us. Come on Rosie girl, it's Christmas or in your case Chanukah and it's time to receive Uncle Walter's present. I'd wrap it up for you but I left my condoms at home. I've wanted to fuck you from the first time I saw you and now my dream has finally come true."

As Walter walked ever closer, Rose ran around to each shower head and turned the shower all the way to the hot setting. She stood in the middle of the room as the twelve shower heads spewed water toward the drain which ran down the entire length of the room in the middle of the floor. A thick cloud of steam began to fill the room. Walter was now at the entrance of the room and was inching closer, moving in on his prey for the kill. When Walter was about six feet away, in a sudden burst of energy, Rose let out a death scream and charged directly at Walter's mid-section and buried her shoulder into his chest cavity. With the wet floor Walter had no traction and could do nothing to stop Rose's forward momentum. With her legs pumping and with Walter securely in her grasp, Rose drove Walter backwards at an alarming rate of speed. When they reached the far wall of the shower room they crashed into the wall and as they did the base of Walter's skull was driven into the cold water control. Rose toppled on to the floor and as she lay there, with water all around her, she noticed that the trial of water running down the wall behind Walter's header was copper colored. When Rose looked up, Walter was looking directly at her with eyes wide open but those eyes were lifeless. Walter wasn't moving. Walter wasn't breathing. Walter was dead. He was hanging on the wall at an odd angle; his entire weight being supported by the cold water control knob sticking in the base of his skull.

After Walter and Sal parted ways, Sal walked towards David's shop and when he was about a half a block away he saw two figures leaving the shop. One was a man, but he couldn't see his face. The other person was a woman and it was hard to make a positive ID due to the mist and snow, but he was sure it was David's daughter, Rose. Sal stopped and watched the couple make their way across the street in the direction of the Show Boat Hotel. They walked directly to the service entrance. By now, Sal was sure that Walter had entered the building through the same entrance and was somewhere in the locker room area enjoying his Columbia Gold. The couple entered the building and less than ten seconds later the male figure appeared at the door and seemed to be looking for something on the ground. He was holding the door with one hand when it slipped from his grasp and closed behind him. He pounded on the door a few times and when no one opened the door he began to walk around the building toward Memorial Avenue. Sal couldn't figure out why Rose was going into the locker room, but if Walter, in his current state, came across her in the same room, something was certain to happen and it would be a very bad something. Whatever was going to happen was going to happen and there wasn't anything he could do about it, so he continued to David's shop in order to take care of his shoe and sock problem.

****

Slim pounded on the door a few times and when Rose didn't answer he felt that due to the thickness of the door, the sound of his pounding would be so muffled that Rose probably couldn't hear it. He had no option other than to walk around to Memorial Avenue and use the front entrance to the Hotel/Casino. From there he would descend to the locker room and look for Rose.

****

Rose stood in a suspended state staring at Walter and confused as to what to do next. Where was Slim? What was taking him so long? He couldn't still be looking for that piece of wood, could he? What if someone came into the locker room now and saw Walter? Should she call building security? How could she explain what just happened? Would anyone believe her story? Just how did a woman end up in the men's shower room in the first place? She was soaked to the skin. Where was she going to get dry clothes? While all of these questions were racing through her mind she heard Slim's voice calling her name and she ran out of the shower room in the direction of the sound of his voice. "Slim, I'm here. Where are you?"

When Slim heard Rose's call he was just one aisle removed from her. The call he heard from Rose was alarming as her voice was filled with fear and that was a sound he had never heard in her voice until now. Slim quickly rounded the corner and as he did Rose ran into his arms and began to sob. "Oh my God, he's dead, he's dead!"

"Dead? Who's dead? Rose, you're soaked, what happened? What is going on?" In between tears and shortness of breath, Rose told Slim what has transpired. "Stay here, Rose and let me go look at Walter. In the meantime, do you have any dry clothes in your locker?"

"Yes, my uniform and I keep a rain coat there as well."

"OK; get a towel and dry off and put on your uniform and your rain coat and wait for me by your locker." Slim took one look at Walter and knew he was a goner. When he got back to Rose at her locker she asked him what they should do. "Rose, I know Walter and I know the kind of people he deals with. They are bad people, VERY bad people. With the connections he has in this town no one is going to believe your story. His father is the head of one of the major crime families in Atlantic City and even if you told your story to the police and they believed you and exonerated you of all wrong doing, Mr. Bruno would seek his revenge. Bruno and his likes operate under the code of an eye for an eye and his people would not rest until the ledger is balanced."

"You mean they'd kill me?"

"Yes, Rose, and if they thought that your father was in some way involved, they'd kill him too."

"Oh my God, Slim. What do we do?"

"First of all, does anyone know you entered this building tonight?"

"No, only you."

"You're positive."

"Positive."

"And no one was in this locker room during the time you were here?"

"No. If they were, they left before we entered. Probably one of the staff wanted to have a smoke before going upstairs, rigged the back door to stay open, had his smoke, came back into the building and went upstairs to work but forgot to kick out the wedge that kept the door open. Tonight there is a big Christmas party being hosted by Mr. Bruno and all available staff are performing their normal jobs or have been assigned to work the suites on the penthouse floor. I was asked to work tonight as well, but I begged off because I wanted to be with you."

"OK; I helped to install most of the cable for the security cameras and I know for a fact that there is no functioning camera at the entrance we used. There is a camera there that will be functioning at the first of the year, but currently the feed to the main monitoring station is not live. Bottom line is that no one knows you came into this building tonight. Even Walter didn't. It was just purely coincidental that the two of you ran into each other so there was no way Walter could have informed anyone else that he was coming to the locker room to expressly see you. From the smell in this place it is obvious that someone was smoking pot. I'll bet Walter came here to have a tote before going upstairs to join in on the festivities."

"Rose listen to me very carefully as what I am about to propose is going to change our lives forever, but it is the only way out of this without you ending up with a contract on your head. Right outside the shower area is a large laundry basket that is used to collect wet towels. I am going to roll that basket into the shower room, wrap Walter's head in wet towels, deposit him in the basket and cover him with a bunch of wet towels. Lucky for us this accident occurred in the shower room with all of the showers running with hot water. Because of that circumstance, just about all of the blood has been washed down the drain. Once I remove Walter's head from the spigot there will be blood and trace matter there but I can wash that down the drain with wet towels and soap. I saw a mop in the corner and I'll mop up the shower floor so that there is no trace of blood anywhere. I'm sure that some CSI team could find blood traces on the floor even after I've cleaned it but why would they even look here if no one knew that Walter was coming here? In the entire city of Atlantic City why on earth would they choose to come and look in this room for Walter? During this past summer I helped with the wiring of a high temperature incineration system for the Show Boat. The room where this system is located is minutes away from this locker room. I am going to wheel Walter down to the incinerator room and throw him along with the mop, the towels, the laundry cart, his clothes and your wet clothes into the incinerator. In a matter of minutes Walter will not exist and all items associated with Walter and you will be reduced to ashes."

"But Slim, depositing Walter in the incinerator is murder."

"Rose, the man is already dead. It was an accidental death; not murder. And disposing of his body is not murder. You can't kill someone who is already dead."

"It will take me 15 minutes, max, to get everything done. While I'm getting rid of Walter, you make your way up to the ground level. The ground level is the level between the lobby level and the parking level. The ground level is generally used by service people and delivery people and it is unlikely that service people will be working at this time and it is much too late for deliveries. Thus, no one should be around. Once on the ground level you will see a door marked "EXIT". Do NOT use that door as that door has a functioning security camera. Two doors down from the Exit door is another door that is marked "CAUTION". That door will lead outside and there is no security camera on that door. When you open the door make sure you put your raincoat around your hand so that your fingerprints aren't left on the door handle. Once outside, pull the hood on your raincoat over your head so that your face is covered and make your way back home. Do not walk straight to your apartment. Walk through a couple of alley ways and circle around to your place. Make sure that no one sees you enter your house. That's very important. If you see someone, keep walking and make another circle until you are sure no one sees you enter your house. Don't tell your dad anything until I get there. After I dispose of Walter and all incriminating evidence I will make my way back to your place as well and then the three of us can sit down and decide what to do next. OK? Do you understand?"

"I understand Slim, but are you sure there is no other way. I feel like a criminal sneaking around and I didn't do anything but try and protect myself."

"Rose, I understand how you feel, but if you want to live and if you want us to have a life together, there is no other way. Now let's get going before someone shows up."

As soon as Rose left, Slim quickly went through the routine he outlined for Rose. His last action was to take a towel and wipe down the door handles on the service entry and each of the spigots in the shower room. He even took the time to wipe down the lockers in the area where Walter was smoking as well as the benches in that aisle. He looked carefully for Walter's joint and found it on the floor next to the entrance to the shower room. He picked it up and put it in his pocket and would dispose of it on this way to David and Rose's apartment. His last action was to grab a wet mop and quickly run the mop in the aisle where Walter attacked Rose. He also ran the mop over the floor back to the service entrance in order to cover up or smudge any footprints that he, Rose or Walter might have made during their time in the locker room. He wiped down the handle of the mop with his handkerchief and stopped to take a deep breath to think of any trace evidence that he could have left behind that would place either Walter or Rose or himself in the locker room area. Satisfied with his job he left the building. No one in the world would ever know that Rose and Walter had been in that room together that night. That is, no one except Sal.

****

David was in the throes of closing for the day and when he spotted Sal walking past the front window of the shop. He felt another shakedown coming on so he rushed to pull the shade down and lock the door but he was too late as Sal was already opening the door. David was very polite since he didn't want any trouble. He was also very afraid of Sal and knew that it didn't take much to upset him. The bad news was that Sal was in the shop. The good news was that

Walter wasn't with him. "I'm about to close so it might be better for you to come back tomorrow."

"Listen you little asshole, I'll tell you when you can close and you're not going to close until you clean my shoes and get me a new pair of socks." After making that statement Sal removed his shoes and socks and slammed them on the counter in front of David.

David looked at the shoes and said, "Size 15. I don't know if I have a pair of socks in that style that will fit you. The biggest size I have in the kind of sock you have is a large and that only goes up to a size 12. I do have some over-the-calf-socks and a large in that style will cover your foot but it won't go over your calf."

"I don't need for you to review your entire fucking inventory of socks. Just get me a pair that will cover my feet and go above my ankle."

David retrieved a pair of socks, and began to clean and polish his shoes. As he was doing his work, David asked Sal, "Where's your pet rock, Walter?"

"Very funny, Jew boy; I thought you Jew boys lost your sense of humor after Adolph torched your asses. But, since you asked, he went on ahead to the party and I told him I'd meet up with him after you took care of my shoes and gave me a pair of socks."

After completing his work David said, "That will be $5.50 for the socks and $3.50 for the clean and polish job."

"Three dollars and fifty cents for cleaning and polishing my shoes? For the price of those cheap socks, you should have thrown in the shoe shine for free. What happened to your Christmas spirit? Oh, that's right, I forgot, you Jews don't have any Christmas spirit. Tell you what Jew boy, just put it on my bill and I'll pay you when I feel like it." Sal walked to the door and as he was leaving he turned and said, "NOW you can close."

Knowing that the service entry door to the Show Boat was locked, Sal walked around to the front entrance to the building and then took the elevator up to the Penthouse floor. When he arrived, some guests were milling around and the waiters and waitresses were scurrying through each suite with trays of hors de oeuvres and beverages. Sal went to each suite, but Walter was nowhere to be found. "Mr. Bruno, excuse me sir, have you seen Walter?"

"No Sal, I haven't seen that worthless sack of shit. Probably out whoring around, getting stoned or spending my money. If/when you find him, you make sure that he is in a civil state of mind because some very influential people will be attending this party tonight and I don't want his dumb ass to embarrass me.

If he's not in a civil state of mind and able to carry on a decent conversation without slurring his words or making a complete asshole out of himself then I will hold YOU responsible. You understand me?"

"Yes sir."

"Fuck," Sal said to himself as he walked away from Mr. Bruno. He knew that Walter loved to rub elbows with all of the big shits and he knew that Walter had been looking forward to going this party. If he was fucked up and if he had to keep him from going to the party, Walter was going to be thoroughly pissed off and he wouldn't take lightly to the suggestion that he couldn't attend the festivities. But Mr. Bruno had given him an order and when Mr. Bruno gave you an order you obeyed without question. If he had to knock out Walter and tie him up he would do so. But he had to find him first.

****

A Cruel Twist of Fate

When Slim got back to David and Rose's apartment, Rose was in the process of taking a shower and David was in a disturbed state and was pacing the floor.

"Slim, what in the hell is going on? Rose rushed in here crying and ran straight to the bathroom, locked the door and turned on the shower. I asked her what was going on and she didn't reply. I thought that maybe you two had an argument and broke up. I've never seen her in such a state in my life. Tell me, what happened, please."

Slim proceeded to tell the entire story to David and as he was finishing the tale, Rose appeared and quickly ran to David and threw her arms around him and began to cry once more. David hugged her and told her that everything was going to be alright. "Remember when your mother left us and how hard that was? We made it through that OK and we will make it through this as well."

David turned to Slim, "Slim, what you think we need to do?"

"OK, let's look at the facts and go from there. Unless Walter specifically told someone that he was going to go to that locker room to have a smoke, there is no way that anybody could place him in that location. Even if they could, by the time anyone looked there, that room will have been used by a number of people dressing and undressing and taking showers. I don't think there is any trace evidence of Walter being there now, but even if there is something I forgot, in a couple of days that place will be so compromised that it will be impossible to determine if Walter was there. The whole world could search for him but they would never be able to find him and that is certainly to our advantage.

But Walter is Mr. Bruno's son and Mr. Bruno and his people will never stop looking for Walter. In their circle every minus has to have a plus. Somehow, someway, somebody is going to pay for Walter's disappearance because Mr.

Bruno can't lose face. It would be too embarrassing for him to chalk up the loss of his son without evening the score in some way. Even if he has to fabricate something, he will so that everyone knows that you can't mess with the Bruno family and get away with it. That also works to our advantage because the Bruno family will be looking to pin this on a competing family or some past enemy. So it appears that we are not in danger. But if, and this is a crucial if; IF Walter mouthed off to someone about his fantasy concerning Rose and IF that same someone saw Rose entering that building and IF that same someone knew that Walter was in the building at the same time, they could put two and two together and Rose would become a primary suspect. David, you've had a number of unpleasant incidences with Walter. Has there been anyone who was with Walter during those events?"

"Yes, on every occasion he has been with that big guy, Sal. In fact, those two are **NEVER** apart. Sal is Walter's muscle man. Walter can act like a big shit and throw his weight around because Sal is there to back him up. Without Sal at his side, Walter is an empty suit with a loud mouth. The ONLY time I have seen one without the other was tonight when that big goon came busting in here just as I was about to close."

"Sal came by tonight? And what time was that, David?"

"Just about the same time the two of you left here to go out for the evening."

"So just after we leave, Sal shows at the shop by himself. And this guy **ALWAYS** travels with Walter? Hmmmmmmmmm. That would mean that just about the time Rose and I were entering the service entrance, Sal would have been coming down the block toward the shop and the service entrance would have been in his direct line of vision. Sal doesn't know me but he knows Rose and if he watched us walk to the service entrance then he knows that

Rose entered in the building. Did Sal say anything to you about Walter when he was in the shop?"

"I asked him where Walter was and he told me that Walter went to the party."

"He didn't say what party, did he?"

"No, he just said 'the party.'"

"The party HAD to be the party at the Show Boat because that party was being hosted by Mr. Bruno," Rose chipped in.

Slim thought hard for a moment and said, "This is the way I see it. Walter and Sal were on the way to the party together and Sal stepped into a puddle and got his shoes muddy and his socks wet. Sal decides to stop at the shop and Walter goes ahead to the party. The weather is foul; Walter spots the service door and sees that it is open a crack, so in order to save the walk around the block he decides to take the shortcut through the locker room. Maybe he tells Sal that he is going to take the short cut and he'll leave the door jimmied for him and will wait inside and have a smoke while Sal takes care of business at the shop and then they'll go up to the party together. Walter enters the building and we come in right behind him. Rose proceeds down the aisle and is spotted by Walter. I lock myself out of the building. Sal watches us go in the building and watches me come back outside, sees the door slam behind me and then proceeds into the shop. He leaves the shop and seeing that the service entry door is locked he proceeds around to the front entrance.

During the time Sal was in the shop and his walk around the block, the entire incident from Walter's attack on Rose to Rose and I leaving the Show Boat occurred. I hate to say this but I think it was too coincidental that Sal showed up at the shop by himself just after we left. It was also too coincidental that Walter was in the locker room at the exact same time that Rose and I entered the building. When I picked up Walter's joint, the burn mark showed that he only finished about a quarter of the joint which means that he lit up that joint maybe two minutes before he spotted Rose. I'm not 100% sure but I think that Sal knows that Walter was in that locker room with Rose. When Walter can't be found, Sal is going to start retracing the events of the evening and it won't take him long to figure out that somehow Rose was connected to Walter's disappearance. In which case he will come after Rose for an explanation and we can't let that happen. We have to stay several steps ahead of Sal and the Bruno family as they begin their search for Walter."

"So what do we do, Slim?" asked David.

"Rose is in grave danger. Somehow we have to find a place where she can hide and then we have to figure out how we can get her out of Atlantic City without anyone seeing her. Just as Walter has been removed from the face of this earth, Rose has to disappear as well."

"Slim, I have to show you something. Follow me down to the shop." David grabbed a small flashlight and he led Slim and Rose downstairs to the shop. When they got to the floor of the shop David made sure that all of the window blinds were down and then he had Slim and Rose follow him to the area in the floor where the trap door was located. When they got to the trap door David said to Slim, "Rose can hide here."

"Hide where, David? I don't see a place where she can hide."

"Look closely at the floor Slim, do you see anything unusual?"

Slim took a very close look and replied, "David I can't see anything unusual. What am I supposed to see?"

"The fact that you can't see anything is good news because if you can't see anything when I'm telling you exactly where to look, that means that Sal or anyone else won't be able to find what I am about to show you." David reached down and pulled on the ring which opened the trap door in the floor.

Slim was astounded. "David, I worked in this shop for several months and never saw that ring. I even sanded the floors and never saw anything unusual. There is no way that anyone would discover this door." David then proceeded to give Slim a tour of the room. After the tour, they retuned upstairs to the apartment. "David, that room solves the major problem of finding a place where Rose can stay safely until we figure a way to get her out of Atlantic City, but we still have to get her out of town unnoticed and I think I know who can help me."

****

Walter never did show up at the party. Old man Bruno was slightly curious about Walter's absence but, truth be known, he was kind of glad that Walter was a no show because you could never predict Walter's behavior. If he showed up sober and not influenced by drugs, he was an engaging fellow and pleasant to be around. But, if he showed up under the influence of some outside agent he could be an embarrassment and a first-class asshole. The trouble with Walter was that the ratio of being sober and drug free versus drunk or high was about 100 to 1 in favor of him being drunk or high. Sal became very concerned when Walter didn't show, but he had to stay at the party until it ended because if he left to look for Walter and Walter showed up at the party a mess and he wasn't there, Mr. Bruno would have his head on a plate the next day for not following his order. Walter was a no show that evening, so the next day Sal checked out every Casino, every hotel, every restaurant, every bar and every hooker in Atlantic City and no Walter. It was time to go to Mr. Bruno and tell him that something was wrong.

When Sal told Mr. Bruno about Walter being missing, the old man ran his hand through the few hairs he had on his balding head and said, "God ah damn that ah little asshole. It ah always ah some ah shit ah going on with ah him. OK, I'll have some people make some inquiries. In the meantime you keep looking." Sal decided not to tell Mr. Bruno about his last sighting of Walter and about seeing Rose and some guy going into the service entrance of the Show Boat Casino/Hotel just minutes after Walter entered the building. He'd let Mr. Bruno use all of his muscle to find Walter and if that didn't work, he was going to take the matter in his own hands. This was personal. If something happened to Walter and Rose was involved, he would make that little Jew bitch pay.

****

Father Raymond Gorman was in very good shape for a 65-year old. Even though he was grey and looked his age, underneath his exterior appearance was a body that was toned and muscular as a result of daily exercising at the local YMCA and swimming in the Atlantic Ocean. Father Ray swam in the ocean every day for 30 minutes and that included winter days as well. As Father was finishing up his laps in the ocean, Slim was walking down the beach to meet Father and it was really bothering him that he was going to have to lie to his good friend. How can you lie to a priest he thought; but he had to in order to keep Rose safe. Rose was his love and his future and he would do anything to protect her.

Father Ray walked up the beach toward Slim and Slim handed him a towel to dry off. "Well, Slim, top of the day to you my friend. And what brings you to my swimming pool?"

"Father, I need your help and we need to talk in private and I thought this would be the best place for that to happen."

"Surely my lad, but it's a wee bit frigid today and I can't be standing out here in my skivvies without risking catching a death of a cold. What say we go back to the rectory, share a warm rock and rye or two and talk in my private chamber? Carol, my housekeeper is off today so they'll be no one there but the two of us."

When they got back to the rectory, Father put on his sweats, mixed up two, double rock and ryes, put them in the micro oven for 15 seconds and then went to his chamber where Slim was waiting for him.

"Cheers and Saints be praised," announced Father. With that Slim and Father clicked glasses and began to sip on their drinks. "Ok lad, now what seems to be the problem and how can I help you?"

"Father, I have a friend who is in an abusive relationship and she has nowhere to turn. Right now she is in hiding for fear that her boyfriend will find her and give her a good thrashing. I know that you work closely with the good sisters of St. Joseph at the St. Bede Sanctuary for Abused Women and I know that you and the good nuns have helped a number of poor souls escape from Atlantic City undetected and begin a new life in an undisclosed location.

From our past discussions you know about my uncle Tim in New York. Tim is willing to help out and provide this woman with a safe haven and help get her started in a new life, but I've got to get her to New York for that to happen. So I'm coming to you for your help in this matter. Understand that this matter is extremely confidential. In fact, this woman doesn't even know I've come to see you. I just told her I would do everything I could to help her in this difficult time."

"Not that it matters Slim, but what is your relationship to this woman?"

"She's a good friend of good friend. I really haven't known her that long. All I really know is that she has been in this abusive relationship for some time and, wants to get out of it but is afraid to try."

"Is she married to this fellow and are there children involved in this relationship?"

"The answer to both questions is no. This guy is married and has a family. During their courtship he deceived this young woman about his marital status. When she found out about his wife she decided to end the relationship but he wouldn't hear of it. He wanted something on the side and he wasn't going to give it up. Furthermore, since this man is an upstanding citizen in the community, he couldn't risk having his affair made public. That's when the relationship turned abusive. He told her he would kill her if she went public or to the police. He warned her not to leave town and reminded her that he was a man of means and if she tried to leave town he could stop her. So the poor girl is in a quite a bind. This guy has turned her into his sex slave."

After completing their discussion, Father Ray consented to contact Sister Jean Cavanagh at the St. Bede Sanctuary and together he and Sister Jean would draft a plan to help this young lady escape from Atlantic City. When Father Ray asked Slim where the young lady was hiding, Slim had no recourse but to tell him of the secret location. Slim pointed out that he had helped David Feltzer remodel the building and during that process he became aware of the secret room.

When his friend came to him and asked him for his help he remembered that secret room and contacted David and asked if it would be OK for the young lady to hide in the room until a plan for her escape could be devised.

"David Feltzer. Don't know the man, Slim."

"You wouldn't, Father. David is Jewish and he is relatively new in the community. He just opened a leather shop right off of the boardwalk near the Show Boat Casino." Slim was telling his good friend one lie after another and it really bothered him, especially because he was a priest and was such a good and caring soul, but he had to do it. He just couldn't say, "Well Father, I am in love with this girl and this guy came after her and she managed to kill him and then I took this guy and threw him in an incinerator and now the Bruno family is out to seek its revenge so I need you to help me sneak her out of town." Actually it was better that Father Ray didn't know the truth about the situation. The less he knew the better off he would be in case somehow the trail of Rose's disappearance was traced back to him.

They ended their session with Father Ray saying that once he talked to Sister Jean and they had a plan he would visit David at his shop and discuss the details and once David had the details he would share them with Slim.

****

Old man Bruno pulled out all of the stops in his search for Walter. Everyone in the family had an assignment regarding a place to search, and/or a person to interview regarding Walter's whereabouts. The police who were on the Bruno payroll were alerted and a "quiet" city-wide search was conducted. Every airline in the airports of Atlantic City, NJ, Newark, NJ, Philadelphia, PA, LaGuardia, NYC and Kennedy, NYC were checked to see if Walter's name was on a recent flight manifest. All bus terminals and train stations were checked as well. All of this activity was conducted without any notification to the press. This was a family matter and family business was never made public. After several days of intense searching, no clue had surfaced; not one promising lead. It was as though Walter walked into the ocean and was carried out to sea. In fact, after not turning up one clue as to Walter's location, Walter disappearing into the ocean became a very logical scenario.

****

The day after Walter's demise, Rose called her shift supervisor at the Show Boat Hotel and told her that she had received word that her mother in Poland had turned seriously ill and that she was going back home to Gdansk to care for her and that she wouldn't be returning to the United States for a long time, if ever, and she was tendering her resignation effective immediately. She requested that any pay earned should be sent to her father and she gave the supervisor the address of the shop. The supervisor was sad to learn of her mother's illness and said she understood her situation completely. She told Rose she hated to see her leave as she was a dependable, bright and a very promotable employee. She wished her luck and bid her adieu.

After leaving Father Ray's, Slim phoned David and told him that he would be stopping by his apartment later that evening. He told him that he had to wait until it was dark and until he was sure no one was casing his shop or apartment because he couldn't risk being seen with David. He said he'd explain everything when they got together.

****

Sal was surprised that the old man was acting so cavalier about Walter's disappearance. He didn't know that old man Bruno was actually somewhat relieved that Walter disappeared since Walter had been a constant pain in his ass for years. The old man knew that Walter suffered from the delusion that he was going to succeed his father when he was ready to hand the reins of the family operation to his successor. After all, he was his oldest son and in matters of the family, the oldest son was always the successor. But that was never going to happen as old man Bruno wasn't about to hand over his life's work to some drunk pot head who hadn't the sense he was born with. Old man Bruno figured that Walter finally mouthed off to the wrong person or may have been involved in a drug deal gone badly. It didn't matter. What mattered was that Walter was conveniently gone and hopefully never to return. To save face and to maintain his reputation, old man Bruno was going to leak out the word that Walter had some back tax problems and before being detained by the Feds he decided to send Walter back to Italy. Everyone would buy that story and that would be the end of it. The only person who wouldn't buy the story would be Sal.

****

That evening Slim arrived at David's apartment well after sunset. Before approaching the apartment he made several sweeps of the area looking for anyone unusual in the area who might be seated on the Boardwalk or standing in the area for an unusual period of time. He did spot one guy sitting on a bench on the Boardwalk seemingly taking a long look at the entrance to David's shop and apartment, but after about 10 minutes he sauntered down the Boardwalk toward the casinos. Once inside the apartment David and Slim made their way in the dark down to Rose's hiding place. David stomped on the floor twice, hesitated for a brief second and stomped one more time. This was Rose's signal from David that it was he who was going to open the trap door. If she didn't hear two stomps followed by one stomp, she was to grab the shot gun he left with her and blow away the first person who descended down the staircase. David pulled on the latch and opened the trap door and he and Slim descended into Rose's secret domain. Immediately Rose ran into the arms of Slim and the two of them shared a warm and long embrace.

"How are you Rose?" Slim asked.

"I'm OK. It's actually very comfortable down here but the days are long and it's hard trying to stay quiet all of the time. I read a lot, watch television using ear plugs and exercise.

Poppa and I eat together each night but he doesn't stay long for fear that someone might come to the apartment unexpectedly and if it took him an inordinate time to answer the door it might make a visitor suspicious. Basically it's pretty boring, but I feel safe and it's good to know that poppa is right here all of the time."

"So what's happening, Slim? How long does Rose have to stay hidden away?" asked David.

"I visited with my friend, Father Gorman, at the St. Bede Rectory. He is closely associated with the nuns who run the St. Bede Sanctuary for Abused Woman. He is going to talk to Sister Jean Cavanaugh at the Sanctuary and the two of them are going to work out a plan to get Rose out of here and out of town. Rose, I've contacted my uncle Tim in NYC and he has agreed to take you in and take care of you until this whole thing is resolved. Tim works in the City but lives in Queens and that will be a safe place for you to spend some time. One can get lost in a big city and there aren't many bigger cities than New York. You'll have to spend some time with Uncle Tim. How long I'm not sure. But we have to be careful not to rush things. Once in NYC with Uncle Tim, you will try to lead a normal life.

Tim says he thinks he can get you a job in the house-keeping department at the hotel where he works. In the meantime I will continue to work here as I normally do but I don't think it is advisable that I be seen coming to the shop. When Walter doesn't show up, Sal is certain to come here looking for you. He doesn't know me and it's better that he can't connect me to you and/or David. He knows that David had nothing to do with Walter's disappearance because he was with David when Walter disappeared. His main focus will be you, Rose, and that's why you have to stay hidden until Father and Sister figure out how to get you out of here. The way I see it, once you are out of here and safely in New York, we wait a few months and when the heat dies down I'll let Uncle Tim know. Spirit Airlines in Atlantic City has flights to Newark, NJ and when the time is right I'll fly to Newark, NJ and meet Rose there and together we'll fly from Newark, NJ to Dublin, Ireland. From Dublin we'll take an Aer Arann flight to Waterford. Once in Waterford, someone in my family will meet us and whisk us away to a new life in Carrick-on-Suir. David, this is going to be very difficult for you. Once the plan for Rose's escape begins to play out you are going to have to say goodbye to your daughter, but understand that it is her best chance to survive and lead a full, normal and happy life. Once we get to Ireland, Rose and I won't be able to come back. I know you just started your business here and it looks like it is going to be very profitable, but you could start a similar shop in Carrick-on-Sur and I know that you'd be successful.

You wouldn't make the money you would in Atlantic City, but you would have a good life and you'd be near Rose. It would be a good life there for all of us, but I can't make that decision for you, especially when you've worked so hard to fulfill your dream of coming to America and start a new life. For now we wait for Father Ray to work out the details of the escape plan with Sister Jean. I assume that in the next couple of days Father Ray will come to the shop and discuss the plan with you, David. I'll phone you in a couple of days for an update. OK? Are we all in agreement as to what we are going to do?" Both David and Rose agreed and now the only thing left to do was to wait for Father Ray's visit.

****

The search for Walter had turned up absolutely nothing. Old man Bruno was convinced that Walter had vanished. To where and how, he didn't know and he cared less. He was just glad that he was gone and he planned to leak his story out about Walter going to Italy in the next day or so. When Sal heard this he knew that he was now on his own in terms of getting to the bottom of what happened to his good friend. He would not rest until the issue was resolved and the score was settled.

It was time to make a visit to Rose and find out how that little bitch was associated with Walter's disappearance. To this end, Sal stopped by the Show Boat Hotel and talked to the manager of Housekeeping to find out when she was scheduled to work. He was surprised to find out that Rose had resigned just a few days prior. When he asked the supervisor why she resigned the supervisor said that she couldn't give him that information because it was personal. After lifting her off of the floor by her throat and slamming her head against the wall, the supervisor told Sal everything she knew. The next visit Sal made was to the shop to see David. He knew that David had nothing to do with Walter's disappearance, but he had to know where Rose was. He wasn't buying that story about Rose going back to Poland to attend to her sick mother. It was too much of a coincidence that Walter disappears and Rose takes off for Poland. If she did go to Poland, Poppa Jew would tell him where she was located and if he declined to give him that information, that would be the biggest mistake he ever made in his life.

****

David was just about to close up shop for the day when he saw a big shadow pass by his storefront window. It had to be Sal. Either that or an eclipse of the sun just occurred.

Sal entered the shop and said, "OK, where is she?"

"Where is who?" David replied.

"Don't give me that shit. You know EXACTLY who I mean. Your little wench daughter, that's who!"

"I don't have a daughter who is a little wench. My daughter is a beautiful young woman and right now I assume she is attending to her sick mother in Poland. She left here several days ago when we got the word from some friends that her mother had taken ill. Even if her mother had not taken ill, it would have been just a matter of time before Rose returned home to Poland since the American life style didn't seem to suit her."

"Where did she go the other night when I came in here to have my shoes cleaned?"

"Ah, let me think. Oh yes, that night she went out of a date with a fellow she met at the hotel."

"What fellow?"

"It was her first date with the man. I really don't know him and I can't even remember his name. I think it was Joe. Or maybe it was Jim? I'm not sure."

"You are a lying little Jew fuck. You know that? Now, you are going to let me search this shop and if I don't find her here, then we are going up to your apartment and let me search there and you'd better hope that I find her."

Sal conducted a thorough search of the shop as well as the apartment and not finding Rose he pushed David into the wall and put his face an inch away from David's and said through his teeth, "I'm going to be watching your fucking Jew ass 24/7. I know that little cunt didn't go to Poland and I know that you know where she is. When I find her, it is not going to be a happy occasion for her or you. I want you to think hard about that. And while you are thinking about that, think about this." As Sal said the word "this" he reared back and delivered a vicious blow to David's solar plexus. As David lay on the floor, he heard the door to the apartment slam shut. It was some time before he could gain enough strength to get up and as soon as he was able to stand up straight he began to cough up blood.

****

Father Ray and Sister Jean conferred and came up with plan to get Rose from David's shop to The Sanctuary. That evening, right before closing time, Father Ray went to David's shop to inform him of the plan.

****

Sal began to spend most of his time sitting on a bench on the Boardwalk reading a newspaper or at least it appeared to any passerby that he was reading a newspaper. In reality he was watching David's shop to see if Rose or any woman who approximated Rose's size left the building. He was watching when Father Ray entered the shop and that visit peak Sal's interest. He thought to himself, "Why would a priest be visiting a Jew? Of course a priest might need a pair of shoes repaired just like anyone else, but this priest didn't have a pair of shoes with him. And why would Feltzer close up the shop and pull down the shades on the window when the priest arrived? And why did the priest stay so long? And when he left, why didn't he have a pair of shoes with him? Maybe the shoes he was wearing were the ones Feltzer repaired? Could be; but something smelled about this visit and it was a rotten smell."

****

That evening Slim called David and David discussed the plan that Father Ray and Sister Jean had devised to transport Rose to The Sanctuary. Slim thought that it would work, but there was a risk factor and that risk factor was directly associated with someone who might be watching the shop. If someone wasn't watching the shop there would be absolutely no risk. If someone was watching the shop the risk would be directly proportionate to the astuteness of the observer.

****

The following day Father Ray stopped by the shop once again to inform David that the plan would be going into action at the close of business that day. He told David that he was to make sure that all window blinds were down at the close of business and that all lights were to be darkened.

****

Sal watched as Father Ray stopped by the shop for a second time. Again, he had no shoes with him. And again, he left without shoes or any leather apparel. Something was going on between the Jew and the priest. About five minutes before David normally closed the shop for the day two nuns went into the store and one of the nuns had a shopping bag with her. As soon as they entered the shop David drew the blinds. Several minutes later the lights went out, but the nuns still hadn't left the shop. What was going on? All of a sudden the door to the shop opened and the nuns left the building. To someone with an untrained eye or to someone who wasn't watching closely, nothing seemed to be out of the ordinary. But Sal wasn't your ordinary person. His antennae were up and he was zeroed in on every detail of the activity. What Sal saw, which an ordinary person might not have picked up, was that two nuns entered the shop and three nuns came out of the shop and the nun who entered the shop carrying the shopping bag wasn't carrying that bag anymore. The third nun who looked to be the approximate size of Rose, stayed very close to the other nuns and she walked in perfect cadence with the other two. If one didn't look very closely it would have been very hard to notice if there were two or three nuns. But Sal noticed. He KNEW that there were three nuns and he knew that one of them was Rose. Even though he was close enough to see what was going on, he was still 50 yards away from the three nuns; not nearly close enough to grab Rose, but if he moved quickly he might have a chance to catch up with them. As Sal started to move toward them, Sister Jean saw the figure of a large man on the Boardwalk beginning to come their way and he wasn't walking. It was obvious that he was pursuing them. Immediately she and the two nuns with her began to run toward The Sanctuary.

As they ran, Sal increased his pace as well. It was only three blocks to the Sanctuary and it appeared that the nuns had a good chance of making it there without being caught. For a large man Sal was very light on his feet and was able to move at an alarmingly fast pace. The distance between Sal and the nuns was decreasing rapidly and much to Sister Jean's chagrin it looked as though they were not going to make it to the safety of The Sanctuary before their pursuer overtook them. Just as it seemed that Sal was about to overtake them, a dark shadow traveling at a high rate of speed and running at a ninety degree angle to Sal, plowed into the big man's right side and sent him sprawling head over heels into the street. As Sal lay on the street with the wind knocked out of him, the nuns sped ahead to safety. It took Sal a few minutes to regroup and he wondered what in the hell or who in the hell had just knocked him for a loop as there was absolutely no one in sight.

****

Just before he went to bed that night, Father Ray applied some mineral ice to his right shoulder. Hitting that big guy had been like running into a wall.

****

Wife beaters or those who abused women and pedophiles were two classes of people for which the law officers in Atlantic City had absolutely no respect. You could count of the law to do anything they could to protect an innocent woman and/or child. In fact, the entire community held the St. Bede Sanctuary for Abused Woman in very high regard. Several electronic firms and firms dealing with home security systems had donated their time and their equipment to outfit The Sanctuary and its grounds. Panic buttons had been installed in virtually every room in The Sanctuary. Should a trespasser attempt to gain entry to The Sanctuary, a surveillance camera would record his/her every move and the feed from the camera would be viewed by a private security firm. At the first sign of trouble a silent alarm would be sent simultaneously to police headquarters as well as to all patrol cars in the area. Should one of the nuns depress the panic button a similar alarm would be sounded. Once Rose had gained entrance to The Sanctuary she was safe from the outside world. Sal knew this and was extremely upset that he hadn't been able to grab Rose on her way from David's shop to the Sanctuary. He also knew that once she was in the Sanctuary, the nuns would devise some kind of clever plan for her to get out of the city. Providing a safe haven for women and children and arranging for their transport was their forte and they were good at it. How could he stop Rose's departure?

Laundry trucks, bread trucks, gardeners, appliance service personnel, mail trucks, furniture vans and a number of parishioners visited The Sanctuary on a regular basis. There was no way he could stop and search every vehicle. And if the nuns chose to declare to the authorities that he was a threat to their safety or one of the women in The Sanctuary, the likelihood was that he would find himself thrown in jail; it wouldn't matter that he was one of old man Bruno's henchmen. There was no way for him to gain entrance to The Sanctuary. His only recourse was to find out where Rose was going once she left the compound. In Sal's estimation, in addition to Rose there were only three people who might know of her final destination; that would be Poppa Jew, the priest or this nun who called herself Sister Jean. Somehow, some way, he would make one of them talk.

****

It was Saturday afternoon about 4:00 P.M. and Father had been in the confessional box for about an hour and he had only heard two confessions. He remembered the good old days when he would enter the church and there would be a number of parishioners in a queue silently praying their rosary as they waited for confessions to begin. In fact, on some of those days he had to secure a priest from a neighboring parish to help him hear confessions due to the large number of folks who would show up. But, in its wisdom, the church decided in the early 1960's to remove some of its most hallowed traditions; the Latin mass went by the wayside, Friday fasting from meat became a thing of the past, the liturgy of the mass changed, people were holding hands and singing, guitars and folk singers replaced the church organ and the choir. Used to be when you walked down the street you KNEW when you went by a Catholic Church because the Catholic Mass was unique in its language, its liturgy and its music. But today, passing by a church and listening to the service, it is difficult to tell the difference between a Protestant celebration or a Catholic Mass. Pope John XXIII and the Church elders during his reign tried to make the religion more accessible in order to gain converts which would bolster the amount taken in on the collection plate. But the strategy backfired on the Pontiff because new members were not attracted to the church and many of the core members of the church became disgusted with "the new ways" and abandoned the Church. Nobody was becoming a priest a brother or a nun anymore and parish churches were dying by the dozen. Regional parish centers were coming into vogue. Just in Atlantic City alone the parishes of St. Regis, St. Philomena and Holy Rosary had combined to form the Word of God Congregation. Word of God Congregation? That didn't even "sound" Catholic.

St. Bede Parish was one of the last bastions of the old church remaining in Atlantic City and as long as Father Ray was alive it would stay that way.

As Father Ray was lost in his thoughts about the deterioration of the traditions of the Church, a large dark figure was quietly making his way up the side aisle of the empty church toward the confessional box. The figure moved so silently it was as if it hovered a few inches above the floor and glided its way up the side aisle. In his hand was a wrought iron chair that he had been sitting in the garden just outside the entrance to the church. Even though this chair was very heavy, the figure carried it with ease. In fact, he had looped two fingers through the ornamental iron work and carried the chair much like someone carrying a light brief case. Without making even the slightest hint of a noise, the figure set the chair down in front of the entry door to Father Ray's confessional box, tilted it back slightly and slid it under the door knob. Then the figure turned and entered the confessional box to Father's left.

Immersed in his private thoughts, Father Ray thought he heard someone enter the church but wasn't sure. Maybe it was the wind outside or maybe it was a sound made by one of the birds who had nested in the eaves of the church near the front stained glass window. He began to listen a bit more intently and even though he didn't hear the telltale sound of footsteps, he felt sure that someone was in the church. Another customer he thought. He opened his missal and turned to a verse which would prepare him to hear a confession and waited for the person to enter the confessional.

As Sal put his full weight on the kneeler, Father Ray opened the small sliding door that separated the two cubicles revealing a screened area which was covered with a white cloth.

"May the Lord be with you," Father Ray said as he greeted his confessor.

"And may the Lord help you if you don't tell me what I want to hear."

Father was taken aback by this response. Who was this person and what was he talking about?

"Who are you and what do you want? This is God's house and the only business conducted here is God's business. If you want to talk about something else I'd be happy to discuss the matter but not in a church confessional. In fact, why don't be both step outside of the confessional box and discuss this matter out in the open?"

"Sorry, padre, you're staying in the box and you WILL talk to me if you know what's good for you."

Father Ray decided to end the little game and leave his box. He turned the knob to open the door and the door wouldn't budge. He pushed harder but the door still wouldn't open.

Just then, with the speed of a striking cobra, a huge hand broke through the screened area of the confessional box and a vice-like grip came to rest on the collar of Father Ray's shirt. A second later Father Ray's face was plastered against the screen. His attacker was so close that he could smell his breath. The grip did not loosen and Father Ray was helpless to move.

"Now you priestly little fuck. I know that you, that nun bitch and that Jew, Feltzer, helped a woman get to that abused woman's shelter and I need to talk to that woman. Now tell me where those nuns are going to send her or, as they say in religious circles, you'd better be ready to meet your maker."

"I don't know where they are going to send her. They never tell anyone. If they did, their whole mission would be compromised. You have to believe me. No one but those nuns knows where she is going when she is going to leave Atlantic City. And even the nuns don't know her final destination. All they know is she is going to leave Atlantic City. After that, family members or the legal authorities get involved."

"I think you are a lying fucking Judas and for now I'm going to spare your life. But, padre, you'd better make your own confession because you are going to be visiting Jesus real soon."

Sal then pulled Father's head through the screened opening, raised his elbow and applied a bone crushing blow to the back of Father Ray's skull. As Father lay unconscious, Sal left the confessional box, grabbed the chair and left the church. As he was leaving the church grounds an old woman was opening the gate on the way to the church entrance.

"Excuse me, mam," Sal said. "Are you on your way to confession?"

"Yes," she replied.

"Well, you are going to have to wait until next week because I just had a confession with Father and he told me if I saw anyone coming into the church to tell them that he wouldn't be hearing confessions anymore today; seems like the poor fellow is suffering from a migraine headache."

"Well thank you young man and I'll be sure to keep Father Ray in my prayers."

"Good idea miss, Father is going to need all of the prayers he can get."

****

Dan VanAckeren was a lucky man. Recently his company, **Dan's One-Hour Dry Cleaning and Uniform Supply,** had captured the bid for supplying and cleaning the uniforms of all personnel in the Atlantic City Convention Center. Added to his existing contracts with several restaurants in the Northern end of town, The Sanctuary for Abused Women and the cleaning staff at the Sheraton, Atlantic City Hotel, Dan was finally on very solid ground financially. He and his wife, Peggy, had worked many years and long hours building up the reputation of the business and securing the uniform contract for The Convention Center was an accomplishment that would insure profitability for years to come. On this particular afternoon Dan had just picked up several large bags of dirty laundry at the Sanctuary for Abused Women, dropped off a dozen bags of clean uniforms at the Convention Center and was pulling up to the service entrance of the Sheraton Hotel to drop off several tall bags of cleaned and pressed uniforms. Dan backed up his truck to the service entrance, got out of the truck and rang the bell next to the door on the loading dock.

Thirty seconds later the receiver for the hotel pushed a button and the large metal door slid to the side.

"Hey there Mr. Dan," said old Bob McClintick, as he approached Dan. "What do we have for delivery today?"

"Two standard bags of clean uniforms and a one special-of-the-day-bag," replied Dan.

"Alrighty my good man; you take care of the two standard bags and I'll get the hand truck for the other bag."

While Dan attended to his bags, Bob retrieved the hand truck, placed the special bag on the truck and wheeled the bag into a dark corner of the receiving dock. He then returned to complete the paperwork for Dan. After exchanging departing pleasantries, Dan returned to his truck and Bob pushed the button and watched as the heavy metal door slid on its track into an air-tight and locked position. Bob then walked back to where he placed the special bag and said, "You OK in there Miss?"

Rose replied, "Yes I'm fine. Is it OK to get out now?"

"Yes indeedy. The coast is all clear."

Bob helped Rose extract herself from the bag and when Rose was fully out of the bag what appeared was not a young, attractive woman, but an older-looking woman with gray hair and a pasty complexion who was wearing wire-framed eye glasses.

The "new" Rose wore a somewhat battered cloth coat, granny shoes and carried a large purse that looked more like a sack than a purse. She was the perfect picture of a senior citizen who was in Atlantic City to spend the day playing the nickel slots and using her free lunch coupon.

"OK Miss; in ten minutes the bus will be at the front entrance to the hotel to pick up patrons returning to Philadelphia. Follow me and I'll lead the way," Bob declared.

Bob and Rose made their way to the freight elevator and then up to the ground floor. From there it was a short walk across the lobby to the front entrance. When they arrived at the front door there were a number of senior citizens in line waiting for the bus to arrive. When the bus arrived, Rose boarded, gave her return ticket to the driver and took a seat in the back of the bus next to an old gentleman who began to snore two seconds after he sat down. Ever so gently Rose looped her arm inside the old man's. He never felt a thing. In fact he kind of smiled and snored a bit louder. To anyone looking at the two of them you'd think it was just an old couple out for a day at the gaming tables spending the proceeds of their Social Security checks.

In about an hour or so the bus would stop at the 30th Street Station in Philadelphia. From there Rose would take a New Jersey Transit train to Penn Station in NYC. Once in Penn Station she would walk over to the Long Island Railway Station and take a train on the Hempstead Branch and get off at Floral Park. Arrangements had been made for Slim's uncle Tim to meet Rose at the station. The good news was that Rose's Atlantic City nightmare was about to end. The bad news was that with Sal on the loose, the nightmare was just beginning for others.

****

Just about every morning Sr. Jean attended 6:00 A.M. Mass at St. Bede Church. She loved going to Mass but she hated walking the three blocks to the church from The Sanctuary. Her dislike of walking to the church had nothing to do with an aversion to exercise and everything to do with the route she had to traverse. Before the rapid growth of the Casinos in Atlantic City, a number of "beautification projects" had begun in neighborhoods throughout the city. Federal funding, as part of urban renewal, had been the main source of the money flow to support these projects. But these funds had dried up in concert with the growth of real estate near the Casinos and the Boardwalk. In a very short time, many of the neighborhoods that were to be "beautified" became nothing more than abandoned urban eye sores.

Block after block consisted on nothing more than half razed buildings, empty lots and broken down store fronts. Some low-income housing had been built, but those homes had been abandoned and once left empty, scavengers had descended on these places, ripped out the wiring and plumbing and took anything that might have any resale value. The empty homes now became shelters for vagabonds, drug dealers and the homeless. Being a nun and wearing the habit insulated Sister Jean from attacks by many of the unsavory characters who populated her route to the church. Even though these social derelicts had no respect for life or the law they still seemed to respect people "of the cloth". But you never knew when one of these cretins who might be on dope or under the influence of alcohol would just snap and lose all control and if that happened it didn't matter if you were the Pope, you were going to be in big trouble.

As Sister made her way down the street she had an uneasy feeling that she was being watched, but that was a feeling she experienced many times before. "Not to worry, just keep moving," she said to herself. Then she was sure she heard a shuffling sound, but that could easily have been a rat or a homeless person turning over in his sleep in one of the broken down store fronts. When she thought she heard another sound she stopped to listen to determine the direction of the source of the sound. Before she had the opportunity to fine tune her hearing, she felt a powerful force around her neck and a wet cloth with a pungent odor being placed over her mouth and nose.

Sister Jean was not sure if she was dreaming or if she had regained consciousness because everything was black. Her mind was racing as she attempted to make sense of her predicament. Wasn't she just on her way to Mass? Where was she? What was she doing here? Where was here? Why couldn't she move? Why couldn't she see? What was in her mouth? Why couldn't she take a deep breath? She was on the verge of complete panic when a she heard a voice say to her, "If you can hear me, Sister, wiggle the fingers on your right hand." Sister Jean wiggled her fingers.

"Good girl. Now listen closely Sister and do what I tell you and you won't be harmed. Right now you are in a place where your screams will not attract attention. You have duct tape around your eyes, a gag in your mouth and you have been secured to a chair. There is no way for you to escape. I am in complete control of your life and your destiny. Not even Jesus can help you. Understand so far? If so, wiggle the fingers on your left hand."

Sister wiggled the fingers on her right hand. She immediately felt a hard slap to her head followed by a searing pain in her temple.

Sal said, "Sister, just as the captain said in the movie **Cool Hand Luke**, 'What we have here is a failure to communicate.' I told you to wiggle the fingers on your LEFT hand and you wiggled the fingers on your RIGHT hand. Now once again, if you understand what I am saying to you, wiggle the fingers on your left hand."

Sal watched Sister wiggle her fingers on the correct hand and then said to her, "I am going to remove the tape from your mouth and just like it says in the bible to give drink to the thirsty, I am going to give you a nice drink of cold water. As I said, your screams can not be heard by others, but screaming makes me nervous and if you make me nervous I will remove one of your teeth with a pair of pliers. That extraction, Sister, will not be accompanied by any anesthetic. Do you fully understand me, Sister? If so wiggle the fingers on both hands."

Sister quickly wiggled her fingers in acknowledgement. With one quick movement, Sal ripped the tape from Sister's mouth and Sister gasped in pain. "Sorry, Sister, but it's better to perform that procedure quickly. Removing the tape slowly is much more painful and the nice guy that I am, I try to be as gentle as possible." Sal then placed a straw in Sister's mouth and gave her the OK to take in some water. Sister almost finished the glass in two draws on the straw.

"I'm not here to rape you Sister or do any harm to you. All I want to do is have you give me a little information and I'll be on my way. Once you give me the information I need, I'll cut the tape away from one of your hands and then place the razor blade in your hand so that you can cut the tape away from your other hand and legs and then you'll be free to remove the tape from your eyes. By the time you have finished that chore I will be out of sight even though I may never be out of your mind. Say yes if you understand me."

"Yes," Sister replied hoarsely.

"Good. Sister, recently you smuggled a young girl out of David Feltzer's leather shop. I know this because I watched you go into the shop with one nun and come out with two nuns. I have heard about the miracle of Jesus turning water into wine, but that was kid stuff as compared to your little caper. I am very interested in finding out the final destination of that girl and that information is all you have to provide and I'll be on my way and you can have the rest of the day to yourself. So, where is the girl now and where is she going?"

"I believe the girl is safely out of Atlantic City but I am not at liberty to tell you anything more."

"Not at liberty to provide more information? Is that a nice way of telling me that you aren't going to provide the information I want?"

"Yes. I cannot and will not under **ANY** circumstances break the trust of The Sanctuary. If I do so, there is nothing to stop the next animal like you from trying to extract information as to the whereabouts of the souls we have taken in and vowed to provide assistance. We guarantee them one hundred per cent confidentiality regarding any of the matters associated with their relocation. You can do anything you want to me but I will **NEVER** talk. God is with me and God will protect me."

Sister felt a crushing blow to her sternum. The blow was so forceful that she and the chair to which she was taped flew back six feet and tumbled twice. Immediately Sal was on top of her and with amazing dexterity he attached his pliers to a molar in the back of Sister's mouth with great force pulled and ripped the tooth from her jaw bone. He then shoved a rag into Sister's mouth and her screams of pain were turned into muffled groans before she passed out. As Sister Jean regained consciousness her first sensation was the feeling of cold water being splashed on her face.

"Wake up you bitch," she heard the voice say to her. "Are you awake?" Sister nodded weakly in the affirmative.

"So much for God protecting your holy ass, Sister; that was one tooth down and thirty-one to go. I'm going to ask you one more time and just one more time; are you going to tell me where that girl has gone to?"

In her entire life Sister Jean had never spat. Not even when she brushed her teeth. Not even when she was told by the dentist to spit, did she spit. On those occasions she released the liquid stored in her mouth in a gentle stream onto the side of the reservoir and watched as the water current carried the contents down the small drain. But, as they say, there is a first time for everything and when Sal poised his last question, Sister Jean forcefully spat out a huge wad of blood-soaked spittle that landed right in the middle of Sal's forehead and dripped down into his right eyelid. Seconds later Sister Jean felt a hand going into her mouth followed by a flash of intense pain and then everything went silent and black.

****

Lead article, second page of the Press of Atlantic City, November 11th edition:

LOCAL PRIEST MURDERED
Early this morning, Ben Johnston, a local retiree, was fishing off of the Atlantic City Pier when he thought he saw what appeared to be a body floating under one of the pier's pilings. The Beach Patrol responded to Mr. Johnston's 911 call and discovered the body of Father Raymond Gorman bobbing in the water about 25 feet from shore. At first glance, Father Gorman's death seemed to be a case of accidental drowning. But Detective Joe Gannon of the Atlantic City Police force reports that the medical examiner has determined the cause of Father Gorman's death to be from blunt force trauma to the head. Father Gorman was well-known throughout the city for his dedication to working with The Sanctuary for Abused Women and his untiring efforts to help organize recreational activities for the youth of the town. Many feel that through Father Ray's efforts a number of the troubled youth in our community reformed their lives and took to a life of sports and/or physical activity rather than pursuing a life or crime and drug dependency. Father Ray also served as President of the Atlantic City Historical Society and was a strong advocate for maintaining some of the historical landmarks in the community. It is a sad commentary on the times in which we live that such a good person could be taken from us in such a violent matter.

Final arrangements for Father Gorman have yet to be made.

****

Eddie Lawrence had been captain of the Atlantic City Police Force for a number of years. Immediately after his graduation from the New Jersey State Police Academy he worked as a correctional officer at the Trenton State Penitentiary. After a 5-year stint in that position he felt he could better serve the public capturing criminals than babysitting them. He submitted an application to the Atlantic City Police Department and because of his excellent performance evaluations at Trenton State he was hired immediately. He walked a beat in almost every precinct of the city and over a 15-year period he worked his way up through the ranks to his current position. Eddie was widely respected by his fellow officers not only because he was tough and fair but because he was consistent in his management style. Nothing served to disrupt a team more than a leader who waffled in his judgments or who constantly changed his priorities.

Eddie was a true-blue cop and a man of good character. Even though "the family" had infiltrated the ranks of the Atlantic City Police Force, Eddie did everything he could to keep honesty in the ranks. But when a person had a family to feed and he/she wasn't making a bundle being a cop, Eddie could understand how it was easy to take a bribe and look the other way. He understood it, but that didn't mean he liked it or that he tolerated it.

Unlike any captain of the police force in a city the size of Atlantic City, Eddie did not always spend his days behind the desk attending to administrative duties. In an effort to demonstrate that he was not only the leader of the team but a player as well, Eddie regularly scheduled himself to ride patrols or walk beats with his front line officers. On this particular day Eddie was on patrol when the dispatcher radioed that a woman had been found lying in the middle of the street about a block away from St. Bede Church. In a flash Eddie and his partner responded to the call. Upon arriving at the scene the EMTs were already attending to the victim. Eddie rushed up the attending EMT and said, "How is she?" Upon closer inspection, Eddie noticed the woman was wearing a nun's habit. "Holy shit; is this woman a nun?"

"Yes sir and she's in very bad condition Captain. She's lost a lot of blood and her vitals are very weak but she's going to make it. We need to get her to the hospital fast as she is going to need immediate surgery."

"What is the cause of her injuries? Stabbing, shooting, beating, rape?"

"None of the above, sir."

"Then what?"

"Close as I can tell, sir, it appears that all of her teeth have been ripped out of her mouth and she's missing a tongue. Gotta go, sir. If you need to talk more, follow us to the hospital and I'll see you there."

Eddie stared in disbelief as he watched the ambulance speed away. Over the course of two days a priest was found murdered and now a nun has been brutally attacked. What in the hell was going on?

When Slim read the news article about Father Ray followed the next day by the report of the attack on Sister Jean, he immediately called David to see if he was OK. He was extremely relieved when David answered the phone and said he was perfectly OK and that Sal hadn't been back since his recent visit and that he hadn't noticed any strangers lurking around his shop or the apartment. David was very concerned about Rose since he hadn't received any word about her whereabouts. Slim told David that he would call him the minute his Uncle Tim called him regarding Rose's arrival in Floral Park. With the recent attacks on Father Ray and Sister Jean, Slim suggested to David that now, more than ever, they both had to lie low and that David had to stick to his normal daily schedule so there was no hint of a connection between Rose and Father Ray or Sister Jean. In addition he told David that there was to be absolutely no physical contact between the two of them. If Sal was watching David's store and noticed Slim going into the store he might recognize him as the person who was with Rose the night that Walter went missing. If that happened, more trouble could erupt and a major monkey wrench might develop regarding Slim's chances of getting out of Atlantic City unnoticed when it was time for him to join Rose and go on to Ireland.

****

Sal was on his way to a late lunch when his cell phone rang. His caller ID feature informed him that he had an incoming call from old man Bruno. "Hello, Mr. Bruno, what can I do for you?"

"Pack your shit, Sal and meet me at the Atlantic City Airport at 6:00 tonight. Our private flight leaves for Reno at 7:00."

"Reno? What's going on in Reno?"

"I'm going to meet with some West Coast family regarding taking over a couple of casinos and a ski lodge. It's time for us to branch out and this could be a big step for us as we've confined our operation to the Atlantic City area. To be a player, you have to have your chips in more than one place."

"When you say pack my shit, how much shit should I pack?"

"Look. I need muscle with me when I'm out there and I also need to have someone with me at all times whom I can trust. I also need someone to stay there and get to know the people and how they operate. Who are the assholes there? Who are the players? Who comes and goes and when they come whom do they deal with? I need a physical presence there one-hundred per cent of the time so that these people don't think they can fuck me over. And that presence should strike a little fear in their hearts and if there is anyone who can strike a little fear in someone's heart it's you."

"You mean I'm going there and not coming back?"

"Once this deal is signed and sealed and I feel comfortable with everything, then you can come back. But that might not be for three or four months or longer."

Sal was not happy to hear this news. It was good news in a way because it showed that the old man trusted him and respected him and looked upon him as an asset to the family operation. Actually that part was very good because if there was anyone you wanted to have on your side it was old man Bruno. Get on his wrong side and you could end up being chum on the next morning's fishing boat. But he still hadn't settled the score for Walter's demise. The priest and the nun had atoned for their sins, but he hadn't balanced the books with Poppa Jew and he was going to find that bitch Rose and teach her a lesson if it was the last thing he ever did.

NEW YORK CITY

FOUR YEARS LATER

Jake had done very well in his classes at NYU. So well, in fact, he graduated Cum Laude in three years. He performed extremely well during his co-op semesters at various hotels in the city. Upon graduation he interviewed and received a number of job offers and finally settled on an offer from the New York City Hilton which was located on the Avenue of the Americas in Mid-Town Manhattan. The Hilton was a grand hotel and having a position in the Hilton family of hotels, the possibility for upward movement in the industry was very promising. After working in the Hilton for only one year Jake was promoted to Manager of Housekeeping Services. When you consider that the hotel has 1,950 rooms you can readily understand Jake's ability to perform and the significance and scope of his new position.

With the promotion Jake received a huge kick in salary and even though he was making very good money, Jake still continued to live in the small studio apartment atop the Sorrento Bakery. Mrs. Sorrento's health was beginning to fail and there was no way Jake was going to abandon her. Even though he worked long hours at the Hilton, before and after work he helped Mrs. Sorrento in every way he could to make life easier for her so that she could keep the bakery open. During the seasonal busy times in the bakery, Jake, out of his own pocket, hired trustworthy students from NYU to help lift trays, maintain the equipment and clean the store in order to lighten the burden on Mrs. Sorrento. During the holidays Jake traveled to Sagamore to spend time with his family. On his way he would always stop and visit Zorb's grave site and pay his respects to Aunt Elsie. On one of his trips to home he discovered that Aunt Elsie had had a stroke and was in the hospice unit of the Coudersport General Hospital. Elsie had no living family and most of her friends had died so she was all alone. Jake stayed at the hospice unit with her until she passed and then paid for and handled all of the arrangements for her burial in a plot next to Zorb's. Other than the death of Aunt Elsie, everything in the last four years had been extremely positive. The most positive aspect was that there had been no further incidents of anyone looking for him in NYC or bothering his family in Sagamore. That entire situation in Pittsburgh was now a memory and he was looking forward, not backward in his life. Everything was rounding into perfect shape. He was young, he was good at his job, he loved going to work every day, he was respected by his employer, he was making good money and his life was touched by wonderful people like the Sorrento family and, of course, his mom and dad and his extended family in Sagamore. The only thing missing was a special lady in his life, but fate would deal him that card when the right person came into his life. Little did Jake know that his special card was right at the top of his deck.

****

It was a sunny and unseasonably warm November day in New York City and Jake had just exited the 6th Avenue Subway Station at West 49th Street and began his four block walk to the Hilton Hotel. As he approached the entrance to the hotel the doorman on duty quickly held the door open and ushered him into the building with a warm greeting. "Top of the morning to you Mr. Stalk and a fine day it is. Not a good day to be stuck inside in an office that's for sure."

"Well, Tim somebody has to stay inside and attend to the dirty work so that folks like you can enjoy the fresh air, feel the sun on your face and exchange pleasantries with all of the good people who come to stay at our hotel."

"That might be true today, Mr. Stalk, but breathing in the fumes from the traffic doesn't do much to keep me lungs clear and once that morning sun leaves so does the warmth. But I'm not complaining as I like the job and the best part is seeing the smile on a person's face or having them say thank you when you have helped them in some small way."

"I'll bet the big tippers make your day as well, Tim."

"Saints be praised, Mr. Stalk, a show of generosity from the public always does warm the cockles of me heart."

"Tim, I'd like to stay and chat but my work is piling up these days. The holiday season is always busy and this is the time when we hire some temporary people. For me, in addition to my normal chores, that means spending time interviewing candidates and making sure the veteran staff properly train the newcomers."

"Speaking of adding to staff, Mr. Stalk, I was wondering if you might find the time to interview me niece who has come to live with me. She's a fine girl and a hard worker. And the best part is that she has experience working in the housekeeping department in a large hotel. In no time she'd be a fine employee."

"Tim, I'm always happy to talk to experienced people and if she's your niece I know she comes from good stock. Here's my card with my office number. Have your niece call my secretary and make an appointment. I need good people and I need them fast so tell her to make that appointment right away."

"I will, sir, and I thank you. I know you won't be disappointed in her."

"By the way, Tim, what is your niece's name?"

"That would be Rose, Mr. Stalk. Rose Feltzer."

"Good, tell Rose I'm looking forward to seeing her. Have a good day Tim."

"Yes sir, Mr. Stalk, and thank you again."

Tim liked Jake. He was the only person in the management group who took time to say hello and spend a minute or two talking. He made you feel like a "person" and not just another hired hand. He felt guilty lying to Jake about Rose being his niece, but the family tie would be sure to strengthen her candidacy and referring to Rose as his niece sounded a lot better than "Mr. Stalk, would you mind interviewing the girlfriend of my nephew who accidentally killed a Mafia don's son and is on the run from some maniac belonging to the Atlantic City mob."

****

When Rose arrived in Penn Station she was so excited about being in New York City she could hardly stand it. She had read about NYC and looked at a lot of pictures in magazines and on the net but never dreamed she would be a short walk from Times Square and Mid Town Manhattan. Her escape from Atlantic City had gone very smoothly. She felt that there was no way anyone could be tailing her at this point, so before heading over to the Long Island Railroad terminal to begin the last leg of her journey she decided to cast fate to the wind and go up to ground level for a look/see at the famous New York City. Upon exiting Penn Station she found herself at the corner of West 34th Street and 7th Avenue. Rose was utterly overwhelmed, as far as she could see there were tall buildings. There were people rushing everywhere. Car horns were beeping by the second and the traffic was very heavy. Even in the daylight she could see the five-story billboards with flashing lights. There were lights everywhere! The city was electric! It was alive! It was everything she dreamed it would be and more. The thought that she would be living just a short train ride away from such a magical place was pure excitement for Rose. For a fleeting moment Rose wondered how she could leave such a magnificent city to live in some boring, quiet little town in Ireland for the rest of her life. As she turned to go back into Penn Station she adjusted her necklace and her locket and thought about the words her mother had inscribed inside the locket, "Always Follow Your Heart." Just like her mother, Rose was going to do just that.

****

    Rose found Slim's Uncle Tim to be a very caring and polite man and he did everything he could to make her feel welcome. Floral Park was a decent community and Tim's house was clean and basic and somewhat spacious. It was a lot bigger than the apartment above the shop in Atlantic City. When Tim told her about the job prospect at the Hilton Hotel Rose was ecstatic. She was so caught up in her dream of working in Mid-Town Manhattan that Tim had to remind her that she'd better call Slim and her dad to let them know that she arrived safely.

When she talked to Slim, Slim told Rose about the death of Father Ray and the beating of Sister Jean. He informed her that she might have to stay in New York longer than originally planned. It was better to be safe than sorry he explained. After Rose ended the conversation with Slim she thought about his words.....better to be safe than sorry…But the way Rose saw it, staying New York City for an extended period of time was a bonus. She missed her poppa and she loved Slim, but maybe there was a new life waiting for her in New York City. The length of the day and the stress of the trip had finally caught up to Rose and she fell asleep on the couch in Tim's living room clutching her locket and dreaming about what journey would be in store for her as she followed her heart.

****

Rose's appointment with Jake was scheduled for 7:00 A.M. Pretty early she thought, but Jake's assistant told her that Mr. Stalk started his days early and ended them late and that he preferred to conduct his interviewing before being distracted by the normal issues and problems that arose as soon as his "regular hours" began. Rose arrived at 6:30 A.M. for the interview and took the elevator up to the floor number indicated on Jake's business card. When she arrived at the reception area no one was there so she had no recourse but to find a comfortable chair and look through a magazine and wait for someone to arrive. A few minutes later the door opened and in walked a very attractive man. She wasn't sure what Mr. Stalk looked like and she wasn't expecting someone this good looking. Rose felt an immediate attraction to this man and was almost embarrassed by the strength of the chemistry.

"Good morning Miss Feltzer. I'm glad to see that you are here early. It's always a good sign when the employee beats the boss to work. I'm Jake Stalk and I'm very pleased to meet you. Please give me a few minutes to plug in the coffee pot and get my wits about me. I'm glad you could come in so quickly and I'm anxious to chat with you. Your uncle Tim had a lot of good things to say about you."

As Jake went about the business of hanging up his coat and preparing the coffee, he was thinking that this woman was strikingly beautiful. He felt a little flutter in his heart and a bit unnerved. He felt like he was on a first date and not in the process of conducting a professional interview with a prospective employee.

The interview went very smoothly and it was hard for Jake to maintain an air of professionalism during the talk. He wanted to ask Rose out on a date, not hire her. But duty called and he put Rose through the usual paces of an interview. At the end of the interview Jake told Rose to call her supervisor at the Showboat and have her fax a recommendation to his office. If the recommendation was positive, Rose could start training the following Monday. The interview ended a little clumsy as both Rose and Jake were in the middle of this mutual attraction thing and neither one knew quite how to handle the situation. Jake finally said, "Rose, I'm assuming that your recommendation will be positive and that you will be on the payroll starting next week. It is not my usual practice, but if you agree, I'd like to have lunch with you in a week or so just to check up on how you are doing and maybe you could give me your thoughts about the effectiveness of our training program."

"Lunch sounds wonderful, Mr. Stalk. I'm sure you can track me down in the hotel, but if you have trouble, feel free to call me at the home number on my resume."

"Rose, when we have lunch, I'd feel more comfortable when we are alone together if you'd called me Jake rather than Mr. Stalk."

"I like the sound of alone together and I'd like very much to call you Jake," responded Rose.

After that exchange Jake's heart skipped a beat and Rose's hands began to sweat a little. Jake bid Rose adieu with a handshake and the mutual electricity in that handshake caused each one to feel a little weak in the knees.

The faxed recommendation from Rose's former supervisor arrived on Jake's desk the next day. Normally Jake's assistant made the call to the new hires, but in this case Jake decided to make the call himself. The following Monday Rose was officially a member of the Housekeeping Unit of the Hilton Hotel.

Two weeks later Jake looked at the Housekeeping master schedule and found Rose's work schedule and caught up with her in the employee's lounge. She was seated in a plastic-covered lounge chair eating a piece of fruit.

"Hi Rose. How's everything going?"

"Hi Mr. Stalk, I mean Jake, everything's great. Cleaning rooms and changing sheets is a bit tedious and the pay is OK, but this is a great hotel and the supervisor of Housekeeping seems to be comfortable with my work and doesn't check up on me much. I think she trusts me to do a good job and that in and of itself is a nice compliment."

"Well I'd like to hear all about your boring job. I see on your schedule that you finish up at 6:00 P.M. on Friday. That's a bit late for the lunch I talked about, but early enough for a dinner. So would you like to have dinner with me Friday?"

"Jake, I'd love to, but I wouldn't have the right clothes to wear. I'd have just my uniform and I wouldn't want people to think you are taking your maid out to dinner. Plus, after working all day stripping beds and cleaning rooms I'd have to shower and do my hair and all of those good things women need to do when preparing to go out for an evening."

"Not a problem. The hotel always keeps extra rooms available just in case a special circumstance presents itself or if there is some kind of equipment malfunction in the room and the guests screams and hollers to be moved to another room. So all you need to do is to bring a change of clothes with you to work and you'll be all set. The rooms have all of the toiletries and a hair dryer so that solves part two of your problem. I'll track you down on Friday and give you the key to the room. So what do you say?"

"Ok, it's a date."

"Great! I'll make reservations for 7:30 P.M. That should give you plenty of time to get ready and for us to cab to the restaurant. Oh, and one more thing Rose, unless something drastic occurs, the room will be available for the night so you'll have the option of staying over if you'd like. Your work schedule calls for you to work on Saturday so staying over would save you the trouble of making a late trip home on Friday night and then having to get up early to return on Saturday. Just so you know; that option is available to you."

"And who pays for the room if I stay over?"

"It's on the house, complements of the Manager of Housekeeping Services."

Friday came and Jake tracked down Rose and gave her the key to the room. In the interim Rose had decided to stay over because the hassle involved in making the round trip to and from home. And who knows how the evening would play out?

Jake pulled out all of the stops in an effort to make a lasting impression on Rose. He made dinner reservations at **The Tavern on the Green** located in Central Park on the upper Westside of Manhattan. Dinner was followed by a relaxing horse and buggy ride through Central Park. The weather had turned colder and was more representative of a late November day in New York City and during the buggy ride Jake and Rose huddled together under the cover of a heavy wool blanket. Midway through the ride snowflakes began to gently fall and lightly dust the landscape. It was a beautiful scene and Rose felt like she was living a wonderful dream. It was as if she was a princess and Jake was her prince and they were riding in their carriage through the woods back to their estate.

Jake was not only handsome, he was bright, a good conversationalist and by all appearances he was in good financial shape. What more could a girl ask for? Jake was absolutely enamored with Rose. She seemed to be beautiful inside and out. She had told him all about her life in Gdansk, her dad and their journey to Atlantic City. But there was one important thing Rose conveniently left out of her story and that was the fact that she was practically engaged to Slim.

****

Slim was in between jobs in Atlantic City and decided to fly home to Ireland for the holidays. He called Rose and suggested that she come with him, but Rose begged off explaining that she couldn't get time off of work. After all, the only reason she was hired was to help through the holiday rush, so how could she even approach her supervisor about taking time off? Slim said he understood and the compromise they reached was that she would meet him at JFK airport when he was changing planes for the second leg of his journey to Dublin.

It was Sunday, December 22nd and Rose had the afternoon off and was in a cab on her way to rendezvous with Slim. She was going to see Slim with mixed emotions in her heart. Since that first dinner date with Jake, she and Jake had been seeing each other on a regular but infrequent basis. He was working long hours as well as she and finding overlapping free time was a problem. Even though their time together away from work was sporadic, Jake always managed to stop by the floor where she was working to say hello. He would also find out when she had lunch break and the two of them would go out for a quick lunch at a fast food place or grab a sandwich at ***Blimpie's*** and sneak into one of the vacant conference rooms in the hotel and eat lunch.

Jake had been a perfect gentleman, and other than a goodnight kiss he had not been sexually aggressive. In a way, this bothered Rose because it made her wonder if Jake was falling for her as hard as she was falling for him. She didn't expect him to try to make love to her on the first date, but how long could he go on being Mr. Nice Guy? And then there was Slim. Two months ago she was ready to marry him, but now since Jake came into the picture she wasn't sure about her feelings for Slim. Absent mindedly she tugged on her locket and thought about following her heart and right now her heart was leading her to Jake.

At the airport Slim was so anxious to see Rose he could hardly contain his emotions. The time between flights was only an hour and fifteen minutes. Even though his connecting gate was in the same terminal, in an effort to see Rose, he was going to have to exit the terminal and then have to go back through security again. This would significantly cut down on the time that they could spend together, but being able to see Rose was a bonus and even if he could only spend five minutes with her it was worth it.

Slim exited the secured area, spotted Rose and quickly maneuvered through the crowd in her direction. Rose spotted Slim coming her way and they met in an embrace and they held that embrace for a full thirty seconds. As they made their way toward the security area closer to Slim's connecting gate, Slim brought her up to date on what was happening in Atlantic City. David was doing fine but was living in fear that someone from "the family" would attack him, especially after what happened to Father Ray and Sister Jean. The investigation regarding Walter's whereabouts was non-existent. The murder of Father Ray was unsolved. With no witnesses, no murder weapon and no known motive, Captain Lawrence and his detectives didn't have one suspect in mind. The newspaper reported that the NJ state CSI unit hadn't turned up a single clue in the case. Sister Jean had undergone several surgeries and was still hospitalized. She would need more surgeries and the reports were that even if she was to make a complete recovery she would never be able to speak again. As with Father Ray, the police had no clues regarding Sister's attacker. Sal hadn't been seen in awhile but that didn't mean he wasn't around. He might have been just laying low until he heat wore down on the investigations associated with Father Ray and Sister Jean. Rose told Slim all about her job and the fact that Uncle Tim was a good man and was doing his best to make her comfortable. She told him that she really enjoyed the hustle and bustle of New York City and how lively the city was during the holiday season. When it was time for Slim to reenter the secured area he embraced Rose and told her that he loved her. Rose hugged him back and as their lips met the thought went through Slim's mind that Rose didn't say she loved him back.

As Rose watched Slim make his way through the security area she was very emotionally confused. She thought she loved Slim and she thought she was falling in love with Jake. She was trying to follow her heart but the road was a very confusing one. Sometime soon there would be a fork in the road and she would have to choose one path to travel. She didn't look forward to that day. For now she'd just play both ends against the middle and see what happened.

****

It was the night before Christmas and all through the house not a creature was stirring, not even a mouse. But that wasn't necessarily true if the mouse was Cameron Mac Kenna (AKA....Squeaky Mac Kenna). Cameron, the only son of Scottish immigrants, was the best second-story man in the business and the best B & E (breaking and entering) specialist on the East Coast. The sound of a pin dropping was louder than the sound Cameron's footsteps made when he was in the act of burglarizing a home or a business. Like the wind, Cameron would be in and out of a house and no one would know the difference until the next day when they awoke to find that all of their good jewelry and their most precious possessions had somehow evaporated into thin air. Cameron loved the Christmas season when people would be out and about buying expensive items to bestow upon their loved ones on Christmas day. These people were his potential "customers". With 10 shopping days until Christmas, Cameron would case the upper tier jewelry stores and furrier stores and watch as wealthy men and women made their holiday purchases. Then he'd follow them out to their cars, take down their license plate numbers and hire an underground computer wizard to tap into the state motor vehicle data base for the names and addresses of those registered to the vehicles. Presto, like magic he'd have his own list of homes to visit before or in tandem with good old Saint Nick. It was somewhat interesting how Cameron got his nickname. It came about on one Christmas Eve as he was slithering to and fro in the living room of an estate in Princeton, NJ. As he was in the process of filling his bag with goodies, he inadvertently stepped on the family pet's favorite chew toy. The family pet in this case was a young and quite muscular Rottweiler. When Cameron stepped on the toy it squeaked ever so slightly, not loud enough to wake any human in the house but loud enough to wake up the dog and old Fido came prancing into the room to see who was screwing around with HIS favorite toy. When the dog spotted Cameron he started the beginning of a ferocious bark, but before the sound of the bark formed in the dog's larynx, Cameron calmly drilled a bullet into Fido's brain.

With the silencer on the gun, two sounds were heard in the matter of a few seconds. First was the Pfffffffffft sound the bullet made as it exited the silencer and second was the sound of wrapping paper crinkling as the dog gently collapsed onto one of the gifts next to the Christmas tree. Cameron continued his shopping spree and before he left he dragged the dog over to the Christmas tree and hid him under a pile of gifts. He even took the time to transfer one of those stick-on bows to the dog's nose. On his way out he put the squeaky toy in his pocket as a keepsake to remind him to be on the lookout for such items in his future endeavors. At the bar the next day Cameron pulled out the squeaky toy and told the story of his recent caper to his gangster buddies. They all hooted and hollered and one of his friends yelled out, "To our new best friend, Squeaky Mac Kenna." Everyone clicked their glasses together and from that day on Cameron was known as "Squeaky" amongst his peers.

When his cell phone rang, Squeaky looked at his caller ID and recognized the number as belonging to his good friend Sal Pappano.

"Squeaky."

"Ay, Salvadore."

Sal always got a kick out of Squeaky because he was the only person in the world other than his dearly departed mother who ever called him by his formal given name.

"And how are the holidays treating you my good friend?"

"The economy is somewhat down, Salvadore, but it's never down for the rich. Business is good."

"Squeaky, I was wondering if you could do a job for me."

"Anything lad, you just name it."

"Thanks Squeaky, I knew I could count on you. OK, I need you to get into the apartment above the "Feltzer's Leather Shop" which is located about a block from the Showboat Casino. Do you know the place?"

"I know it well. Some of my newest customers buy custom-made leather gifts from that place. High-grade leather and the man is a talented craftsman. I can usually fence one of his custom-made purses for a couple of C notes."

"I'm not interested in leather, Squeaky. What I'm interested in is his phone bills for the last few months. Phone bills is what I want, nothing else but phone bills."

"Not a problem lad. How quickly do you need me to do the job?"

"No rush Squeaky, anytime by the first week in January. When you get them, just pop them in mail."

"Your wish is my command, Salvadore. Give me your address and before you know it the bills will be in your mail box."

"Squeaky, you didn't ask me how much this caper is going to cost me."

"For you, Salvadore, I'll extend a holiday discount. I think three C notes would be reasonable."

"Tell you what, Squeaky, I'll give you the cash when I see you and if one of the numbers on that list turns out to be a winning number, I'll give you a five C note tip."

"Spoken like a true gentlemen, Salvadore, and one who is full of the Christmas spirit."

****

A Cruel Twist of Fate

Over the holiday season Jake and Rose didn't see much of each other as they both were working extended hours. A couple of times they arranged to meet in a vacant conference room for lunch but that was the extent of their social life. After the holidays Rose's employment was to end as the holiday rush was over and the need for part timers had been exhausted. But Jake interceded on Rose's behalf with Human Resources and the Housekeeping supervisor and arrangements were made for Rose to start as a full-time employee at the beginning of the new pay period in January. The new pay period began January 15th so that meant that Rose had about two weeks off before she had to go back to work. Jake hadn't taken a vacation day since he started with the Hilton Corporation. Truth be known, he hadn't gone on a vacation his entire life. Knowing that Rose had off for a couple of weeks, Jake arranged to take a vacation week and he hoped to spend it with Rose.

On Rose's last day before her time off, she and Jake had arranged to have lunch together at the Carnegie Deli. As they shared a huge corned beef sandwich Jake proposed the idea of taking a week's vacation together. Rose was overwhelmed by the invitation and her answer was a resounding yes. Anticipating a positive response Jake brought some brochures with him of potential sites. With great excitement they perused the brochures and settled on the Aruba Hilton and since Jake was a level 23 employee in the Hilton organization he was eligible to secure a 2-bedroom hotel suite at a very generous discount. Very quickly plans were made and when they got back to work Jake went to the hotel concierge and asked that she make all of the necessary flight and room arrangements for him.

On January 5th as Rose and Jake's flight was bounding down the runway for its departure to Aruba, Sal was opening his mail in Reno, NV and low and behold his package from Squeaky had arrived.

Squeaky had delivered as expected. The last 3 months of David's phone bills were included in the package and Sal was surprised to see how many calls David made each month. In the month of December David had made over 150 calls that were not local! The area code numbers were from all over the United States as well as a few in Europe. Sal had underestimated the fact that many of David's customers came to Atlantic City from all over the United States as well as foreign countries and that he had so much interaction with those people. Somewhere in these numbers he felt sure one would lead him to Rose. The first step in narrowing down the numbers was to find a number that had been called multiple times and a number that had been called more than once in every month. After the narrowing down process, Sal had ten numbers on his list. He opened his phone book to the page which listed the area codes for each state and he found that one of the numbers was in the New Mexico area, two were in the Boston area, one was in Chicago, and the remaining six were in the New York City/Long Island area. One fact that came out loud and clear to Sal was that on all three bills there wasn't one call to Poland. This fact just confirmed his belief that both David and Rose were lying through their teeth when they told that story about Rose going to Poland to take care of her sick mother. Those filthy lying Jews had tried to make a fool out of him and for that and for what they did to Walter, Rose would pay dearly.

The next day Sal began making his calls. If the number was a business number he would just say, "Sorry, I dialed the wrong number." If someone at a residence answered he would ask for Rose and then launch into his cover story. His cover story was that he was an employee for an auditing firm who had just completed a year-end audit of the books for the Showboat and it had come to their attention that there were some inconsistencies in the payroll for the month of November. It seemed that due to a programming error, too much money had been deducted in Federal Taxes and that the Casino was now issuing reimbursement checks. On his list of people to receive a supplemental check was one Rose Feltzer. Would they be so kind as to confirm the address for Rose so that a reimbursement check could be sent post haste. Sal decided to work from West to East and the first number he called in New Mexico turned out to be a leather supply house. In Chicago, the number belonged to a customer of David's who had placed multiple orders for merchandise and he had received a number of follow up calls from David checking to make sure the items had been received. Two calls to the 212 area code in New York City were uneventful. When he dialed the 516 area code a man answered the phone and when Sal asked for Rose the man said she was out of town and wouldn't be back until the end of the week. **BINGO!** At that point Sal launched into his story and after the story the man on the other end of the line asked why the Showboat didn't just send the check to the forwarding address Rose left which was her father's shop. Sal responded that he was an employee of an outside firm and didn't have access to Showboat employee files. All he had was a list of names who were supposed to receive checks and his job was to make sure that they had the correct address for the recipients before the checks were sent out. The man on the phone said that he would not give out the address on the phone and that his firm needed to go back to the Showboat Casino personnel files and retrieve Rose's forwarding address. Sal thanked the man, hung up the phone and then threw it so hard against the wall that it broke into a dozen pieces. He was so close to getting that address. But he knew that Rose was living in the 516 area code which was some place in Western Long Island. Was the man who answered the phone the same man who was with Rose the night that Walter disappeared? There was no way to know. Since the man wouldn't give the address he'd have to make contact with his underground resource, give him the phone number and have him break into the phone company's data base and get the address. For an accomplished hacker the job wouldn't be very difficult, but Sal would have to pay for the time it took to get that information and people who hacked into systems for a living didn't come cheap. But, no matter what Sal had to pay, Rose was going to end up paying a much higher price.

    The Aruba trip was akin to a honeymoon trip for Jake and Rose. They toured, snorkeled, lay on the beach for long stretches of time and took great delight in counting Divi Divi trees. Each afternoon the hotel offered a happy hour for drinks that was actually three hours in length. Following the happy hour(s) Jake and Rose retired to their suite and made love until it was time to get ready for dinner, clubbing or perusing the shops in down town Oranjested. Even though Rose was seemingly head over heels in love with Jake, deep down she felt guilty and couldn't seem to get Slim out of her mind. How could she be making love to Jake and thinking about Slim? During the day, as she lay on the beach, she constantly made comparisons between the two of them and wondered which one would provide her with the most happiness in life. She realized how unfair her display of emotions to each one had been; but neither one was the wiser as to the charade she was playing and as long as she could keep it that way the more time she had to figure out what she wanted to do. Eventually she knew that there would be a loser and a winner, but Rose only cared about one person in this love triangle and that was herself. She was following her heart just like her mother had and if someone got hurt it didn't matter, just as long as it wasn't her.

****

It took Sal's friendly hacker less than an hour to marry an address with the 516 exchange he investigated. The house was owned by a Timothy McGraw of 7395 Daisy Avenue in Floral Park, NY. When Sal received this news in Reno he broke out into a huge smile and said to himself, "Gotcha, you little Jew wench."

On the 1st of February Sal received a call from old man Bruno. Everything was falling into place regarding his business deal in Reno. He was very pleased with Sal's investigative reporting and his work in Reno and told him that the deal would be wrapped up during the first week of the month. He went on to say that once the deal was consummated, Sal could take a month off and go on a vacation anywhere in the world he chose and he would foot the bill. Sal thanked Mr. Bruno for his kind gesture and as the two of them were culminating the phone call, Mr. Bruno said, "Any first thoughts on where you might want to go on your special trip?"

Sal responded "I've always had this fascination with Long Island. Maybe I'll stop there and do a little business and then tool out to the Hamptons."

"Long Island and the Hamptons in the dead of winter doesn't sound like a fun trip to me."

"Oh, you'd be surprised at the fun I plan to have," replied Sal.

****

After returning from the trip with Rose, Jake was clearly one-hundred per cent, head over heels in love with Rose. He was committed to her and was planning to ask her to marry him. But, before he popped the question he wanted Rose to meet Mrs. Sorrento and he wanted to take her to Sagamore to meet his parents and the rest of his extended family in his home town. It would be up to Rose, but Jake was hoping that she would consent to having an old-time, small-town wedding in Sagamore. That place was so special to him that he couldn't imagine celebrating an event of that magnitude in his life anywhere else. But if Rose was set on having a wedding in Atlantic City or even Poland that would be OK with him. Of course all of Jake's plans were based on the fact that Rose would say yes when he popped the question. From Rose's perspective, the trip to Aruba had been great. Every day was a new adventure and Jake spared no expense in trying to make her happy. Each time they strolled down the streets of Oranjestead, Rose led Jake to a jewelry store, "just to look", but she knew that Jake would break down and she wouldn't leave empty handed. It took less than a week for her to be able to manipulate Jake and Rose loved having that power over a man.

****

The house at 7395 Daisy Avenue in Floral Park, Long Island, sat at the corner of Daisy and Atlantic Avenues. It was a 1950 vintage, two-story home constructed of yellow brick. There wasn't much of a front yard and the street was not tree lined. Every window was complete with a brown and faded-white aluminum awning which made it somewhat difficult to see into the windows from the street level. But, being a corner property, every entrance to the house was in full view to the public. The house was situated only three blocks from the Floral Park train station and due to that fact; there was a constant turnover of cars parked on the street as daily commuters scrambled to find an available parking space in order to avoid having to pay the daily parking fee at the train station. NYC commuters worked long hours so it was not unusual to see cars parked on the streets around 7395 Daisy Avenue anytime during the day or night.

A Cruel Twist of Fate

Sal used his computer to search for a decent place to stay in Floral Park. From the limited choices available Sal chose the Floral Park Motor Lodge on Jericho Turnpike. One review of the hotel stated, "Good value, clean, good place for a short stay"; just what he wanted. On the map it looked like the Jericho Turnpike was just on the other side of the train tracks from Daisy Avenue. Again; just what he wanted as he wanted to be far enough away as to not attract attention, yet close enough that he would have no traffic problems negotiating to and from the hotel. What sealed the deal on the hotel for Sal was the fact that nearby you had Arturo's Restaurant, Ciro's, Fiore Italian Cuisine and the Stella Ristonante. He could eat at a different Italian restaurant every night! How could you beat that?

The drive up from Atlantic City was uneventful until he crossed the Verrazano Bridge and exited onto the Belt Parkway. From the moment he entered the Belt Parkway to the time he turned onto Pulaski Road the traffic was a nightmare. More than once Sal pounded on the steering wheel and asked himself, "How in fuck do these people drive in this shit every fucking day? Why in the fuck would anyone want to live on Long Island? The whole fucking place is just one big parking lot!" But, what kept him going was the thought of a good dinner and several bottles of wine at one of those Italian Restaurants on Jericho Turnpike. After he checked into to his room, Sal took a quick ride over to Daisy Avenue just to get a feel for the drive. It was an easy trip, maybe a five-minute drive. But it was seven o'clock at night and traffic was dying down. "Who knows," he thought, "with the amount of traffic around here tomorrow morning it might take a fucking hour to get there." But that was tomorrow and that worry would have to wait. For now, it was on to Arturo's.

At 6:00 A.M. the next morning Sal was cursing often and loudly as he cruised up and down Atlantic Avenue and

Daisy Avenue looking for a parking space. "Jesus H. Christ," he said to himself, "you can't drive in the place and you can't park here either. What kind of fucking place is this?" But luck was in Sal's favor as he spotted someone leaving a space on Atlantic Avenue almost at the corner of Atlantic and Daisy. From there he would have a bird's eye view of the house at 7395. Upon settling in, Sal grabbed his copy of the Long Island Press and began to pretend to read the paper. To the casual observer he was just another morning commuter killing some time before meandering over to the train station. As Sal sat there he couldn't have been more pleased with the location of the house. It was a perfect set up. He could park here all day and all night and not draw the attention of anyone in the neighbor; how lucky for him and how unlucky for Miss Jew of Atlantic City.

At approximately 6:30 A.M. the front door of the house at 7395 Daisy Avenue opened and out stepped an older man. He looked to be trim and fit but he was definitely not a young man. He wasn't the guy Sal saw with Rose the night the two of them entered the service entrance to the Show Boat. He was followed by a young lady and that young lady was none other than the Jewish American Princess, Rose Feltzer. As the two of them sauntered up the street, Sal exited his car and followed at a safe distance. He followed them into the train station and watched as they descended to the train platform below. From his research on the computer he knew that Floral Park was the last stop on the Hempstead Branch Line of the Long Island RR so he assumed that they were heading West to NYC. They could be going to Bellrose, Queens Village or Hollis, all stops before Penn Station, but his gut told him that they were going to The City. There wasn't enough time to get in line for a ticket so he just went downstairs to the platform to await the train. He could always pay the conductor on the train. The cost of buying a ticket on the train versus buying it at the ticket window was higher, but what the fuck, old man Bruno was picking up the tab. Sal kept his distance but always kept his eye on Rose. She certainly wasn't expecting anyone to be following her, but at his size, if Rose noticed him she might get spooked. As the train doors opened everyone starting pushing and shoving in order to get on the train first. "Fucking animals," Sal thought. "Well if that's the game you want to play, count me in," Sal said to himself. With that thought in mind, Sal barreled ahead and pushed people aside like a giant bowling ball smashing into the head pin. Some guys didn't know what hit them and they got really angry and were ready to swing at the guy who just displaced them, but upon seeing his size and the look on his face, they meekly grabbed their brief cases and went about their business.

At Penn Station Sal watched Rose and her friend exit and he followed along as they made their way underground to the 6th Avenue Subway Station. Luckily there wasn't anyone in front of him waiting to buy a token, so Sal shoved a $10 bill under the glass and the agent returned the favor by shoving some tokens and change in his direction. Sal was just exiting the turnstile when he heard the screeching of the brakes of the train; he hustled ahead and got to the door just as it was closing. He heard the double tone followed by the recorded message, "Watch the closing doors," but ignored it, grasped the door with one hand, gave it a mighty heave, reversed its direction and bounded into the train car. He spotted Rose and her friend in the car ahead. So far so good. At West 53rd Street Rose and her companion exited and began to walk north on 6th Avenue. Sal kept a safe distance and stopped when they entered the Hilton Hotel.

Today had been a great day for Sal. He saw where Rose lived and now he knew where she worked. He thought twice about following her into the hotel but he decided to wait until later; first things first, right now he was really hungry.

Before the end of the week Sal found out that Tim McGraw, the guy who owned the house was a doorman at the Hilton and also worked as a nighttime security cop several nights a week at the McGraw-Hill Building in Rockefeller Center. He couldn't figure out the connection between Rose and this guy. Maybe he was a just a "Do Gooder" who supported the Sanctuary for Abused Women and provided a room for those kind of women. He discovered that Rose worked in the Housekeeping Unit at the Hilton Hotel and she had lunch most days with a young man who also worked at the Hilton. Based on his size, Sal felt that this was the guy who was with her the night Walter was wasted. When Rose was out of the picture, Sal managed to get into the elevator with the guy and got close enough to read the name on his Hilton ID badge……Jake Stalk. He looked up the name in the phone book to see if he could get an address, but there was no listing under that name. But, if this guy was the same boyfriend he saw in Atlantic City, wouldn't Rose just shack up with him? Why was she staying out on Long Island with the old guy? Still some unanswered questions but at least he had a good feel for Rose's daily movements. He knew everything he needed to know about Rose in order to make his move. The only unanswered questions regarding his move on Rose were, when, where and how.

****

After the holidays in Ireland Slim had returned to Atlantic City and was not a happy camper. When Rose first got to New York she used to call almost daily, but as time passed her calls became irregular. Added to this fact was he still hadn't forgotten that she didn't tell him she loved him at the airport that night. Something was going on and he wasn't sure what. He talked to David to see what he knew, but David wasn't able to shed any light on the issue. Uncle Tim said he saw Rose going to lunch several times with the Manager of Housekeeping Services; but it wasn't unusual for Managers to have lunch with employees; especially new employees. Uncle Tim reported that to his knowledge, he couldn't recall Rose receiving phone calls from any men. The only behavior out of the ordinary was the week she went to Aruba in January. But, as Rose explained, that was a "girl thing" with some of the people with whom she worked. As far as he could tell, Rose didn't do much other than go to work and spend time at the house.

"But you have to remember Slim, I work 10 hour shifts every day and then I work part time at night as well; anything could happen and I'd be none the wiser. She is a young woman in need who just happened to be attached to my nephew so I agreed to help out until she got on her own two feet or until the two of you go off to Ireland. I didn't sign up to be her babysitter."

After talking to Uncle Tim, Slim thought to himself: There hadn't been any signs of any trouble since Father Ray passed and Sister Jean was beaten. Nobody had accosted David or bothered him in any way. Months had passed and there was no sign that anyone had followed Rose to New York. If there was ever a good time for he and Rose to make their way to a new life in Ireland the time was now. If he waited much longer, he felt that he might lose Rose altogether.

Of course the possibility existed that Rose had fallen out of love with him. If that were the case, he'd have to deal with it, but he wouldn't deal with it in Atlantic City. He was going home to Ireland with or without Rose.

The next day Slim phoned Rose and laid out his plan. At the end of the week he would be leaving Atlantic City. He would buy the air line tickets to Dublin for both of them. On the second leg of his flight, she would join him and together they would make their way to Ireland. He would make flight arrangements so that there would be ample time for him to deplane in JFK, leave the secured area, meet with her and then have the both of them proceed through the security checks and to their departing gate on time. Rose was quiet during Slim's conversation and afterwards didn't express overwhelming joy with the plan Slim outlined.

"Rose, I thought you'd be happy that we are leaving. Our life together in Ireland was all we talked about when we were together in Atlantic City. The whole plan of getting you out of Atlantic City was so that you could be safe until I would join you and then together we'd leave the country to start a new life. Aren't you excited? Do you still love me? Do you still want a life with me?"

"Yes, Slim. Yes is the answer to all of those questions, it is just that this all seems to be happening so quickly. I do like my job and I do like the excitement of being in New York City but yet I do want to leave with you. I guess I'm just mixed up right now."

"Rose, is there someone else in your life?"

"No Slim. How could you think that? I love you and only you."

"I could think that there is someone else in your life because things have been very different between us since you went to New York. I can't explain it, but I just sense there is something wrong. Maybe it's just me. Maybe I want this life with you so badly that I'm worried that it won't happen and I focus on every little thing, always thinking negatively, always worried that I'll lose you."

"Don't worry my Slim. You won't lose me. I'm yours forever."

"I want to believe you more than anything, Rose. But I have to tell you that if you change your mind and don't show up to meet me, I am going on to Ireland myself. I don't mean for that to sound like an ultimatum, but there's nothing more for me Atlantic City or this country. I want to spend the rest of my life at my home in Ireland and I want to spend that time with you. I hope to see you next Saturday my love."

"I will see you then, don't you worry."

After hanging up the phone, Rose said to herself, "I've known since the beginning of my relationship with Jake that this day was going to come. But I thought I would have more time before deciding which fork in the road I want to take."

After work the next day Rose went shopping for some new clothes and as she passed by the men's department she decided to pick up a few things: A monogrammed belt with an **S** on it, a pair of monogrammed cuff links; again inscribed with the letter **S**, several pairs of dress jeans, several shirts and a bottle of cologne.

****

Sal called Squeaky and said he needed his help one more time. He discussed his plan regarding Rose and explained exactly what part Squeaky would play in this drama. Sal explained that if everything went as planned, when he got back to Atlantic City he and Squeaky would go out for an evening on the town and it wouldn't cost Squeaky a nickel. In fact, in addition to the night on the town, Sal would pony up two G's for his assistance.

In responding to Sal's proposition, Squeaky responded, "Salvadore, count me in. Your generosity reminds me of a famous quote; 'No person has ever been honored for what he has received; always, for what he has given.'"

"Squeaky, any more quotes like that and you might just bring me to tears. Remember, when I call you and say "NOW", that's your cue to spring into action."

"Count on it, Salvadore, that's me; a man of action."

****

At lunch the next day with Jake, Rose told him that she had some bad news. She had received a call from a doctor in Poland and was told that her estranged mother had taken seriously ill and had been admitted to a hospital in Gdansk. Her mother had asked the doctor to call her daughter in America so that she might be able to come to Gdansk and spend some time with her before she died. The doctor said that death wasn't imminent, but the sooner she arrived, the better. Thus, she would be leaving on a flight from JFK airport on Saturday. When Rose began to tear up, Jake held her close and told her that everything would be OK. He told her not to worry about anything at work. He would make the necessary arrangements with her supervisor for emergency leave. In addition, he would rent a car and take her to the airport. As a big tear rolled down her cheek, Rose looked up into Jake's eyes and said, "I'm so lucky to have you."

****

On Saturday evening Sal stopped at the Dunkin' Donuts and ordered two large coffees, two pecan rolls, two Boston Cream donuts, two Barvarian cream donuts and two jelly roll donuts and headed for Daisy Avenue. Tonight could be the night he unleashed his havoc and he wanted a lot of sugar and caffeine in his system to keep him alert. Based on his previous surveillance he knew that the old man would be leaving for his rent-a-cop job around 7:00 P.M. That would leave Rose in the house all alone which is exactly the way he wanted it. True to his schedule, at 7:00 P.M. sharp the old man appeared on the front porch with Rose and she kissed him and they both embraced for a good 30 seconds. That hadn't happened before; what was going on? Such a big show of affection just because the old fart was going off to work? Maybe he underestimated Rose. Maybe she was banging the old guy AND the young guy. A little fucking Jewish slut is what she was. Shortly after the old guy left, a car pulled up in front of the house and Jake walked up to the front door, knocked and Rose let him in the house.

As Sal watched Jake enter the house he thought to himself that he couldn't have planned this more perfectly himself. Part of his master plan was to bring Rose and her lover together and he wasn't quite sure how he was going to accomplish that feat. But with Mr. Lover Boy showing up on his own, it was the perfect ending to a perfect day. Sal pulled out his cell phone and using the speed-dial feature he called Squeaky. When Squeaky answered, Sal said, "**Now**" and hung up. As Sal was getting out of his car, he saw Jake and Rose exiting the house and each was pulling a suitcase. Holy shit! Were they going on a trip? This development was unexpected and Sal figured he'd have to get control of the situation fast. After all of the time he spent planning his move on Rose and all of the sleuthing he did to locate her, he couldn't let her go off someplace. Who in the fuck knew where she was going? And if she got away, how long would it take him to find her again? When Jake and Rose got to the car, Rose left her suitcase behind the trunk, walked to the passenger side door and got into the car. With the swiftness of an attacking hawk Sal shot across the street. Just before Jake closed the trunk lid he felt a searing pain in the back of his neck. He didn't lose full consciousness but he was temporarily paralyzed and in less than ten seconds Sal put his hands behind him, placed handcuffs on his wrists and his ankles, slapped a piece of duct tape over his mouth and shoved him into the trunk.

During the time Sal was disabling Jake, Rose sat in the front seat staring straight ahead in a trance-like state, lost in her thoughts about the situation she had created with Slim and Jake. She realized that in a couple of hours her double life was about to come to an end. "Too bad," she thought as she had hoped to play the game a bit longer. But when Slim threw a monkey wrench into her plans with his unexpected timing of his request that she accompany him to Ireland, she had to play along.

Sal slammed down the trunk lid, went around to the driver's side door and slid into the driver's seat. Rose was still grossly involved in her thoughts and didn't look to her left until Sal was sitting next to her. As she started to scream Sal reached over, grabbed her by the neck and pressed his thumb on her Adam's apple. Rose was trying to scream but nothing more than a garbled sound was being emitted from her voice box. In fact she was now having trouble breathing and began to struggle to get air into her lungs. "Now listen to me you filthy little murdering fucking Jew, I could kill you right here and now but I have a better plan in mind. I'm going to take my thumb off of your throat and you are not going to make a sound. If you start to scream again it WILL be the last sound you ever make. Nod your head if you understand." Rose nodded her head and Sal released his hold on her throat.

"Let me introduce myself. I'm Walter Bruno's best friend. The Walter Bruno I'm talking about is the one you murdered in the employee locker room of the Show Boat Casino."

"What did you do to Jake?"

Sal slapped Rose across the mouth and said, "Fuck Mr. Lover boy. He's fine and very comfortable in the trunk. Now as I was saying, you murdered my friend Walter."

"I didn't murder him. It was an accident. He tried to rape me and he slipped on the floor in the shower room and hit his head."

"And then you used your cell phone and called 911 so that someone could come to his aid, right?"

"Not exactly."

"Meaning what?"

"Meaning that someone came into the shower room and checked his pulse and determined that he was dead."

"And that someone was your lover boy?"

"Yes."

"And once you and your lover boy determined that my friend died from accidental causes you called 911 to report that to the authorities, right?"

"Not exactly."

"What in the fuck does not exactly mean? I thought you Jews were supposed to be smart people. Even a dumb Jew could answer that question. You either reported the accident to the police or you didn't; simple as that."

"Ah…..I got real scared and ran out of the hotel. I don't know what happened after that."

Sal reached over and grabbed Rose by her hair and slammed her head into the dashboard. "You lying little Jew fuck; I should kill you right now but I won't because that would be too easy on you."

Sal pulled out his cell phone and called Squeaky. "Squeaky, are you with the old man?"

"He's right here next to me, Salvadore. He's tied up at the minute, if you get my drift, but he's anxious to talk to his little girl."

"Ok. Put the phone next to his mouth and tell him to say 'Hello Rose.'"

Squeaky put the phone next to David's mouth and Sal held his phone to Rose's ear while David said hello to his daughter.

Sal moved the phone away from and said, "Squeaky. Hold tight and I'll be back to you."

"Now Rose. One word from me and my friend Squeaky puts a hole in daddy's forehead unless you tell me exactly what happened to my friend Walter. So let's try this again.

What happened to Walter? This is your last chance to fess up or Poppa Jew's brains will be splattered all over his little shoe shop. That would be bad for business, don't you think?"

Rose then told Sal the truth and the whole truth about the events that occurred that fateful night in the employee's locker room.

"So you torched my friend's ass? Is that what you are saying?"

"Well, yes, but he was already dead and frankly he deserved it."

"If you had just left the scene, Walter's dead body would have been discovered the next day by some employee and reported to the police. You did such a good job of eliminating fingerprints and any traces that you were at the crime scene, that a police investigation would never have been able to connect you and your lover boy to Walter's untimely demise. So why torch the poor son of a bitch?"

"We couldn't take any chances and that animal deserved to be eliminated. The way I see it, we just saved someone the expense of burying or cremating that monster."

"That monster was my best friend and the way I see it, a good friend of mine didn't even have the opportunity for family, friends and loved ones to provide a proper burial. What you took away from Walter was the greatest theft of all. You stole his respect from him. That fucking priest lied to me and he had to pay for his sins. The holier-than-thou nun wouldn't talk to me so she had to pay as well. Seems to me that the only one who hasn't paid a price is you, but that's all going to change because tonight is "collection night."

As Rose sat there wide eyed, Sal began to fiddle with the GPS system on the car. After completing his task he turned to her and said, "I've just programmed this system to guide you to Lefferts Blvd. which is several miles from the

JFK terminal. When you get to Lefferts Blvd. you will see the signs for remote parking for the airport. There are two lots, lot A and lot B. You will turn into Lot A. When you get to Lot A keep driving to the rear of the lot; all the way to the very last space in the lot. I will be following behind you all the way. If you vary one fucking iota from the prescribed route I will call my friend and he will take care of your father. He has been instructed to put a bullet into his head but I've also given him the leeway to "play" a little before wasting Mr. Shoemaker. Squeaky loves to hammer nails and work with wood and shit like that. Who knows, he might even crucify his old wrinkled ass. Of course, you could always decide to sacrifice the old fart and make a break for it, but be aware that I attached a tracking device to your car when I packed junior in the trunk so there is no way you can get away from me. As I said, I will be right behind you. Keep me in your rear-view mirror. If I flick my high beams once that means I want you to slow down. If I flick my high beams twice that means pull over to the right side of the road immediately. Make sure you abide by all traffic laws; no running red lights, going through stop signs, etc. And lastly give me your purse." Rose handed Sal her purse and he removed her cell phone.

    The trip to the parking lot went smoothly. Rose kept driving to the rear of the lot as Sal had directed. She pulled in to a very remote spot and Sal pulled in next to her. The closest car to them was at least twenty spaces away. They were also about 10 spaces away from the nearest light standard. It was a dark and lonely spot; just the kind Sal had dreamed about. Sal got out of his car and motioned for Rose to get out and join him as he stood behind her car. Sal said, "Gimme you keys." Rose handed him the keys and Sal popped the trunk. Jake was lying there much in the same position as he was when Sal threw him into the trunk.

"Ok lover boy; listen carefully, I'm going to remove the tape from your mouth, but if you make a sound, I will put a bullet into your crotch and one more between your eyes for good measure and then Mrs. Lover boy will get one in the back of her pretty head.. Nod if you completely understand what I said." Jake nodded his head and Sal ripped the tape from his mouth.

"Rose told me all about your escapades in Atlantic City and how you personally shoved my best friend into an incinerator." Jake was astounded by these words.

"What are you talking about? I've never even been in Atlantic City."

"Don't lie to me you prick. I'm sick of all of this fucking lying!"

"No, really mister I don't know what you're talking about. I love Rose and we are a couple, but I never was with her in Atlantic City and tonight I was just giving her a ride to the airport."

"And where was Rose supposed to be going without you?"

"Her mother in Poland is ill and she was going home to be with her."

"Oh fuck; don't give me that shit again. That's an old story, pal. Certainly you could have come up with a better sounding lie than that."

"But it's the truth. Tell him Rose." But Rose kept silent.

Sal then said, "And you weren't going with her, right?"

"Absolutely, I was just being nice and offered her a ride."

Sal pulled the suitcases out of the trunk and said to Rose, "OK, Miss Poland, open up the suitcases."

Rose opened the smaller suitcase first and Sal began to go through its contents. The first item he pulled out was a man's flannel shirt. "What's your shirt size lover boy?"

"Large," replied Jake.

"Surprise of surprises; I see several men's shirts both size Large."

Then Sal asked Jake, "And what's your pant size?"

"36 X 32," responded Jake.

"Another incredible coincidence; both of these jeans are 36 X 32. Not yours, right?"

"No. No. Not mine. I don't know whose clothes they are, but they are not mine."

Sal fished around once more and came up with the belt and cufflinks. "What did you say your name was?"

"Stalk, Jake Stalk."

"That would be Stalk with a letter "S", correct?"

"Correct." And then Sal showed the monogrammed items to Jake.

As Jake stared in horror at the items, Sal said, "Let's recap what we know so far. The shirts are sized large and you wear large shirts. Strike One. The jeans are 36 X32, just your size. Strike Two. And low and behold, two monogrammed items coincidently have the same initial as your last name. Strike Three, pal. You are fucking out."

"Rose, **YOU HAVE TO TELL HIM THAT THIS IS ALL A MISTAKE**. Please Rose." But Rose remained silent.

Sal pulled a gun from his pocket and screwed on a silencer. He shoved the gun into Jake's mouth. "Rose, get your little ass over here." As Rose came around to Sal's side, with his free hand Sal pushed the speed-dial digit for Squeaky.

"Squeaky, how are things at the shop?"

"The situation here is absolutely under control, Salvadore."

"Good. Now Squeaky I want you to take out your pistol and place it next to the old man's temple, but don't shoot until I say the magic word. OK?"

"Right you are boss man."

"Rose, you took away a loved one from me and now I am about to return the favor. The dearly departed Father Ray would say something like "an eye for an eye and a tooth for a tooth". The easiest thing for me to do right now would be to blow your lover boy away followed by your old man and then yourself. But that would be too easy on you. You'd only experience the pain of losing a loved one for a few moments. I want you to spend the rest of your life in mourning just like I will mourn the loss of Walter until my dying breath. So, I'm not going to waste you, but I am going to waste one of your loved ones and it's going to be your choice. The choice you make you will think about every day for the rest of your natural life and I hope it drives you fucking crazy with guilt. Someone once said that sometimes it's better to be dead than alive and you will know how that feels in just a few minutes. So here we are Rose; we've come to the end of the journey; the ball is squarely in your court."

Rose could have spoken up for Jake when he asked for support, but as she listened to Sal it became obvious to her that he was operating under the impression that it was Jake who was with her in Atlantic City and not Slim. In fact, it was blatantly clear that Sal didn't even know Slim existed. As the wheels turned in her devious little mind; Rose felt that her best chance to survive this ordeal would be to keep her mouth shut and let Sal keep thinking that it was Jake who tossed Walter in the incinerator. Maybe he'd take his vengeance out on Jake and leave her alone? As Sal rambled on, it was becoming clear to Rose that by keeping her mouth shut she had made the right decision. She was going to get out of this deal alive! The choice she had to make between losing Jake or her dad was an easy one for Rose. If Sal shot Jake, her father would be allowed to live and a bonus would be that the love triangle she created would be conveniently eliminated. She has always worried about how long she could keep one from finding out about the other and what might happen when that occurred. She didn't want to run the risk of losing both and being on the outside looking in. So, even if this was a tragic ending for Jake, it certainly provided an upside for Rose and she was going to take advantage of it.

"It's past my dinner hour, Rose and I'm getting real fucking hungry, so let's end this shit and call it a day. You make the choice or I will."

Rose tugged on her locket, thought of her mother's words and said out loud, "I'm sorry Jake."

Sal said into his phone, "Squeaky, don't shoot the old man." He depressed the 'end call' button on his cell phone, looked at Jake and said, "Tell Walter I send my warmest regards," and pulled the trigger. Sal wiped down the gun and handed it to Rose. "Don't think about shooting me Rose as there was only one bullet in the chamber." Sal carefully removed the handcuffs from Jake and was sure to pick up the piece of tape that he had ripped from his mouth. He took off his surgical gloves, put them in his pocket and said to Rose, "All is well that ends well. The score is now even Rose." Suppressing a laugh, Sal said, "Please give your sick mother my regards when you get to Poland." Leaving with a huge smirk on his face, Sal got into his car and drove away.

After taking a minute or two to think things through, Rose removed the suitcases from the car. She opened one of the suitcases, took out a cotton sweater and wiped down every conceivable part of the car she had touched. She carefully wiped each key on the key ring and threw the keys into the trunk. She carefully removed Jake's wallet from his pants pocket and removed his cash and credit cards. When the police found him they would be led to believe that this was a robbery that went tragically wrong. She shoved the gun into her purse and walked up to the shuttle bus pick up.

About 5 minutes later the shuttle arrived and Rose was on her way to the terminal. When she arrived at the terminal she went into the first women's room she could locate. Lucky for her, the room was empty. She went into the stall and took the pistol out of her purse and unscrewed the silencer attachment. If the gun was found, it couldn't be traced to her, but those CSI people were really smart and if they got a hold of the gun they might somehow be able to trace it to Sal and then Sal could provide an avenue for the police to come looking for her. Better to be safe than sorry. Using a cloth, she carefully wiped down the silencer and the gun. Holding the gun with the cloth she proceeded to wrap the gun in toilet paper. She kept wrapping until the gun was well padded. Some cleaning person might notice the gun easily if it was just lying in the open in the receptacle, but with it wrapped, the possibility of it being found right away was remote. Who knows? It might never be found. She performed the same procedure on the silencer. She deposited the gun in the trash receptacle and then went to another women's room and deposited the silencer in that trash receptacle. After exiting the second women's room she proceeded to the ticket level and looked at the board listing the departing flights. She noted the gate for Slim's connecting flight to Dublin and was on her way.

As she approached the screening area she saw Slim waiting by the entrance. He waved and she waved back. He ran to her and said, "You are a little late, I thought you weren't coming. Oh my God, Rose, I'm so happy you are here. What took you so long?"

"The friend who brought me to the airport had some car trouble and he had to pull off and fool around with the engine for a bit."

"Well thank God he knew how to fix the car or I might have left without you. By the way, he must be a real nice guy to take time out on a Saturday night to drive you all the way out here."

"I guess you could say that about him Slim. In fact, if there is anything you could say to describe him it would be that he was a nice guy. One of the nicest guys I ever met."

AFTERMATH

When Jake failed to report for work his supervisor, Mr. Lynn, called Mrs. Sorrento and made an inquiry as to his whereabouts. Mrs. Sorrento reported that she hadn't seen Jake since the previous Saturday afternoon and she was very worried about him. It was very unusual for him to just disappear without saying a word. Maybe there was a family emergency and he rushed home and was so involved with family affairs that he had just forgotten to call into work? Knowing Jake that was very unlikely, but Mr. Lynn made the call to Jake's parents and was told that they hadn't talked to Jake in over a week. Knowing Jake's "Pittsburgh background", Jake's dad suggested to Mr. Lynn that he was going to call the police in NYC and file a missing person's report. After making the phone call, John and Lucy drove to NYC and met with the supervisor of the missing person's bureau. John explained the entire background associated with Jake's situation in Pittsburgh. After listening and taking copious notes, the supervisor told John and Lucy that his department would do everything they could to find Jake. But considering the circumstances and the background facts, one could not rule out that Jake's sudden disappearance might have been caused by professionals and if that were the case, they had better prepare themselves for bad news. He reassured them that where there is life there is hope and he reaffirmed his promise to follow up on every lead that surfaced. After John and Lucy left, the supervisor had little to no confidence that Jake would ever be found, at least not in one piece.

The car rental company called Jake on the final day of his the 3-day grace period following his rental. The car was now past due and they were going to charge his credit card with the cost of an additional week's rental plus a late fee.

Mrs. Sorrento answered the phone and explained to the car rental people that Jake had been missing for a week. The car rental people cared nothing about Jake's disappearance; and everything about getting their car returned. They told Mrs. Sorrento that they were going to charge Jake's credit card with a week's rental charge plus the late penalty and were going to file a report with the local authorities of a possible stolen vehicle.

****

Detective Don Robbins was reviewing recent missing person's cases when "perky" Patti Gannon from the motor vehicle theft division walked in holding a sheet of paper that listed the most recently reported stolen tags. Patti was wearing a fairly sheer silk blouse and the temperature in the office was cold. One look at Patti and it was obvious why the boys in the office had nicknamed her "Perky".

"Hey Patti, how goes it? What have you got there?"

"The most recent list of reported stolen tags; sometimes a cross reference between your missing persons and those registered to stolen vehicles can turn up a hit for you guys."

"Thanks Patti. By the way, are you and Joe still heading to Ireland for your anniversary?"

"You bet. Next week. Joe's been taking orders for Irish whisky for the last month. Want a bottle?"

"Nah, I'm a beer guy. I can't afford good Irish whiskey on a cop's salary."

"I hear you on that score, Don. When we get back I'm going to have to take all of the overtime I can get to help put a dent in the cost of this trip."

"Thanks again for the list Patti, have a safe trip and a good time. If I don't see you before you leave; 'Erin Go Bragh' and all of that good stuff."

After Patti left the office Don was thinking that he was glad he didn't slip up and say 'Erin Go Braghless' to Patti.

As Don perused the list he saw that **Discount Car Rentals** had reported that one of their customers, a Jake Stalk had stolen one of their vehicles. They listed the make, model, VIN and tag number of the missing car. After making a cross reference, Don went to his supervisor's office to report that they had their first lead in the Jake Stalk case.

The listing of Jake's missing rental car went out to all agencies in the tri-state area as well as the FBI data base. Every state and local cop in a radius of 500 miles would have the information regarding Jake's rental car in their patrol car computer. Meter maids and beat cops would be on the lookout for an abandoned car carrying Jake's identifying tag number.

In many missing person's cases the people aren't missing because of foul play, rather they became missing because they decided to disappear on their own. Maybe they ran away with a lover. Maybe they owed a debt they couldn't pay. Maybe they got involved in some kind of a bad situation and felt that the only way to resolve it would be to get out of town for a week a month or permanently. In missing person's cases it is common to check parking lots of train stations, bus depots and airports for vehicles owned or operated by a missing person. These were common stash points for people on the run.

****

A year ago, Ron Harbour lost his job as a financial analyst for a big firm on Wall Street. After years of making big money, all of a sudden he was out on his ass. He couldn't believe it when it happened. But, with his skill set he felt very positive about the prospects of getting another job within the industry. Maybe he wouldn't be making the bucks he had in the past, but certainly he'd be able to "do alright". Much to Ron's dismay and surprise he couldn't find any work in the financial world. In actuality, he couldn't find work of any kind anywhere. Oh yeah, there was always McDonalds or Burger King or some other fast food chain where he could flip burgers, but how in the world could he go from making six figures a year to six bucks an hour? Pete Fewster, a buddy of Ron's, was the Supervisor of Parking and Concessions at JFK Airport and one night while playing cards with Ron and the boys in the neighborhood, he mentioned to Ron that he had an opening for a Security Patrol Officer. The job wasn't very challenging and the hours sucked, but it paid $15 an hour, included free food at any of the airport concessionaries and came with paid holidays and "minimal" health benefits. Ron felt so worthless after not working for so long that he jumped on Pete's offer.

On Ron's first night on patrol he was riding shot gun as his supervisor was giving him hints and tips about the job.

"Ron, the tag on every car that comes into this lot is photographed and stored on our main computer. On a regular basis we receive reports from local, city and state municipalities regarding tag numbers of stolen or missing vehicles. Our computer people scan these reports into our computer and then the computer compares our recent data base with these listings. When a match occurs that means that somewhere in our lot a stolen or missing vehicle has been parked. The problem with our system is that vehicle tags are photographed when they enter the lot but are not photographed when they leave the lot. So even if a stolen or missing car was parked here, it could be gone by now. When I came into work tonight I was informed that we have a new "hit" in our system. Our job right now is to see if we can spot a dark blue Honda Civic with a NY tag number SDB-1983. We'll start at the rear of Lot A and work our way forward. If no luck there, then we'll go over to Lot B and follow the same procedure." As they approached the last row in Lot A, Ron's supervisor turned on the high intensity search light and slowed the car down to a crawl as they passed each vehicle.

When they were about 10 yards from the end of the row Ron exclaimed, "Isn't that a Honda parked down on the right past that light standard?"

Ron's supervisor inched his way toward the car and stopped next to it. As he shone his light on the tag, SDB-1983 was staring him in the face. "This is it, Ron. Let's get out and take a look."

As they approached the car, Ron said, "What's that smell?"

Ron's supervisor said, "I know that smell." He then pulled out his cell phone and called dispatch. "Dispatch, this is Security Patrol. I'm in Lot A, at the very end of aisle ZZ. We have a 'stinker'; you'd better call the Port Authority cops."

A Cruel Twist of Fate

****

When Detective Robbins arrived at Lot A, the scene was somewhat chaotic. Parked at various angles in the rows around the Honda was an ambulance, several police cars from nearby localities, an NYPD cruiser, an unmarked Crown Victoria, a Port Authority cruiser and a Hummer marked 'NYPD Bomb Squad'. He signed the crime sheet report provided by the officer in charge and approached the rear of the car. Standing at rear of the open trunk were two Port Authority Detectives and leaning into the trunk was the Nassau County Medical Examiner.

"Good evening gentlemen, I'm Detective Robbins from NYPD Missing Persons. Do we have any confirmation on the victim and any determination as to cause of death?"

"Vic is one Jake Stalk. There are powder burns around the victim's mouth which indicates that a weapon was fired either at close range or placed in the victim's mouth. There is an exit wound in the back of the victim's head the size of golf ball. I'm ruling out suicide because there is an absence of a weapon in this trunk as well as clear evidence of cuts around his wrists and ankles. Obviously this poor soul was bound in some manner. For how long I won't be able to tell without running some lab tests. There is a residue of tape around his mouth and on his cheeks which indicates he was silenced. Techs have been dusting for prints but can't find a single one anywhere on this vehicle. Not one print anywhere! His wallet is empty with the exception of his NYS driver's license, an AAA card and a few restaurant discount cards. Whoever did this was hoping to pass this off as a robbery gone bad, but in my opinion this wasn't a simple robbery. No, this smells to me like a kidnap and murder done by professionals."

When Don got back to headquarters he reported the grim news to his supervisor then he said, "Captain, I'm going to get a large cup of coffee and then I'll be on my way."

"Where are you going, Detective?"

"Sagamore," replied Don.

****

Jake's funeral was attended by the largest number of people in the history of the Armstrong County. UMW members from all over the state of Pennsylvania and West Virginia came to pay their respects to the Stalk family.

Jake was laid to rest in a plot next to Meta and Big John.

Following Jake's passing, Lucy became somewhat of a recluse. John was often sullen and both seemed to be in a constant state of mourning. A year to the day after being notified about Jake's death, Lucy passed away in her sleep. Prior to her passing she had no known health issues. Her death certificate stated, "cardiac arrest," but her family physician knew better. He said it was simply a case of a broken heart. John lived on mourning the loss of his son and his "Lucy" and continued working in the mines until he retired at age 70. The state of his health declined rapidly and he became afflicted with Alzheimer's disease. John continually rebuffed efforts by his friends to be admitted to a nursing home. Finally, due to a mixture of sheer frustration and love for the man, a number of the women in Sagamore decided to just let John live out his life at home and they took turns every day attending to his daily needs until he passed. John was reunited with his Lucy and his son at the age of 90.

BACK TO THE FUTURE

Jake's case remained unsolved and all of its files were eventually transferred to the Cold Case division of NYCPD. To this day no new leads have surfaced.

The murder of Father Ray remained unsolved and like Jake's case file, it was eventually designated as a "cold case." After the death of Father Ray, St. Bede Parish dissolved.

Sister Jean underwent 16 oral surgeries to repair her jaw structure and fit her with a complete set of false teeth. Between her first and last surgeries, 14 months passed and during that entire time she had to eat all of her meals through a straw. She was never able to speak properly again and she eventually learned sign language. With cuts in federal funding, combined with a lack of support from donations, The Sanctuary for Abused Women became defunct and the nuns who worked there were dispersed to other communities across the country. Instead of accepting a reassignment, Sister Jean left the community of nuns and moved to a life of peace and solitude in the northern part of the state of Maine. Today she works in a small private school in Caribou, ME which specializes in helping children who were born deaf and/or blind.

Sal remained a faithful and trustworthy employee of the Bruno family. He was never questioned or became a suspect in any of the investigations regarding Father Ray, Sister Jean or Jake. For years he lived in Atlantic City and vacationed at the Hamptons. On one fateful evening at a **Kentucky Fried Chicken** restaurant, as Sal began to devour his third bucket of fried chicken, he got a chicken bone stuck in his throat and subsequently died from asphyxiation. At the time of his death, Sal weighed in at a rotund 376 pounds. At his funeral there were no takers when the funeral director asked for volunteers to be pall bearers.

Until his knee replacement surgery, Squeaky remained a top-flight second story/ B & E man. After the surgery he decided to retire. He was always very frugal with his money and a few years previous to his retirement he had paid cash for a small place on the Jersey Shore. He spends his days fishing and taking walks on the beach. To avoid loneliness, he bought himself a Rottweiler puppy. He named the dog "Mister Squeaky."

On the night of Jake's death, David did not escape unscathed. Per Sal's instructions, Squeaky did not put a bullet in David's head, but he did use one of David's leather knives to remove his thumbs and forefingers. Unable to continue in his work, David sold his shop and moved to

Ireland to join Slim and Rose. He helps out at the farm and the tavern in whatever way he can.

Slim and Rose got married six months after arriving in Ireland. Two years later, she and Slim had a daughter and they named her Margaret Ann McGraw. They called her Maggie. When Maggie was 10 years old she awoke to find a necklace with a locket around her neck. On the one side of the locket was a picture of her mother and on the other side was an inscription that read:

Always Follow Your Heart

When she went downstairs for breakfast that morning she asked Slim where mommy was. With tears in his eyes, Slim told her that mommy had left. Maggie never saw her mother again.

CPSIA information can be obtained at www.ICGtesting.com
232605LV00001B/34/P